EVERY

LITTLE

SIGN

MICHELE PACE

Every Little Sign

9 8 7 6 5 4 3 2 1
First Edition

Printed in the United States of America.

Book cover design by Olga Grlic
Book interior design by Lisa Gilliam

ISBN: 979-8-370-21595-7 (paperback)

For Michael, who always encourages me to take chances.

For Jane, a fearless warrior.

CONTENTS

PART ONE

PART TWO

PART THREE

PART ONE

CHAPTER ONE

Emma

The little silver box, delicate and sleek, sparkles when the light finds its smooth finish. I flick the clasp and watch the lid rise, exposing seven oval pills. Seven enticing bits of temptation that require my undivided attention just to avoid them. I exhale and blink away the moment, snapping the container shut, then slip it back into my bag.

As I step outside the Pru, a looming storm churns overhead. Spidery blades of lightning crackle, trailed by a growling barrage of thunder. I catch the scent of dense, moist air, and almost as if on cue the sky begins to wail, sending heavy pearls of water to blanket the city. I hurry up Boylston, my black leather tote hoisted above my head, puddles of wetness leaping onto the jeans I changed into just a half hour earlier. As I cross the street, the spiked heel of my boot catches a groove in the pavement and I hastily twist at my ankle, prying the peg from the deep crack. The *O'Malley's* sign beams just ahead, and I sigh in relief.

I follow a gaggle of Bruins jerseys into the warm pub, immediately seduced by the aroma of brisket and freshly baked soda bread. A film of moisture instantly builds beneath my layers of silk and wool; I remove my coat and drape it over a hook near the door. The crowded room with its Irishy-green walls and vintage sports memorabilia rumbles with voices and laughter—lively clusters of patrons huddle at high-tops, drowned out by the occasional roar of zealous fans applauding their teams.

Claire spots me from across the room and beckons with an enthusiastic raise of her hand, loose golden waves skimming her shoulders. She's not the type of girl you miss—with her creamy skin and striking blue eyes, she has an uncanny ability to grab attention wherever she goes. We've been friends since we met during our second year of law school at Boston University. She was a transfer student looking for a study partner in our research and writing class, and although I was more comfortable working independently, she convinced me to join her. From that point forward we've been close, and now we work together at Parker, Hill & Lee, a midsize law firm in downtown Boston.

I snake my way through bodies, each nestled together in a space not meant to hold half this many people. Sweeping my dark hair into a loose ponytail, I fan my blouse to keep it from sticking to my skin. When I finally reach Claire, she stands with her arms swung wide, the scent of her signature perfume enveloping me before she does. She has two inches on my five-foot, six-inch frame, but tonight my boots put us eye to eye.

"Oh my God, Emma—what took you so long? I've been guarding this seat with my life—at one point I even bought a couple beers to keep a completely lit but arguably hot townie from stealing it," she says.

I drop onto the open stool beside her and scan the room, hoping that some kind soul will appear with a cocktail in hand. Claire takes a sip from her drink and looks at me with a probing arch of the brow.

"I know, I know ... Dean asked me to finish a motion before I left."

"I'm guessing you had more time than you thought," she says, gesturing over her shoulder. I curl my head to the right and spot him standing at a table with a group of colleagues, his light brown hair neatly parted on one side and a slight shadow framing his jawline. Dean is undeniably handsome—it's easy to stare when you should be listening. *I digress.* Sadly, for his admirers—and there are many—he is a happily married man. It's one of the things I love most about him, actually—it gives me hope that good ones *do still* exist. At the moment, though, I admit to being a little perplexed; Dean always takes on more work than he delegates to the associates, so it's curious that he asked me to stay late while he came here to socialize.

I consider walking over to say hello, but then Claire reaches out, the tips of her soft fingers guiding my chin back in her direction. "Do me a favor—just for tonight, let work go. Talk to me about that beautiful anesthesiologist you had dinner with," she says, tilting a tiny straw into her mouth and sipping the last golden drops of a whiskey sour, another one already nudged up against it.

I bite at my lip and lean into the bar, attempting to order a drink. "I canceled," I whisper, hoping that she lets the thought pass.

Claire sighs. "Oh, Emma, tell me you didn't."

"I had to work late," I respond, glancing at the nearest screen to avoid the eye roll that I know is coming.

"You do realize that you sabotage any chance at a relationship, don't you?"

"When I meet a man who makes me want to look twice, I'll let you know," I respond.

"I know you will. It's just that …"

"It's just that, *what*? Why is being alone so unthinkable? I like being by myself—taking bubble baths with Taylor Swift streaming on a loop and no one to judge. I enjoy not worrying about feeding someone else—if I want Lucky Charms for dinner, only my gut will complain. Most important, though, is that I love the work I do. Making time to coddle a man simply doesn't fit into the schedule right now."

"Oh, Em, you're about to turn thirty-two, and most of your friends are headed to the altar. In fact, some even to the maternity ward. I just don't want time to get away from you," she says, her hand gently stroking my arm.

I love everything about my friend—*except this*. The constant volley of reminders that time is fleeting and I'm destined to miss the wifey train, even though she herself is not yet married. I know she means well, and in a sisterly way she just doesn't want me to end up alone eating bags of cookies with a herd of kittens wearing tiny little kitty jammies in my bed. I get it—*I really do*. But justifying my life choices time and again *is exhausting*. I take her hands in mine and smile. "Love is a glorious thought, but it's not a priority for me. Right now, work makes me happy," I say, hoping the conversation shifts to her.

"Fair enough. But just remember this—work will never listen to your stories. Work can't break your fall—and you know we all tumble from time to time. And when you grow old, work will still be young and ready to move on to a fresh new victim."

I offer a warm smile. "You're right. Work may not do that for me—but you can."

Claire leans forward, her perfectly manicured fingers threading into mine. "What if I marry a handsome doctor and we decide to buy a vineyard somewhere in Tuscany? Then who will be there to catch you?"

"I guess I'll just land on the ample padding God gave me and order another cocktail," I say, pivoting my stool toward the bar, my arm high and swaying. I try to catch the attention of one of two bartenders—the *ooooh, you could use a cheeseburger* skinny girl with shoulder-length auburn hair doesn't seem to notice me. Despite my best efforts, the bristly-jawed guy at the end of the bar has apparently cast a spell on her and I might as well be a breadstick waiting for a drink.

I turn back toward Claire, but she's busy on her cell. I look over and notice a photo on her screen. "Oh, that must be the Walgreens guy. How are things going with him?" I ask.

Claire looks up and hastily tucks her phone back into her purse. "He's a definite maybe," she says with a wink.

"Only you could find *Mr. Maybe* while buying condoms at a drugstore."

She smiles. "You could walk out of here with a man right now if you wanted to—look around, every guy in this place has had his eyes on you since you walked through that door."

"I could string Edison bulbs across my naked body and no one in this room would take their eyes off of you," I say, believing every word of that statement to be true.

Dean glances over, and his gaze lands on me. He shoots me that dimpled grin and I'm easily disarmed, forgiving him instantly for making me work late. As he swims through the crowd in our direction, his untucked denim shirt slips over a pair of tan five-pocket pants. I'm startled when Claire leaps to her feet just as Dean approaches. "I'm gonna go say hi to the others," she says, disappearing into the throng of half-baked millennials.

Dean watches her walk away, and as the distance between them grows, he raises a brow before pivoting his attention toward me. He takes Claire's empty seat and leans in. "I'm glad you came," he says.

I raise my voice above the background noise. "I almost didn't make it—my boss asked me to finish the Davis motion while he was out playing with his adoring new recruits."

Dean smiles, but something about him seems off. "You know how much I appreciate your work, Emma. To be honest, I didn't plan on joining this little soiree, but I noticed the other partners huddled up in the conference room and thought at least one of us should be here."

I sigh. "How can I tease you with a comeback like that?"

"Believe me, only my body is here—my head is back at the office."

"I thought you seemed a little preoccupied tonight," I say.

He stares down for a minute, then returns his gaze to me. "That's probably a fair observation." Dean isn't easily rattled, but tonight I see something that I don't recognize—he's unnerved. I stiffen in my seat. "What is it?"

"I was reviewing documents for Silverstone Development and came across something that struck me as peculiar. I've been digging into it for a while now, and it just keeps getting worse."

"How bad is it?"

"It's bad. I've been going back and forth with our client contact; I'd like to confirm my suspicions before I take it any further, but if I'm right, this thing is gonna explode and it's not just heads that are gonna roll—entire bodies will be dropping after everything comes to light."

"Can I help?" I ask.

He rakes through his hair and I notice his throat rise and fall hard. "Let's talk after I hear back."

"Of course. I left the brief on your desk, including the three affidavits. I'm guessing they're ready to sign and file as is."

"I'm sure they are. There's a reason you were promoted to senior associate, and someday you'll be a partner heading up your own team. And when you do, no one will be more proud of you than me."

It's difficult to conceal my excitement at the mention of making partner—a goal that would never define me, but one that's important all the same. Dean gets up as Claire returns. She reclaims her seat, then spins toward the counter.

"Can I get you two a drink?" he asks, looking down at his cell and typing a message.

I lean into Claire. "Dean's offering to buy us a drink."

"I'm good," she says, without looking our way. She doesn't appear to be upset really, but there's something going on. I look down and notice her foot rattling on the edge of the barstool.

Dean's forehead furrows, and I feel as if I need to apologize for her strange response. "The Tillaman case has her preoccupied," I say. *That's a lie.* The truth is, I have no idea why she's avoiding him; I suppose it could have something to do with my promotion. I know she wanted the position, but I'm sure she doesn't hold it against him. Even she would admit that her attention to detail is a little less sharp than mine. *No, this is something else.* Dean's eyes drift as if his mind has traveled away from our conversation.

I tap his shoulder, and he returns his focus to me. "I'll have what she's having," I say.

Dean made his way through law school as a bartender, so he can identify any drink you put in front of him. He makes eye contact with the female bartender. "One whiskey sour and a Sam Adams," he calls out. The redhead nods in acknowledgment, appearing to move just a little faster for him than she did for me. Moments later his outstretched arm passes the amber-filled tumbler with a slice of orange and a cocktail cherry. There's a fragrant waft of honey and oak as I take the first sip, a calming warmth rising inside me.

"Oh this is good. *Really good*," I say.

Dean manages an unconvincing smile. "I'm gonna take off in about twenty minutes, so I should get back to our table. You may want to stop by and say hello."

"Absolutely, I will."

He taps the counter then walks off. I watch him maneuver through the busy room, sliding onto a stool and nudging in between two junior associates. I've been working with Dean since I started at the firm; we met years earlier while I was at BU and he volunteered to lead our moot court team. Sometimes I think I learned more from him in that short period of time than I did in all three years of law school. I peer over at the cluster of young attorneys, the way they look at him with such admiration. I envy those kids just starting out, all the time they've spent seeing the law through his brilliant eyes. He has left a mark on them already; they just don't know it yet.

Over the next few hours Claire and I catch up on our college friends, the various proposals, some breakups, and the typical girly gossip. We talk about what's trending, her favorite influencers, the new additions to her purse collection, and the apartment she rented in Cambridge.

"How's your dad doing, by the way?" she asks.

"He's good, actually. He spends a lot of time tutoring these days; last time I saw him he talked about writing a book."

Claire smiles. "I would definitely read that book."

I grin and reach for a cocktail napkin. "Didn't you say you had friends coming to town for a visit?"

She nods. "Already did. Jessie was here last week. We went out for sushi, got mani-pedis, and stayed in one night to re-watch the fourth season of *Ozark*—which by the way, was just as good the second time."

"I was hoping to meet her in person this trip," I say, my buzz strangely amplified.

"I love Jessie dearly, but having a guest is like taking care of a child—expensive and exhausting," she says, finishing her drink.

Smiling, I dig through my tote for a tube of gloss and swipe a layer over my lips. "So you decided to have another visitor right away then?" I ask with a wink.

Claire giggles. "Allie was just here for a photo shoot. I was only able to pin her down for one day—we had drinks together and spent a couple hours at the Museum of Fine Arts. Then off she went to climb some new mountain or sail across the ocean—as I've explained, she's a bit of a vagabond."

"When are you finally gonna introduce me to these girls?" I ask.

Claire takes another sip from her straw, then leaps to her feet and grips my hands. "Hey, why don't we go shopping this weekend?"

My idea of shopping is hitting Target, but that's miles away from my trust-fund bestie's appetite for five-thousand-dollar purses and nine-hundred-dollar boots. It's not that I don't love splurging from time to time—*I do.* But in some ways we couldn't be more different—I'm a Southie girl who loves a bargain; she's a South Carolina mansion type who's never met a fad she didn't want to follow. But she doesn't flaunt her wealth-by-birth status. We may have been born into opposite worlds, but when we're together, we're the same—Hallmark Christmas movie junkies with a flair for sushi, chai tea lattes, and long walks by the river. Besides, she's always been willing to help me with my pro bono cases, never missing a meeting with the inmates. That has been invaluable to me.

"Shopping sounds amazing," I respond. *I'd rather walk on broken glass, but for her I'll make the effort.*

"It's a date, then," she says, falling back onto her stool and tipping her glass to clink mine.

I finish off my drink and then stand. "I need to visit the little girls' room," I tell Claire, watching as she turns to flirt with the bartender. I make my way down the narrow hallway and am only a few steps away from the door when I feel a *woosh* of dizziness. My body rocks and I tip sideways, leaning into the wall. Regaining my balance, I quickly punch through the door and prop myself on the sink, splashing water onto my face. The image staring back at me in the mirror is blurred. I manage to steady myself, and get out of there as quickly as possible.

When I return, Claire is leaning on the bar still chatting away. I take a seat and place my hand on her arm. She turns my way and smooths a lock of hair behind my shoulder. "Are you okay?" she asks.

"No, not really. Aren't you feeling this too?"

"Feeling what?"

"Like we're back on the Green Line after finals, drinking vodka from Mountain Dew bottles," I say, signaling to the bartender for a glass of water.

"This is what relaxing feels like," she says.

"This is more than just relaxing—I think I may have passed right over buzzed and entered shit-faced," I say, reaching for the glass, cubes of ice clanking in the cold liquid. I glide my hand along the back of Claire's buttery tan leather jacket; she reaches around and gives me a tender squeeze. Getting to her feet, she walks to the end of the bar and plants her elbows on the counter— her eyes fixed on the guy behind it. Over the last five hours I've consumed two whiskey sours and several shots of Fireball, and I'm feeling boozy for sure. But it's more than that—somehow this sensation is different. The music stops, and something inside me shifts. I hadn't noticed until now that the crowd has dispersed, only a few diehards still slouching at the bar. The jubilant chatter has evaporated, leaving an uncomfortable silence in its wake. As I rise to my feet again, the walls begin to whirl, and sweat beads at my temples. I tuck my head down and firmly grip the table, pleading with it to stop. When I look up, I see Claire stumbling away with erratic steps. I call out her name, my voice reduced to a breathy hiss. She turns back and smiles, then pivots and continues down the hall.

The bartender is busy behind the counter, sleeves of tattoos on both arms wet with soap as he moves glasses from one sink to another. He swipes steam from his forehead, his tousled blond hair bright against his olive skin. He seems to sense me watching him, and glances upward.

"You need some help?" he asks.

"I'm good," I reply, studying the slosh of water in my glass as it moves from side to side in my nervous grip.

Claire totters back my way, her right arm sliding along the shiny walnut bar. "I ordered an Uber. Let's go to your place," she slurs.

I turn toward the exit, and the doors expand and contract like mahogany lungs—*this can't be the alcohol.* I snap back toward the bar where we had last been sitting, my gaze finding the two empty glasses. A loud *clank* snatches my glance and plants it back on Claire. She ignores the glass lying on its side oozing water onto the floor and scoops up her pink Himalayan Louis Vuitton bag, drapes it over her shoulder, and nearly trips when she catches a stool with her camel suede bootie.

I reach for the door; the slick curve of the metal handle feels cool to the touch. I know what this means—the temperature has dropped, and the air on the other side of the heavy wood will sting.

❦

Claire stumbles to my side and pushes ahead of me, the early-evening rain now replaced by a chilly wind that grabs hold as I step out into the night. I hustle to catch up, my arm swinging into hers. We stagger along half a block, propping each other up as we look for the car. A dozen wobbly steps later and I see it—a silver Range Rover, sleek and important-looking, backed into a small alley, just where the corner bends.

"This can't be our Uber, Claire." *Anyone who can afford to drive this car isn't working their ass off picking up strangers from bars, driving them to homes they wish they could live in but can't yet afford.*

"We're good," she responds.

Stepping closer, Claire reaches for the chrome door handle, her purply-black fingernails glistening in the reflection of the streetlamp. I watch her hand wrap around the metal and grip, jerking it open. Peering inside, I strain my eyes to focus. I make out the silhouette of a man sitting in the driver's seat, but his face is obscured. As he turns our way, he appears vaguely familiar, but searching my alcohol-impaired brain doesn't help put a name to the face. *Why would someone I know just happen to be driving our Uber?*

As I lean in to get a better view, a shadow climbs from behind me. I twist to my right, startled by a clenching grasp coiling around my arm. A violent thrust sends me reeling backward, screams wedged in my throat. My head is slammed into the wall, shoulders scraping along the rough stone as I slide half-conscious to the ground. Startled and in pain, I pry myself upward, a catlike arch to my torso. I can make out blurry swaths of blonde hair and arms flailing in the distance. The piercing shrill of a terrified voice pleading for her life wrings at my heart and I know I need to get to her. I struggle with my own damaged body, desperately trying to move. Hunching back onto my knees, I lean forward onto my palms and then with one arm I reach out, but as I lift myself upright, cufflike fists grip my legs and wrench me back, my body twisting from side to side as I'm dragged away facedown. Even the shock of it all doesn't mask the sting—I feel every scraping slice across my tender flesh. Kicking frantically, I thrash and flail, trying to shake free; but then one last vicious swing connects, and my body slumps to the ground as if every bone has been removed, and my screams go quiet.

CHAPTER TWO

SIX HOURS LATER

My eyes whip open and I wince. I drag my weighty legs over the side of the bed; my toes feel cool against the slick wooden floor. A slaying ache radiates down my spine as I struggle to twist the lid off a water bottle, droplets spilling onto my lap. I take a hefty gulp to quench the dehydration pasting my tongue to the roof of my mouth. The rumble of a trash truck outside the window makes my head throb, and I search my battered brain for what day it is. *It's Tuesday. No, maybe Wednesday. Is it Sunday?* I reach for my cell and tap the screen, then focus on the date—*it's Friday*. I stare over at the chair next to my dresser and notice the clothes I wore yesterday folded neatly in a pile, but typically I undress in the closet and leave my garments there. *Exactly how much did I drink last night?*

Spooked by a tiny flare of anxiety rising inside me, I fight against gravity to launch myself upright, my hand whipping toward a pulsing soreness just above my ear. Squinting away the angry glare of the morning sun, I slink into the bathroom, one pain-filled step at a time. I hunch over the sink and splash water onto my face as my head searches for answers. *Why does my body ache?* Reaching for my toothbrush, I notice the translucent brown prescription bottle taunting me and pry it open. It's nearly empty—*how is that possible?* I study the contents for another few seconds, then flip one of the remaining tablets onto my shaky palm. Angst crawling through me now, I study the small peachy pill, craving its calming effect. I know this will do the trick. But then I think better of it and watch as it slips from my fingers back into the container. I quickly brush my teeth instead, but just as I slide the toothpaste into the cabinet, my reflection comes into focus and I lean in, studying my face. There's a purplish-blue lump jutting from the right side of my forehead just below my hairline, and my eyes expand. *What the hell?*

The guest bedroom upstairs is next to mine; I gently nudge the door to see if Claire is awake, anxious to find out just how hard we partied last night—surprised to discover the bed neatly made. *Did she already leave?* I continue toward the stairs and wrap my hand over the sleek wood. The downstairs hallway appears darker than usual from up here. Gripping the smooth railing, I gingerly make my way down the steps, carefully navigating each one until the landing steadies me. Every shade is pulled, which I don't remember doing; but my fatigued, unusually sore legs have neither the energy nor the desire to travel the extra distance to raise them. I teeter my way to the kitchen, fill a pot with water, and toss a scoop of organic roasted beans into the machine. The house is silent except for the faint rumble of the coffee brewing. As I pop a slice of sourdough into the toaster, my fingers discover and then probe an unexpected throb in my right arm. Looking down, I'm startled when I notice another fresh bruise, this one peeking from below my short cotton sleeve, just above the elbow. I walk over to the hall mirror, lift my top, and stare at my bare rib cage, twisting to check my back. Stripes of red snake from my stomach to my spine, and I stagger back. Dropping the soft fabric, I slide my finger along the globelike welt above my elbow, fiercely searching my memory for any sort of details.

I reach back to the last certain recollection I can piece together from the night before. I remember meeting Claire at O'Malley's at eight o'clock. We drank whiskey sours, and at some point I think we moved onto Fireball shots, which might explain the dull pain expanding behind my eye sockets. But after that, things haze up, and I lose time. I grab my phone and check the messages, then send a text.

Claire, where are you? What happened last night?

I tug the cord raising the kitchen shade, and watch the city appear. A UPS truck hovers outside, a horde of vehicles stretched along the road like schoolkids lined up, anxious for recess to begin. Several coffee-gripping pedestrians scurry to unknown destinations like any other day. I check my phone again, but Claire hasn't responded. I dial her cell and it goes straight to voicemail. I leave a message. *Claire, I need to talk to you. Call me. Please.*

A half-empty bottle of vodka glowers from across the counter, teasing me as I refill my mug with coffee. I glare back at it, pleading my case for avoiding a morning cocktail. Fortunately, the lurch of my stomach wins that battle and I grab a piece of buttered toast instead, mentally congratulating myself for the second good decision I've made so far today. Sliding into the breakfast nook near the window, I notice a small russet-gray song sparrow sitting on the ledge, clattering a soft tune, and manage a weak smile.

My cell chimes and I jolt upright, snatching the phone from

the counter, my eyes attached to the new message. It's a doctor's appointment confirmation—disappointment wraps around me and I collapse inside myself. Steadying the mug with both hands, I move toward the staircase; but just as I raise my leg to head upstairs, something grabs my attention and pulls me back down. It's my olive-green coat, slouched on the floor next to the side door. Two things about this image tug at the signals traveling to my brain—first, I could never be drunk enough to drop a six-hundred-dollar coat I couldn't afford, but purchased anyway, onto the floor. But more importantly, I never use that side of the house to enter when I come home at night. My routine is unwavering—I unlock the front door; then once inside, the first thing I do is latch the dead bolt and flip on the light. I twist my head to the left, and my eyes dart over to the light switch. My pulse accelerates when I notice that it's in the *off* position, and the dead bolt is *unlocked*.

I turn back toward the side door and take a few hesitant steps, but as I get closer, my pupils grow wide. The smooth fabric is covered in scrapes, and spatters of something so deep red that it's almost black. I rock backward, catching myself on the distressed black console. *Did I drink that much last night? Could I have spilled an entire glass of cabernet on myself? Did I even have any wine?* I step closer, and an unexpected creak from a loose floorboard makes my chest bounce. I hesitate, then move even closer. A stale stench rises toward me and I swing my hand over my mouth. I bend down and grasp the coat with two fingers, pulling it toward me. And then it hits me—*this isn't wine.* The tacky syruplike spots stick to my fingers and I release my grip, watching the material sink to the thin oak slats. Barely able to control my growing unease, I grab my cell and swipe, dialing

Claire's number one more time. I'm disappointed when I hear her recorded voice again, and end the call.

It's eight o'clock now; the firm will have just opened. I call Ronni, hoping to catch her at her desk. As usual, she answers cheerfully after the first ring.

"Good morning. Parker, Hill & Lee."

"Hey, Ronni, it's Emma."

"Morning, Emma, how can I help you?"

"I was wondering if Claire is at the office yet."

"Just made my rounds and I didn't see her. She doesn't typically arrive before ten though."

"Right. I just thought maybe she headed in early to get some work done."

"Sorry, I haven't seen her. Do you want me to have her call you when she arrives?"

"Yes, please. That would be great."

"Will do, then. Let me know if you need anything else," Ronni says.

"I will," I respond, ending the call and placing my plate and cup on the counter. I slink over to the staircase, my hands clamping the railing as I crane my damaged body up each step. I hurry to shower off the night, flinching as the hot water sprays over each raw wound. I gently towel off, then step out and twist my long brown hair into a smooth wet bun. Fumbling through my drawer, I grab a tube of tinted moisturizer, my hand jittery as I smooth two droplets onto my face, then apply a thin layer of mascara and swipe a light pink blush on my cheeks. Standing naked in front of the closet, I quickly drag my finger along the stretch of mostly muted garments, stopping on a pair of black ankle pants, a pale blue blazer, and nude flats.

As I'm wrapping the soft tweed around my body, I hear my cell chime again. Clambering over to the bed, I hectically toss the comforter, searching for the phone. I can hear it, even see its glow, *but where the hell is it?* Flinging the thick white duvet to the floor sends it flying and I scoop it up—deflated when it's not Claire on the other end. The call is from my assistant, but I have no time right now to deal with anything other than my missing friend. I hit *Decline* and instead send a quick text letting her know that I'll be in late today and to message me with any urgent matters. I slip the phone into my pocket, grab a pressed juice from the fridge, then scoop my bag to leave.

Stepping outside, I lock the door and drop the drink on Frankie's porch, then make my way to the subway. I usually walk to the office in the morning, but I need to check on Claire first. Her place is in Cambridge, so I head in the other direction toward the subway.

—✦—

Her building smells expensive. I can't really explain it, but it's as if there's a high-end staff following residents throughout the day, making sure that every speck of the glossy marble is pristine at all times. Modern chandeliers hang from towering ceilings, their flawlessly polished crystals dangling overhead. Sometimes I get the urge to spill something on purpose, just to find out if little cleaning fairies will appear out of nowhere. But this morning I'm not in a playful mood. *I need to find Claire.*

I take the elevator up and hustle down the hallway, anxious when I finally knock on her door. I stand back, hoping I'll hear the tap of her steps coming to greet me. After a long minute I ring the bell, realizing that if she's in there, I'll most likely be waking her from a drunken sleep, and she'll be irritated. *She should be at work like the rest of the world by now; I'm probably doing her a favor.* I stand outside in the hallway wishing I'd remembered to bring the spare key she gave me, *just in case.* I lean back against the wall for a few more minutes, then try again— knocking, ringing, calling. I finally concede that she isn't home and find myself praying that she is with her new beau, although I have no way of getting hold of him to check.

⸏⸏⸏

I'm on the train heading back toward the office when new messages appear on my cell, growing more frantic when none are from Claire. I respond to a couple work emails, then glance at the local news, not all that interested—until something unexpected yanks at my attention. The bold letters that stretch across the tiny screen are so alarming that they might as well be a shrill voice clamoring for my attention. *Body found at the Charles River off Memorial Drive. Authorities working to identify the victim.* Cupping my jaw, I read on in horror until the most terrifying thought of all shoots through my brain like a sparked flare. *It can't be Claire.*

CHAPTER THREE

From my office I can see the path that stretches from the hallway to the lobby, and this morning I can't peel my eyes away for more than a moment or two. I have a strict filing deadline to meet before noon, but every time I start to read a document, I stop and look again. *And then again.* I listen for her—but every voice that enters is another disappointment. The office is buzzing with staff members wrapping up projects, getting ready for the weekend—and meanwhile, tiny bits of dread keep entering my brain like little building blocks of fear. I'm about to call her again when Ronni appears.

"Sorry to interrupt, Emma, but you were asking about Claire earlier."

I stand anxiously. "Is she here?"

"No, she's not, and her ten o'clock meeting has been waiting in the lobby for nearly an hour. None of the partners are here to take her place, and I'm not sure what to do."

My chest thuds, and I look at my cell—*it's almost eleven.*

"What do I tell the client?" she asks.

"I'll make something up and ask them to reschedule."

"Thanks, Emma," Ronni says, scrambling back to her desk.

I hastily pull up the calendar on my computer and realize that this is not just any meeting Claire is missing—this is a potential client the firm has been pursuing for more than a year. Claire would never pass up an opportunity to bring in business that could elevate her chances for a promotion. Suddenly everything is coming together—the scrapes and bruises on my body, Claire not responding or showing up. *Oh God, this is worse than I thought. I have to report her missing.*

⁂

The Boston Police Department is located in a multistory brick building on the South End. When I arrive it's nearly noon, and I'm met by an energetic young officer with sandy-blond hair and a generous dousing of cologne. He escorts me to a room at the end of a wide hall, then disappears, leaving me alone in a tiny cubelike space as a slow explosion of fear blooms inside my belly. The cinder block walls are painted white; the room is featureless and empty except for a rectangular metal table with thin legs and four chairs. I sit down, flinching when one of my mysterious injuries rubs against the back of the uncomfortable chair. I fumble through my bag for a packet of Tylenol and a tube of lip balm, first popping the tablets, then slathering gloss on my chapped lips.

It's nearly noon now. I wrap my arms around each other, searching the space for a thermostat but see nothing. I slip my coat over my blazer and check my cell again, the continued absence of any messages adding to the wild thumping in my chest. Sitting here in a windowless box staring at a sad gray door while precious time ticks by feels wrong—*I should be out there looking for her.* I consider leaving, but then I notice the door handle twist. The man who enters appears to be in his mid-thirties—he has thick brown hair with a slight wave, a square jaw, and is dressed in a light blue button-up shirt tucked into slim-fitting black pants. As he steps forward, I stand.

"Good morning, I'm Detective Luke Mason. Please, have a seat," he says. I drop back into the chair, and he sits across from me.

I watch him flip the cover of his notebook and click his pen. His fingernails are clean, prompting me to remember what Nana once told me—*you can tell a lot about a man by his hands.* I need the person who is about to hear my story to pay attention and to take what I say seriously. So maybe this is a sign that he cares, at least about his hygiene.

"I see you've provided a preliminary statement about a friend of yours, someone you think has gone missing," he says, looking up at me for confirmation.

"That's right," I respond, adjusting uncomfortably in my chair.

Detective Mason skims the report. "You're referring to Claire Ryan?"

"Yes," I respond, pressing my hands into my thighs to keep them from bouncing.

"What makes you think she's missing?"

"We were together last night at a work event, and this morning I can't reach her. I have no memory of how I got home, strange welts and bruises are forming on my body, and the coat I was wearing has something on it that quite possibly could be blood." When I finish talking I notice Detective Mason's posture rise.

"Let's start from the beginning. Tell me what you do remember about last night's events."

I chew at my lip, knowing I have to be careful not to color or twist the memories I do have so that he can do his job. I grip the edge of the table and work to recall what I can. "We were at O'Malley's on Newbury celebrating some attorneys who had recently joined our firm. We spent most of the evening sitting by the bar and catching up; plenty of cocktails and shots were involved. Typically if we've had too much to drink, we'll Uber to my place and Claire will sleep over—that was the plan last night. Anyway, this morning she wasn't there, and she didn't show up to work either. Strangely, though, I don't remember arriving home myself or changing out of my clothes, but both happened because I woke up in my bed this morning like any other day."

"Maybe she went home with someone else, or went to her own place?"

"We left together, and other than a brief conversation with the bartender and our colleagues, she hadn't been talking to anyone other than me for most of the night."

"What attempts have you made to reach her?"

"I've texted her several times, left voicemails, and I went to her apartment."

"Do you have a key to her place?"

"Yes, but I was in a rush and forgot to bring it with me. I knocked for a while, though, so if she was in there, she definitely would have heard me."

"Why don't you give me her address? I'll have a well-check visit performed now," Mason says, sliding his pad toward me. I work to steady my hand as I write the address, but it's nearly impossible to control the pen in my skittish grip, and his perceptive glance tells me he notices.

"Have you talked to her parents? Maybe she had a family emergency and took off to be with them—forgot to notify you?"

"She wouldn't leave without texting me. Her father passed when she was a child, and her mother lives somewhere in South Carolina; I've never met her. But if something urgent had come up, it would have been while she was at my house and she would have left a note."

"You two are close but you've never met her mother?"

"No, I haven't. I'm a Boston native, and for years I've been paying off student loan debt—that pretty much keeps me planted in the city. She's from the South, and to my knowledge her family hasn't traveled here, at least not that I was told about."

"So, I assume you don't have any phone numbers for friends, a boyfriend maybe?"

"Detective Mason, I was with Claire last night; she was trashed. I'm one hundred percent certain she didn't pack up and take off to South Carolina in the middle of the night or leave me to hook up with a guy while she was in that condition. But the answer to your question is no, or I'd be calling them myself."

He stops writing and taps his pen on his chin, his expression unreadable. I notice a jagged scar climbing from his jaw toward his ear. He catches me looking and whips his hand over it, but then slowly lets go and we look at each other for a long moment. He breaks the silence. "How long were you at the bar last night?"

"Five hours maybe. At some point the place emptied out, and I started feeling strange, so I knew it was time to go."

"Tell me what you mean by strange."

"Well, I had plenty to drink, but this was different—it was as if my brain was crawling. I remember struggling to focus—feeling confused and dizzy."

"And how about Claire, was she also confused?"

When he says it, his tone is flippant, and I want to flip him something right back. "Yes, she was behaving strangely as well."

"Had you two smoked anything, taken a drug, anything out of the ordinary?"

"Nothing," I respond.

Detective Mason grips his chin while he studies his notes. "I need to ask you a sensitive question, Ms. Gray." The words loiter in his throat for a moment, but I know what's coming. "Do you think you might have been sexually assaulted last night?" he asks.

My eyes pool at the thought, knowing that the same question could be asked about Claire. But the answer for myself is clear. "No, I do not."

Mason continues writing and I clutch the chair handles harder, fighting the urge to bolt out of here and search for Claire myself. He finally looks up and I release my grip. "Can you tell me anything else about last night? The smallest detail could be the most critical in a case like this."

I continue to recount each moment as muddled fragments emerge from the abyss of what should be my memory. The pummeling of questions keeps coming, and with each one the room seems to shrink and the air feels thicker, until I finally get to ask my question. "Have they identified the body that was pulled out of the Charles this morning?"

Detective Mason tips back in his chair, swiping through his thick brown waves. "I can't discuss that investigation, not yet, anyway. I take it you're making a connection between that incident and your friend?"

"Can you at least tell me if the victim was female?" I ask.

Seeming to read his uneasy audience, Detective Mason stands, slipping his pen into his pocket and sliding the folder under his arm. I rise and look at him with my mouth agape. *Wait, is this it? He isn't gonna say anything else or give me any information?*

He moves closer to the door, then turns back. "I'd like to get your injuries photographed, Ms. Gray. And, since you describe feeling out of the ordinary last night, I'd like to get a blood draw as well. I'll also need a description of Claire, anything you can tell me about her habits that may help us locate her," he says.

"If you give me your cell number I can send you a recent photo of her," I say, tapping on my phone to find the images from last month's office holiday party.

"I'd appreciate that," he says, handing me his card. "Oh, and, Ms. Gray—I'm going to need to send a team to your home today to collect the coat you described, as well as print your place."

I look up. "Print my place?"

"You said you can't remember entering your home or changing out of your clothes. I need to cover all bases."

"Right … right … I get it," I respond. I tap his number into my contacts, then attach two photos and hit *send*.

"Got 'em, thank you. I have your information, so I'll be back in touch as soon as I know anything," he says with a smile, his deep dimples and light olive skin so distracting that it's almost unfair to have to look at him while I'm dealing with this nightmare. And just like that, the interview is over. I walk out the way I came in, passing below the high-arched doorway without any answers.

Climbing the steps toward my townhouse, I'm engulfed by an uneasy feeling, faced with the tragic realization that Claire would never avoid responding to me for this long. As I twist the key in the lock, my phone chimes—it's Ronni. This time I pick up.

"Emma," Ronni says, her voice cracking on my name alone.

"Sorry I had to leave without telling you. I'll explain later."

Silence fills the gap between us until I hear a faint whimper. *She's crying.* She continues, and the tremor in her voice can be heard again. "Emma, have you *heard*?"

A spark of fear detonates inside me. "Heard what?"

"The body they pulled from the Charles this morning."

"I read about it earlier," I say, terrified that the next thing to slink out of her mouth will crush all hope that Claire is okay.

"Emma, it's Dean—they just identified his body."

Her words assault me like a punch to the skull; I stumble backward, catching myself on the unsteady railing. "What do you mean, it's Dean? *What's Dean?*"

"The body in the Charles."

I plunge through the door, close it behind me, and stand motionless for several seconds. The voice on the other end fades, growing more distant as I lower my arm and the cell along with it. I relax my grip, dropping it to the floor. How am I supposed to hang on to my sanity when one person I care so much about is now gone forever, and another one is *missing*?

CHAPTER FOUR

I t's been nearly seven hours since I left the police station, and almost that long since my appetite vanished. I change into joggers and a black tee, then start a fire and skim the mail. The kettle whistles; I drop a jasmine tea bag into a red mug and fill it with boiling water. Just as the heat from the ceramic cup finds my lips, the doorbell clangs. I clench up, imagining who could be there, still convinced I didn't walk into my place alone last night. I tread lightly, then peer with one eye through the tiny pewter hole, surprised to see Detective Mason standing on the other side. There's another man with him, his head dipped down, the tip of his finger nudging his glasses back toward the bridge of his nose. I pull the door open, exposing my swollen green eyes to the two men.

The grim look on both of their faces makes my chest gallop even though I already know what's coming next. "Detective Mason, I didn't expect to see you again so soon," I say, swallowing hard.

"Sorry to drop by without notice, but we had some developments and thought it best to talk to you in person. Is this a good time?"

"Well, you can imagine the exciting night I'd be having if it weren't for you coming by," I say. "And please, call me Emma."

"This is my partner, Detective Mike Foley. Mind if we come in?" he asks.

Yes I mind. This is the part where I mourn my friend. I don't say that, of course, because another is still missing. Rather, I play nice and motion for them to come in, then close the door behind them. Detective Foley immediately begins scanning the room, a natural cop instinct, I imagine. I watch him tick on his cell, maybe typing notes to himself. His smooth bronzy-black skin creases when he gives me an obligatory smile.

They follow me into the kitchen. "Can I get you anything to drink?" I ask, and take a sip of tea.

"No, thank you, I'm good," Foley responds.

Mason also declines, shaking his head with a tight-lipped smile. "Can we sit?" he asks.

Contrived pleasantries now behind us, I gesture toward the table, watching as they each take a seat at the dining nook. I remain standing, leaning back against the quartz countertop, my palms gripping the cold stone surface.

"Emma, you said you attended the work get-together at O'Malley's last night and then went directly home—correct?" Mason asks.

"I told you, I was at the bar until sometime early morning. I remember leaving, but I don't remember arriving home."

"Do you often have gaps in your memory—especially after drinking a bit too much?" Foley asks.

"Never," I fire back. "Someone was in my house last night uninvited, and that person made sure that I wouldn't remember."

Mason types into his phone, then looks at me again. "You asked me about the body that was pulled from the Charles this morning. Why did you ask that question?"

Hearing him mention the accident reignites the ache that has been building for hours. "Because my friend just happened to be missing on the very morning that a body was found in the river. Is that a hard one for you to put together?"

Mason grins ever so slightly, as if to acknowledge my verbal punch has landed. "Right. It's just that you were the last person with Ms. Ryan before you claimed she went missing, so I was curious as to why you jumped to that conclusion."

"It wasn't a conclusion, it was fear. It doesn't much matter now anyway, does it?"

"Why do you say that?" Foley asks.

My grief-stricken vocal cords attempt to resist forming the syllables, as though refusing to let them go will somehow reverse his fate. But then I manage to say them. "Because my office called just after I left the station. I know it was Dean Wolfe that they found in the river," I say, biting at my lip, my lids filling with moisture.

Detective Foley's head lowers, his hands twisting tightly into each other as his partner continues.

"Emma, a second body was pulled from the river this afternoon." Mason watches me closely, probably concerned I didn't hear what he just said.

I heard him just fine. My body whips around until I'm facing the sink, and I clutch the edge of the counter to steady myself. "What are you saying?" I whisper.

"A positive identification hasn't been made yet, but we believe there's a good chance the second victim is Claire Ryan."

The room sways as the shock propels through me, but the emotional stream that soaked and swelled my face all day has dried up, and there are no tears left to shed. I crawl my fingers toward the half-full mug of tea, slowly gripping the handle, and fling the warm liquid into the white porcelain sink. Tipping the cup upright again, I reach for the bottle of vodka and pour.

"Is that a problem for you?" Detective Foley asks, pointing toward the nearly empty bottle.

I turn to look at the two men. "No problem at all," I say, taking a gulp.

Detective Mason chimes in. "I think what my partner is asking is if you have a problem with alcohol generally."

"Not generally," I respond, tipping the mug toward my lips again.

"I know this is a lot to take in, but we have limited time to make sure we do a thorough investigation while the evidence is undisturbed," Mason says.

"You said a positive ID hasn't been made, but you wouldn't be here if you weren't pretty sure," I say.

"The general description is consistent with our victim. There was a handbag recovered in the SUV near the body, and an ID was found inside the wallet. We haven't been able to make contact with next of kin, so a warrant has been issued for Ms. Ryan's residence—we will be collecting some personal items from her place tonight that will allow us to do a DNA comparison."

"What kind of items?"

"Things that only she would use—a toothbrush, maybe a

hairbrush, a used glass if there is one. We're also looking into dental records."

I was wrong. This new information ignites a fresh flurry of tears, and through them I begin asking my own questions. "I know Dean left the bar earlier than we did. He was headed back to the office to finish reviewing a motion. Claire and I left together hours later to meet our Uber. No one else was with us. How is it, then, that Dean and Claire ended up in an SUV alone at the river this morning?"

"As you said before, there are pieces of last night and this morning that are unclear or missing for you—maybe Claire went to meet with Mr. Wolfe. Right now neither of us really knows what happened after you left O'Malley's."

I slide my fingers into my hair and grip at my skull, a chill whipping up my spine.

Mason steps closer. "Are you in any state mentally to look at a photo?"

"Of a body?" I jerk back. "No fucking way," I say, swallowing another large gulp.

"Did Ms. Ryan have any tattoos?" Detective Foley asks.

My mind drifts back to a vivid memory of the morning Claire had called in a hysterical tizzy after a drunken night of partying had ended with a tiny red devil permanently affixed to her pelvis. "Yes," I say quietly with a tremor in my lips.

Mason gently slides his cell toward me. An enlarged but muted red image appears on the small screen. "Do you recognize this?"

Cupping my face, I release an agonizing screech—the pain so raw it's as if he cracked my chest wide-open, exposing my beating heart. "Yes," I manage to say in a gravelly whisper.

Detective Mason leans in, his hand on my shoulder. "I'm really sorry," he says.

Foley's expression is blank. "I need to make sure I have this right. You claim that you and Ms. Ryan left the bar alone last night, and you end up at home, in your own bed, without any memory of how you got there. You were not attacked sexually, and Claire ends up in the river. So that would mean that you were the last person to see her alive."

I set my mug down. "I'm covered in bruises and scrapes. The last person to see Claire and Dean alive did this to me. If you think I did anything to my friends, you're wasting your time."

"You didn't get those injuries in a struggle with Ms. Ryan, did you?" Foley asks.

I throw him an angry glance. "Excuse me?"

Mason breaks the tension. "We have a team arriving soon. They'll fingerprint your place and take some elimination prints from you. I believe a DNA sample was taken from below your fingernails while you were at the Department, so no need to repeat that test here tonight."

"Am I a *suspect?*" I ask, first looking at Mason, then back at Foley, shooting him a dagger-sharp glare.

Foley steps closer. "I'm gonna leave my card," he says, pointing the small white rectangle toward me. "Please let me know where you'll be staying, and what time works for you to come in for an interview."

"I'll be right here," I respond, swiping at my cheek with the back of my hand.

Foley appears to read my expression. "I'll call you tomorrow so we can set up a time to meet."

I nod, then slink into the living room, crumpling onto the

leather couch. Lying back, I close my eyes to the detectives and to the world—a tempest of fatigue and heartbreak whirling inside me. But just as I begin to drift off, I feel something and look up. Mason is standing over me—his big brown eyes lingering on mine. He pulls the blue throw from the edge of the couch and lays it over me. I sit upright, stunned, wondering what just happened. But then a team of officers arrives and he disappears.

The forensic team swarms in, the heavy thump of uniform boots in rhythm with a pulsing ache building inside me—the alcohol dulling my nerves just enough to keep me from climbing out of my skin. I stare into the fire, embracing the hypnotic sway of the flames as if turning my back on the intrusion will make everything I just learned go away.

CHAPTER FIVE

I f I've learned anything in my thirty-one years of life, it's this—when things get tough, slipping into the clutch of despair is nothing more than an act of futility. Doing something about it has always made more sense to me.

I hinge upright on the couch and stretch my back—*God, how I miss my bed.* I haven't found my way back to sleeping in my room—the thought of a stranger sliding me between my sheets while I was unconscious has kept me firmly planted on the downstairs sofa. The emotional tug of my new reality has become routine—the morning sunlight greeting me with an explosion of sobbing and sadness that squeezes so tight I fear my ribs will crack. This morning is no different.

I hear a tap and turn my head toward the front door. *Please tell me Detective Foley isn't on my porch this early in the morning.* He's been calling me for the follow-up interview I promised him, but I haven't been in the mindset to give another rendition of the events at O'Malley's, so I've avoided his calls. I walk over to the front window and bend the shade to one side so I can view the porch, but no one is there. I open the door—delicate flakes of snow tumbling toward a thin blanket of white powder that has coated the timeworn steps. I breathe in deeply, the fresh air numbing my lungs. Looking down, I notice a white bag resting on the mat. Scanning the street, I have neither the energy nor the desire to worry about who might have left it, so I grip the handles and take it into the kitchen. Inside, there's a small pink box with a note attached.

If not now, I don't know when warm donuts are warranted. Let me know if I can help you, kiddo. Frankie.

The tension in my shoulders melts away. There's something comforting about having a protective former Navy pilot like Frankie living next door. I really should call and thank him, but even something as mundane as good manners feels like a chore right now. I lift the lid and inhale the teasing scent of cinnamon and glaze. I tear off a piece of fried dough and drop it onto a napkin, then pour a cup of coffee and stir in vanilla creamer. I return to the living room, set down my breakfast, and switch on the TV above the fireplace. I'm about to fall back onto the couch exactly where I woke up this morning when I catch a glimpse of myself in the mirror and stop cold. I'm wearing the same clothes I had on the night Foley and Mason were here to inform me about Claire—two coffee stains settled just above my bra line. I swipe at a glob of old mascara collecting at the corner of my lid, and drag my hands through my hair—a film sticking to the tips of my fingers. I look closer—my cheekbones seem more pronounced today, and my complexion appears pallid. *I hardly recognize the girl looking back at me.*

Sinking into the soft cushion, I flip to the local news. It doesn't take long before the incident at the Charles is on display again. A reporter is perched next to the riverbank, and images of the SUV being dragged from the icy waters flash on the screen. My eyes go right to the chyron at the bottom, and my palm whips up, covering my mouth as if it's the first time I'm seeing it. *Murder at the Charles River.*

The story that's being spun makes zero sense to me. It's not just that I lost two of my best friends, but it's the maddening way the media are portraying the events, as if they know something the rest of us do not. I still can't wrap my head around how Dean and Claire ended up together that night in the first place. He left hours before us, that I'm sure of. And Claire and I were definitely together the entire night, at least until those final moments when my memory was put on pause. I'm one hundred percent certain Dean didn't call Claire up to come help him with the motion he was working on. She was a good enough lawyer, sure—meaning, she was smart and the clients loved her. But if I'm being completely real here, Dean didn't have the confidence in her that he did with some of the other associates. It defies logic that he was with her at that hour to solve a critical work issue. What brought those two together that night and how they ended up in an SUV below the Charles is a mystery that keeps me up when the rest of the world is sleeping.

I lean back and take a bite of the donut but my stomach protests. I haven't eaten much of anything since it happened, so a deep fried ball of dough bathed in sugar is definitely a bad idea. I look at my cell and notice that it's nine o'clock; that familiar tug to grab my laptop starts up again. I connect to the office server and answer a few emails, then review two contracts and sign in to check the court docket for a hearing I have scheduled next week.

But then I notice a new email addressed to all firm members. A therapist who specializes in tragic and sudden loss has been made available to staff members who may need his services for the foreseeable future—all sessions charged to Parker, Hill & Lee. Right now, I for one am teetering on the edge of sanity, so *sign me up.*

I stand and watch as a dusting of powdered sugar floats to the floor. Rather than avoiding it, I watch as it covers my bare feet, and then step aside, admiring the clear print I've left on the rug like a piece of art. *I am seriously messed up.*

It's about this time every morning when my last conversation with Dean hacks through my brain like a guillotine, keeping me on edge. I worry Dean and Claire are now dead because of what he learned; it's a thought that lurks inside me like the Ghost of Christmas Past telling me that I need to go back and retrace his actions. I lie back, wishing I could return to the office if only to gather information and for the needed distraction my colleagues can provide. The truth is, I'm not sure how I can ever go back to that place; too many good memories have morphed into wide-open wounds.

I stand and toss my throw blanket over the chair, when I notice a sliver of white jetting from below the front door. I bend down and grip the corner, pulling it through—it's an envelope. I slide my finger below the gummed adhesive and open the flap. Inside is a business card. I pull it out and my eyes widen. *Alex Ford, Silverstone Development.* I stare at the shiny black embossed lettering. *Oh God, this must be who Dean confided in about what he learned!* I continue to work, but my eyes return to the tiny card time and again, and my mind is stuck on one thought. *I need to talk to this man.*

CHAPTER SIX

A sharp *clack* snaps me awake. *Someone is here.*

Springing to my feet, I stumble over the chenille ottoman, spilling onto the thick area rug. I grope through the blackness, hands feeling blindly for a makeshift weapon. Remembering the corkscrew I left on the end table, I scurry over, quickly smoothing my hand along the distressed wooden surface, the sharp point pricking the tip of my finger. I clasp the steel handle with a savage grip and hunch upward, pressing flat against the wall. As I pause to listen, the only sound I hear is the violent thump of my heart bouncing in my chest. Dwindling embers from last night's fire provide a hint of amber light, scarcely illuminating my path. Edging along the wainscoting, my long-sleeved tee sticks to the surging wetness building with each step that I take. Slinking quietly, I wrap my body around the corner and look into the kitchen, the glow of the oven clock just enough to see that it's empty.

Creeping forward, I scan each visible inch of space until a wisp of cool air caresses my neck. *Something's open.* I peer up to the second story, but the coolness now grazes my right arm—*it's coming from down the hall.* I crane to the side and look toward the back entry, panic clutching my lungs as my eyes focus on the dusting of moonlight sneaking through the open door. I wheeze in a breath that I can't seem to catch, my bare feet cautiously inching ahead. I keep moving until I'm close enough to lunge forward, slamming the door shut. My trembling hand grapples with the lock, twisting it tightly into place.

I glance at the closet where I know protection is tucked away, but then I hear another noise—the flank of a hefty branch slapping at the window. I raise the shade and glimpse into the dark, the howl of a steady wind ticking at the glass. I pull my cell from my pocket to check the time—it's almost two o'clock in the morning. The phone judders in my hand, slipping through my fingers, but I catch it. Tightening my grip, I touch 9, 1 … and then I stop. *Think, Emma, think … could you have unlocked the door? Did the wind blow it open?* Or is it worse—an uninvited guest trespassing between these walls—*again?* I summon calmness and reason while I argue with my own thoughts until I convince myself that I am alone.

I flick the switch, and the kitchen lights flash on, bright as the afternoon sun. I pull a vitamin water from the fridge and drink in a large mouthful, swallowing hard. Detective Mason's card is on the counter; I lay my finger on it and slide it closer, staring at his number. *Do I call him this early in the morning? Will he think I'm insane? Or paranoid?* More fatigued than frightened, and now unsure of my own thoughts, I flip on all the downstairs lights except for the living area and plop back onto the couch. Sleep taunts me, threatening to show up, but it doesn't come easy.

⁂

Morning finally arrives—the sun's first rays trickling through the shades, rousing me awake. My body feels heavy and thick with fatigue. I can hardly make out the time on my cell—it's no small effort just to keep from slumping back over. I force myself up off the couch and fold the blankets for the first time in nearly two weeks. I fluff the pillows and put them in place, then stumble upstairs and into the bathroom before I can change my mind. *It's time for me to face my fears.*

My usual morning routine of coffee and emails is pushed aside for a quick shower. It feels like an epic effort, but I manage to utilize a razor and a blow-dryer—two inches of dark roots framing my ashy highlights, a reminder that even my hair has been neglected. The zipper on my black pencil skirt catches my finger, making me flinch, but I ignore the twinge of pain, tugging on a pair of suede boots and a gray wool coat, then head outside.

Just as I close the door behind me, I see Frankie in the driveway working on his car. He has lived in the brownstone next door for as long as I can remember. At seventy, he appears as fit and strong as any forty-year-old I know. After he retired from the military, he made some lucrative investments in the stock market that left him financially comfortable—although by most measures, he lives a modest existence. He's tall with thick white hair cut tight near the scalp, and begins most days with a morning run. His mind is as sharp as cut glass, and no one wants to get into a debate with this man.

When my grandparents were still here, he used to visit them on Friday nights to play cards and drink cabernet, and on occasion they would go to his house for his famous beef tips and a glass of whiskey. He and Gramps were proud Irish men and devout Catholics—they attended mass together every Sunday, after which they would eat lunch and recount stories about their time in the service. After Nana passed, I would do my best to help Gramps as he became less mobile, but I'm not sure what I would have done without Frankie during those years. And now I need him as much as they did, so I encourage him to stay on the healthy path, which includes delivering a pressed green drink to his porch most days.

"Morning, Emma," I hear him call out.

"How can you work on that car in this weather?" I ask, padding down the steps, walking toward him.

He chuckles. "Well, I can't feel my fingers under these gloves, so it's tricky. But I need to get this thing to start so I can put it in the garage. I sure could use your grandfather's advice right about now," he says.

"Me too, Frankie. Me too. Sorry I didn't get a chance to drop a juice on your porch this morning; it's been a rough week."

He smiles. "Don't you give it a second thought. Besides, today I need my big boy mug of black coffee to keep me warm out here while I try to get this ole girl running," he says, tapping on the flawless mist-blue paint. "I talked to your dad by the way; he wanted to make sure I'm checking on you. You haven't been answering your phone."

"Sorry, I haven't been in the talking mood lately."

"I getcha. Grief is a mysterious creature—it grips your chest and squeezes, and never really seems to let go."

"You do know how I feel."

"I've lived that pain for many years," he says, hunching over the engine and twisting his wrench. I worry that I may have just sparked memories of his late wife and decide to change the subject.

"Frankie, do you still have the camera on the side of your house?"

"Sure do, but it's turned off right now. Jacob's workers were setting it off all day, so he disabled it until the remodel was done. It should be up and working again soon, though. Why?"

"It's probably nothing."

"Tell me what's going on, kid."

I flick a nail between my front teeth knowing that Frankie and my dad will talk, and I don't want to upset my father. But since I've decided to stay home against the detective's advice, I want Frankie to know the truth. "Last night a sound woke me up and my back door was open. I figured it was the wind, but then ... well ... you know."

Frankie straightens upright again. "You think someone was in your house?" he asks, swiping the tool on a soiled white cloth.

"I don't know what I think anymore."

"Listen to me, Emma—you can't take chances like that; if you hear something again call me or dial 911 right away. Criminal minds don't operate the way we do—they'll destroy a life with no more thought than they'd give to blowing out a match. I realize you know how to protect yourself, your grandfather made sure of that. But if someone can get into your house while you're sleeping ... that's another animal. You need a better alarm system, and new locks."

"I'm learning that," I say, noticing the time on my cell. "I should get going. Why don't you come over Saturday night and we can start a new game of chess? Unless … you're afraid you'll be destroyed by a girl … again."

Frankie nods in agreement. "I'd love to, Emma."

I smile and blow a kiss, then lift my hand to wave good-bye. He shoots me a playful wink, then quickly buries his head back under the hood.

CHAPTER SEVEN

They're watching me.

Returning to the office for the first time, it feels oddly empty considering the slew of bodies I notice milling about. Clandestine scrutiny hovers as if I'm the only float in the loneliest parade and my co-workers can't help but gawk. Curious eyes lurk, then flit away, trying to appear preoccupied; until I pass by, that is. But then I feel them dart toward me again, riveted to my back—following each of my hesitant steps as I make my way down the marble hallway, the scent of freshly brewed coffee and muted chatter lingering behind me. I have become the human aftermath of a wreck you don't want to look at, yet can't tear your eyes away from.

Approaching Dean's office, I tug at my coat collar, my stomach contracting. I hurry by, resolved to look straight ahead; but my defiant legs first slow and then stop, and I'm unable to keep my head from turning. In an instant, the anxiety I'd fought so hard to suppress comes barreling back. I stare inside and notice Dean's files stacked in neat piles on the small round table in the corner. Photos of his wife and annual guys' trips still line the shelves. Plaques for various achievements are displayed on every wall—and there are many. His chair is swiveled toward his computer, as it usually is when he steps away. Everything about his office screams that he'll be back, but of course he won't be—not today, not ever.

I avoid the kitchen—too many memories of my morning coffee with Claire. My own office is almost exactly as I left it that night—pale gray walls lined with my diplomas from Brown and BU, my desk clear of new files, and my in-box still empty. Three new vases with freshly cut flowers are sprawled across the credenza with tiny rectangular notes perched on plastic sticks. I imagine myself catapulting each beautifully arranged cluster of roses, lilies, and gerberas through the window, desperate to make every scarring reminder of the friends I've lost disappear. But Logan Parker walks in, sliding the door shut behind him, and the thought passes. When a senior partner appears this early in the morning, you just know something else in your life is about to change.

Handsomely mature, Logan is in his early fifties now, the skin around grass-green eyes mapped with light grooves from years of summer waterskiing with his family at their place on Lake Winnipesaukee. His hair is a blend of coffee brown and streaks of sterling white, cut short with a modern flair that somehow makes him appear younger than his age. He's not the micromanaging type, although he demands high-level work. I sense he's uncomfortable today, much like most people who come in contact with me now. The sad truth is that there is no easy way to absorb this new reality, and roaming the same halls that Dean and Claire walked just a couple weeks ago only intensifies the torment.

"Emma, it's good to see you. How are you doing?" he asks.

Working behind closed doors on my first day back should have sent a message—that's what I imagined, anyway. I had hoped to be alone for a while, to have some time to adjust. But recognizing that he too lost colleagues to a tragic, watery grave—I lie. "I'm fine."

He adjusts his rectangular black-framed glasses, one hand raking through his thick hair.

"Do you mind?" he asks, pulling a chair out from under my desk.

I motion for him to take a seat as I tap rapidly on my laptop, trying to connect to the internet.

"Problem with your computer?" he asks.

"Just an issue with the server; I'll figure it out," I say, fidgeting in my chair.

Logan leans in. "Emma, stop. Take a breath," he says, typing a message on his cell. "I just sent a message to the IT Department; they'll send someone to help you."

"It'll be fine. I'll figure it out when we're done talking."

"Kyle just responded. He'll stop by in twenty minutes."

"Kyle is an accounting clerk," I say.

"One of our IT members took a leave of absence. Kyle is good with computers, and understands the system. He's splitting his time and filling the gap for now."

I lay one hand over the other on my desk and inhale slowly. "That would be great, then," I say.

"Now, I need you to be honest with me. Are you sure you're ready to come back to the office?"

"I think so. I've been working from home the past two weeks, so I'm pretty well caught up." I leave out the small detail that I've also been authoring a resignation letter and updating my résumé.

"We have lawyers willing to pitch in and help if you need it, with your guidance, of course," he says.

"I appreciate that. But being at home alone hasn't been the healthiest option either."

"I'm not here to give you advice, but we've made professional help available, someone who specializes in traumatic events. The firm has agreed to absorb the costs," he says.

"Right, Ronni gave me his number. I've made an appointment to see him."

"Good, we can all use a little help right now."

I shift the subject. "So, you said you have something to talk to me about?" I ask, a gentle prod to let him know that I'd like to move on so I can return to my pathetic state of silent suffering.

"I do." He removes his glasses again, pinching the area between his brows. I hear him breathe in and hold the gulp of air a little too long, then sigh. "It's about Claire."

"I told HR yesterday that I don't know when her services will take place. Her family hasn't contacted me," I say, dreading the image of my friend being celebrated for who she was, never to know who she could have become.

"Right ... but there's something else," he says, shifting in his seat, adjusting the sleeves of his lavender shirt.

"What is it?"

"Before the incident at the Charles, we had been dealing with a sensitive internal matter."

"Not something that involved me, I hope."

"No. It was Claire. She filed a harassment complaint not long before it happened. Given how close you two were, I'm assuming that you learned about the problem firsthand."

"This is the first I've heard of it," I say, pushing back in my seat, my chest galloping.

"We had been put in a very difficult position, Emma. Claire provided us with a written statement, emails, text messages, and a timeline of when it began. She also indicated that a client was present at a lunch meeting and witnessed the behavior toward her."

"I don't believe it. I know her too well; I would have noticed something like that."

"You think Claire would make something like this up?" Logan asks.

"Definitely not," I say.

"If her accusations had proven to be valid, we would have become the defendant in a very serious lawsuit."

Taking a moment to digest what just spilled out of Logan's mouth, I lean forward. "She never said a thing to me," I say, my hands cupped below my face to keep my jaw from unhinging.

Logan huffs out a breath and continues. "She claimed that shortly after the client observed the behavior toward her at lunch, the files she was handling for his company were transferred to another associate. She felt that the client chose to look the other way. That was the breaking point for her and why she finally came forward."

Thoughts wind and spin, every new revelation a dizzying knock to the brain like a club connecting with my skull. I lift myself up and step toward the window, mindlessly observing the city from above, the hordes of cars and people hurrying here and there, all with somewhere they need to be. I'm struck by how *ordinary* it seems—how everything appears so normal, as if all is right in the world. And I guess that's because to them, it is. That's how it goes, after all—people just go on, trudging through their lives, oblivious to everything that's gone so wrong—while others are left to grieve alone, trapped in their own suffocating bubble of agony. "Who was it?" I ask, dropping back into my chair, a simmering charge percolating inside me.

Logan's head dips.

"Who did she say did this to her?"

He pauses again, his throat visibly rising and falling before his mouth manages to form the words. But then they come, and when they do they bite, as if the words themselves have teeth. "It was Dean."

The name echoes in my brain like an orchestra playing the wrong symphony and I'm the only one hearing it. "Whoa, whoa, whoa—there's no fucking way Dean would have done something like that to anyone, let alone Claire."

"None of us wanted to believe it, Emma. But Claire kept copies of everything. I demanded that we report his behavior to the authorities and let them start an official investigation. My fear was that we had been put on notice of this behavior, and if he were to hurt someone in the future, they would look back at how we handled this matter internally."

"Dean was one of your closest friends—you can't seriously believe he would have risked everything, including his marriage, for a fling with an associate."

"Everything inside me says no, but the proof appeared to be undeniable."

I raise my hands and press them into my head as if doing so will unwind what I just heard—any meaningful response lodged in my throat.

Logan continues. "Claire didn't want to hurt Dean's career. She insisted that we not report him to the authorities, or the bar. We planned on confronting him the day of the incident. I wanted to hear his side because I had a very difficult time accepting it. But the other partners were more decisive and ready to make a move. If it proved to be true, he would have lost his job, and his reputation. Financially it would have ruined him. We can only assume he figured it out and became desperate."

My mind zips at an exhausting pace, my own questions coming faster than my brain can process them. I'm sure he's wondering how I could have missed something this tragic happening to my friend, something so hurtful that she couldn't even tell *me*. I reach down, pull the black tote to my lap, and rummage through it, digging for the only thing I know will keep my heart from rocketing out of my chest. My fingertips probe and feel, but I can't find it. Finally I open the bag wide and look inside.

"Are you okay?" Logan asks.

"No … I mean yes … I mean, I just remembered that my office pass card didn't work this morning. I need to have HR reprogram it, and I just didn't want to forget." *Probably not a good idea to tell my boss that my pacifier, the tiny silver box of Xanax I keep close at all times, is missing.* "Sorry, you were saying?" I ask, continuing my hunt, scanning the floor, feeling along my desk, sliding drawers, terrified that the anxiety climbing inside me will soon manifest into a full-blown panic meltdown. That little box is always with me, always in the same pocket of my tote. Somehow just knowing it's near me is usually enough to steady my nerves. *It's gone.* I blow out a breath and gaze back at Logan, my mind going back to the last discussion I had with Dean. "Which client did she say observed Dean's behavior?"

"She hadn't yet shared that information with us. What she told us was that if a deposition was necessary, she would fill in the details."

"None of this makes any sense to me," I say, taking one more look under my desk.

"Emma, there's more."

I jerk back, returning my focus to Logan. *Oh, for the love of God, how much more shit can he throw at me today?*

"The timing of this is gonna be less than optimal, but it's necessary. If you can handle it."

"Timing of what?"

"You were next in line to make partner. And, well, with all that has happened …"

My insides twist as if a vital organ was just yanked from my body. I've been waiting for this moment since I started with the firm seven years ago, and *now* it happens?

"I don't want it," I insist. *God, how I want it.*

"We can promote someone else; they'll take the position, no questions asked. But, Emma, it's not just that you're the most qualified, and the most deserving. To be honest, we're in a bind, and we could really use your help at the partner level. No one else will be able to jump in and carry his caseload."

"You have plenty of experienced associates, and I'm not sure my head is in the right place to take this on."

"You're right, we have seventy-two of them to be exact. But none as savvy as you, with your work ethic. So listen, if you think you have it in you, then just give it a try—and if it doesn't work out, then we'll make a change."

"I think you could do better than me right now."

"The associates respect you; they've looked to you for answers for years. Right now I worry about them, especially the few that recently joined the firm. They need someone who is familiar and equipped to handle Dean's cases right out of the gate. Say what you will about the man, but he was a talented lawyer, and he taught you to practice the same way."

My posture stiffens; I swipe the corner of my eye, pushing back a rogue sign of emotion threatening to be followed by a full watery explosion. "I need time to work on my pro bono cases; I'm not willing to give that up."

"I heard about the Kenny Lake case. You did a masterful job—that man will walk out of prison because of you."

"He'll be freed because he's innocent," I say.

"That's right. It's no secret that I wasn't a fan of using resources for the pro bono program when Dean first introduced it to the firm, but I've come around. I'd like to invest more in the project to help you succeed if you're willing to keep going with it now that Dean is gone. We can assign three associates for a certain number of hours each week, lightening your load, and that way you can focus on running your own team. Does that work?"

I glimpse down, my eyes tracing diamond shapes in the blue carpet. And then the envelope with the Silverstone business card crawls back into my brain. If I take over Dean's cases, I'll have access to everything. Maybe then I can figure out what it was he discovered before he passed. I clear my throat and straighten in my seat. "I'll do it, but I can't guarantee how long I'll stay."

"That's all we can ask. Let's meet with the other partners tomorrow morning at ten o'clock. We'll get an agreement ready and go over specifics with you then," he says, standing to leave. He pauses in the doorway and holds my gaze until his cell alerts him to a call, and he quickly slips out of sight.

After he leaves I peel a Post-it from my computer screen and linger on the words written by Claire just days before she passed. *Movies, tea and me. Saturday girls' night at my place.* Below the words are two tiny hearts. Sadness pricks at the corners of my eyes and it occurs to me that so many things I thought were true just weeks ago may not have been. First, Claire and I shared everything—but apparently, she had a secret so profound she couldn't even tell me. And maybe I didn't know Dean as well as I thought I did. Most difficult of all, though, is that my dream of becoming a partner has finally come true—but the price of success might just be murder.

CHAPTER EIGHT

I pop a Tums and lean back, the remnants of a ginger green drink slipping down my throat. I've been back to work less than a week and already the demands of my new position have left me stretched thin, my days a dizzying blend of *Emma, I need this* and *please review that.* I'm about to run a file down the hall when my cell rattles and I glance over, an unknown number flashing on the tiny screen. I let it go to voicemail, and consider ignoring it, but curiosity wins the day and I click to listen. *It's Amy Wolfe.* Dean's flawless, bougie wife. Or widow now, actually. *God, what am I saying? Those words feel so wrong.* She wants to have dinner tonight, which would be strange under any other circumstance because we've never socialized outside of an occasional work event. I don't even know her, not really. But it's different now, of course. My guess is that she's just one tiny revelation away from a straitjacket after learning what her husband's been accused of doing. I have no desire to meet anyone for dinner, or to face the one person who quite possibly may be in more pain than I am. But for whatever reason I pick up my phone and play back the voicemail for her number before sending a quick message.

Hi, Amy, of course I'll meet you for dinner. Text me with the time and place.

⚬⚬⚬

There's a stretch of road that slices through the Boston Common, sweeping into Beacon Hill—a charming neighborhood clustered with quaint little shops and restaurants, and tiny reminders of lives gone by. Narrow gaslit streets lined with brick sidewalks, and ornate iron boot scrapers perched beside random entryways— leftover relics from a time when streets were unpaved and public transportation involved horse-drawn carts. Gramps used to take me to a small bakery on Charles Street for warm blackberry scones and tea, and then we'd wander through the public garden looking for seasonal flowers—witch hazel's yellow blooms just as winter fell asleep, cherry blossoms and magnolias in the spring, and roses in the summer. Being here again brings back glimpses of those simple, ordinary days my conscious mind abandoned long ago, ones that at the time had seemed so forgettable, but are now like little treasures stored in my memory, ready to be summoned on nights like this one.

I slip the loop over the highest button on my coat, the wool tickling at my neck. My bare hands absorb the frigid air, so I cup them toward my mouth and blow as I approach the black aluminum storefront doors. Di Bucco's is a small Italian restaurant known for its paccheri with beef ragu, and freshly baked focaccia brushed with imported olive oil. Inside, a cozy warmth greets me, the sweet scent of basil and garlic wafting my way as I take in the spacious room. Italian stone walls and walnut floors are dimly illuminated by silver-scrolled chandeliers. Amy is already here, seated at a small table in the back corner. At thirty-five, she appears to be in her mid-twenties—high cheekbones and full lips accentuate her pretty face. Her vanilla-blonde blowout skims her shoulders, and a thin white gold chain with a large diamond pendant shimmers against her black, formfitting turtleneck dress.

"Amy, I hope you haven't been waiting long," I say.

She rises to embrace me. "Not at all, I just arrived a few minutes ago. Thank you for coming, Emma."

I toss my coat on a hook next to the table and slide into a chair, my legs skimming the white tablecloth. Amy sits back down, her chin settled on intertwined fingers. She takes me in, thick long lashes framing her violet-gray eyes. The waiter appears, his button-up white shirt neatly tucked into his black slacks. He introduces himself and then offers to get us some bread and olive oil.

"No, thank you," Amy says, turning toward me.

"None for me either," I say.

"Are you ready to order?" he asks.

This restaurant is familiar to me, and I'm sure to her also, since she lives nearby and suggested it. I don't even look at the menu—I order the risotto ortolano with extra asparagus and a glass of water, and Amy chooses the chicken marsala and a green salad with balsamic.

"Anything to drink?" the server asks.

Amy glances at the wine list. "A glass of Antinori Tignanello. Emma, should I get a bottle?"

I smile. "I'm good with water." My lying eyes shift toward the bar, stopping at the bottle of Ketel One. It's not hard to imagine myself swigging straight from the tubular glass, but I think better of it. I have no idea why she asked me to dinner tonight, but sensing the *what the fuck was happening with Claire and my husband* conversation might be coming, I decide that I need to stay lucid.

"I'll be right back with the wine," the server says, reaching for the menus. He removes the bread dishes and disappears through the arched hallway toward the back of the restaurant. Amy sits up straight, one hand folded over the other, her glossy almond-shaped nails painted a blushy nude, nearly identical to the shade of her knee-high suede boots.

"I'm glad you called," I lie, staring down at my fingers, the cuticles neglected and nails bare of color. In the past couple weeks I've hardly managed to dress myself, but Amy looks perfectly put together.

"It's strange how quickly it happens—the poor unfortunate widow becomes the leper. The phone stops ringing, the invitations stop coming. It's almost as if my inner circle thinks this murder thing is contagious," she says flippantly.

"I should have made an effort to see how you were doing," I say, now questioning myself for coming. *What if Amy was involved? Could she have learned of Dean's obsession, and taken both of them down in a fit of rage? Oh God, what was I thinking? Maybe I do need a drink.*

The server returns with a glass of wine and my water. Amy fidgets with her napkin, waiting for him to walk away. I slurp from the rim of the glass, choking gulps of water down my quickly drying throat, nervously waiting for her to splay her inner angst. She hesitates, then slides her hands along the table, dropping them onto her lap and looking at me with an intent eye.

"Emma, I didn't reach out to you because of loneliness—I've been by myself for years. You can imagine with Dean's work habits the days were long, and with all the failed IVF sessions—well, to be honest, life was a little tough even before my world crashed. The reason I called you was that I wanted to talk about Claire. I assume Logan spoke to you?" she asks, lifting the glass to take a sip.

So I was right … Amy knows. I contemplate my next words as if I'm giving an inaugural speech, but then I just say it. "Yes, he did," I respond.

"Is it true, then?"

The vague nature of the question catches me a little off guard, but her expression appears genuinely distressed, which begins to erase my previous concern that she may have been involved. I'm not exactly sure what Amy knows at this point, and I really don't want to volunteer any fresh dirt, so I decide it's safest to play dumb on this one.

"Is what true?" I ask.

The scarlet liquid sways in her unsteady grip. "The media is now reporting the incident at the Charles as a possible murder-suicide. You knew Claire better than anyone. Do you believe my husband developed an unhealthy fixation on her, and then took both of their lives? I mean *really?* Dean worked too many hours and gave away much of his time, but a killer? There wasn't a desperate cell in his DNA—he was one of the most confident men I'd ever met. That's why I fell in love with him."

"No, I don't," I say, fighting the emotions prickling behind my eyes.

Amy clears her throat nervously. "Could Dean have been so masterfully manipulative that neither of us knew the real him?"

The server returns with a salad, placing it in front of Amy, then slips away.

"What have the police told you?" I ask.

"They've described the actions of an unstable, desperate man; it's as if I buried a stranger." Amy leans forward, her voice low and deliberate. "The detective showed me the emails, Emma."

There it is—those fucking emails again. The second Logan told me about them, I called BS and now the knowledge of their existence is spreading like a virus. I adjust in my seat and clench my hands together, looking over at that same bottle of vodka with a pleading glare. I'd rather spread my body across the bar and pour that liquor down my throat in front of the entire restaurant than revisit what Dean's accused of doing. But I can sense her despair, and something inside me feels the need to ease her pain, or at least do what I can to placate her for now. "Dean was a brilliant lawyer, and the truth is, he would never put those desperate thoughts in writing, knowing it would leave an electronic trail. You must know that."

"I wish there was another way to interpret all of his messages to her. *Claire, I need to see you. Claire, you're ignoring me. Claire, I can't stop thinking about you. Claire, meet me for a drink. Claire, we belong together.* If I wasn't so sad, I'd be cursing the man who meant so much to me. But even knowing what I now know, *I still love him.* I think I'll always love him," she says, with a fractured voice.

"I doubt this will help much, but you should know that I was with Dean the night before they were found. I was with both of them. They barely spoke to each other," I say. *And that was the truth.*

The vitriol in her voice tells me she's unconvinced. "My husband sent fifty-nine text messages to a young pretty colleague the day before she was murdered, apparently at his hands, and

I didn't know anything was wrong with our marriage. I had to have missed every little sign."

Amy's words catch in my throat and for a second I think I might be in need of the Heimlich maneuver. The server reappears at the perfect moment, setting our entrées in front of us. *Thank you, God.* Then he removes her salad plate and slinks away.

Amy nudges at her meal without actually taking a bite. "There's something else—one additional fun fact that was unveiled this morning," she says, sipping from her wine.

I adjust in my seat, bracing for what I'm about to hear.

"Seems as though my husband used his corporate American Express card to purchase a pair of two-carat diamond earrings one week before he died."

I toss out a Hail Mary pass. "Maybe he was planning to surprise you?"

Her face twists. "I already have diamond earrings, Emma. He gave them to me for my birthday two years ago. Those were a gift for someone else," she says, tipping the goblet to her mouth, the deep red liquid rapidly disappearing from the glass. I watch as tears spill over her cheeks, onto her lips, and below her chin. I see the vulnerability in her and realize that her flawless facade has melted away, exposing who she really is—just a broken girl who loved her husband.

We sit quietly for a while, neither of us saying much, our dinners going mostly untouched. It's funny really, seeing Amy this way. I've always thought of her as this perfectly beautiful, and perhaps spoiled, upper-end girl without a worry in her little utopian existence. But seeing her now, exposed and raw, I realize how wrong I've been. Perhaps if I find the answers I've been searching for, it will somehow solve the puzzle of her marriage as well.

"Have you thought of seeing a professional? The firm hired a therapist. He's available for anyone who needs him; I'm sure that includes you."

"Therapy won't fix this," she says. "I was hoping you would tell me what you witnessed, Emma. Did you notice Dean working late while she was there? Perhaps spending a little more time in her office?"

"No, I didn't." That was also true.

Amy's face drops. "I've been a fool," she says.

"You've been a loyal wife to a man I've only ever known as incredibly thoughtful and kind. If Dean was as they are describing him now, then I've been just as foolish as you."

"We're quite the pair, aren't we?" she says, another tear tumbling down her cheek as she sips from her glass.

"Dean loved you; you have to know that."

"Hard to see it that way right now," she says, twirling at the pasta with her fork. And then she stops and looks at me with wide-open orbs so bright I can almost see through them. "Oh God, I'm so sorry—I haven't even thought to ask about you. I imagine returning to the office and walking among the ghosts will be difficult for a while," she says, pushing away her sobs.

"I went back this week, actually. And you're right, I had planned to leave. But they asked for my help, and I agreed to stay. For a while, anyway." I don't mention that I made partner, filling the vacancy that her husband left behind.

"You're a good lawyer, Emma. Dean always said that. I'm sure they need you there."

My chest crackles with remorse. Not only is Amy nothing like my perception all these years, but through her own grief and tears she finds the character to compliment my work; *she's trying to make me feel better.* "Thank you for saying that, but if I am any good at what I do, it's because of Dean."

She manages a smile.

"And what about you, what will you do now?" I ask.

She finishes her glass of wine, streaks of black smudged below her lids. "I might practice law again. I don't much care about the big house or the fancy car. If I need to sell them both, I will. But first, I'd like to figure out who I was married to," she says.

The server stops by with a water pitcher; I wave him off and request the bill.

"Can I get you some to-go boxes?" he asks, glancing at the barely touched dishes. We tell him we're done, no boxes necessary. I hand him my credit card.

"I wish we had gotten to know each other better before everything happened," I say.

"Me too," she responds.

I look at my cell and notice the time. "It's getting late; I have work to finish tonight and should probably get going. I want you to know that I'm here for you if you ever need to talk, or meet up, whatever I can do to help," I say.

"My brother is waiting for me at my house; I should get going too." Amy reaches across the table, squeezes my hand, then slowly slides her fingers back and stands. She lifts her coat from the hook and slips it on, then loops the silver chain of her quilted leather purse over her shoulder and stares down at me. "I can understand why he liked you so much," she says, lightly tapping my shoulder. And then she walks away, and it occurs to me that I feel the same way about her.

CHAPTER NINE

My appointment with the therapist arrives not a minute too soon; after meeting with Amy I'm so confused I don't even know what I believe anymore.

The steps leading up the narrow staircase are slippery. Grasping the well-worn banister to steady myself, my fingers dust away flakes of white paint chipped from the old piece of hickory. The house is a small Colonial from the early 1900s. It was renovated and split into four office spaces sometime in the past when the area was rezoned from residential to commercial. I maneuver six more steps, then reach for the door with a freshly painted white sign that reads *Mark Bradley, PhD, Psychotherapist*. I've dealt with enough loss in my life not to curl up in a ball and roll into crazyville, but lack of sleep and a missing block of time were enough to send me here for a visit. Besides, this isn't the first mind-bendy professional I've seen in my life.

The room is uncluttered and dripping with character. Ornate crown molding, beautiful white wainscoting, and restored wood-plank floors with a soft navy rug. I sit down next to the window and read from my Kindle until I hear the door squeak open, and Dr. Bradley appears. He's younger than I thought he would be, nice-looking and perfectly bald, a head made to be on display. His beard is thick and dark with a hint of auburn, neatly cut close to the skin. He's wearing jeans and a black sweater with a white collar peeking through, and he speaks in a masculine yet relaxing tone. There are some voices that just get to me, and his is one of them.

"Emma, come on in."

I remove my coat and drape it over the rack next to the door. His office is clear of personal effects with the exception of a Clemson mug, a stack of paperback novels, and a silver MacBook resting on a black desk pad. There's a large abstract painting with ribbons of blues and cream hanging between two narrow windows, and a similar piece hung above the fireplace. I settle into one of two leather chairs; a candle burns on the end table, filling the room with the calming scent of vanilla. Dr. Bradley pulls out a yellow pad and sits down across from me, flipping to a clean page.

"You hurt yourself," I say, gesturing toward a bandage on his hand.

He examines the white gauze wrapped around his palm and smiles to himself. "I've been restoring a '63 Ford Galaxie, and a socket wrench bit me."

A fond memory wiggles in, and I find it soothing. "My grandfather was an old car guy, so I get it—he had plenty of battle scars from his tools over the years."

Dr. Bradley begins asking me mundane questions about my education and medical history—we talk about my love for the city, and how he's dealing with the weather as a Boston transplant. And then he dives right in.

"So, when we spoke on the phone you told me about the nightmares; how are you doing with those?" he asks.

"When I allow myself to sleep, they come."

"Tell me about them, if you can remember."

"They're always the same … I'm running away, but I can't see who's chasing me."

"Sometimes dreams are a result of unresolved conflict in our lives, and maybe the fact that you see yourself as being chased means you need to come to terms with what happened the night your colleagues died—survivor's guilt is a common reaction to tragedy."

I let his words settle in, silently asking myself if it could be true. I'd be lying if I said I don't thank God every day for allowing me to live through that night, but it's not guilt that haunts my thoughts—anger maybe, but not guilt.

"Emma?" Dr. Bradley breaks my trance and I redirect the topic.

"I went back to work a few days ago."

He starts scribbling on his pad. When he looks up again, his expression is blank, and I can't tell if he thinks this development is good or bad.

"How did that go?"

"I wasn't sure if I could return to the place that held so many memories of my friends, but the managing partner made a plea for my help, and I agreed."

"What kind of help?"

"They asked me to take over the team of one of my dead co-workers—imagine that surprise. They even offered to make me a partner," I say, my words exiting with a hard exhale.

His hand swipes along his square jaw. I fidget in my chair, then turn my gaze toward the window. He brings me back into the discussion. "So, tell me how it's going now that you're back at the office."

My brows lift and then lower slowly. "The office crows are starved for gossip, and you can imagine how tasty I am, being the last person to have seen Claire alive," I say.

"It's natural for people to be curious, but it's probably best to avoid discussing what happened with your co-workers until you're ready," Dr. Bradley says, his face down as he writes busily on his pad, and once again, silence fills the room. When he looks up this time, he smiles in such a way that I know he's about to start digging further into what makes me tick. "Emma … let's take a step back. I'd like to visit your childhood."

I blow out a breath. "No one wants to be a guest in that place. Trust me, I was there."

"We can be shaped by our childhood experiences, and the choices we make later in life can often be traced back to the moments that impacted us most. Either repeating behaviors or rebelling against them and creating a new path."

"Well, let's put it this way—if I had any siblings, we would have been a pack of wolves roaming the streets. Thankfully for the world, I'm an only child."

"Is that really how you see yourself, Emma? As if the world is better off because your parents only had one child? Because what I see is an intelligent woman—you got through law school and passed the bar, which is quite the accomplishment. And apparently, you're good at your job. Good enough that they didn't want to see you leave."

The silence drags by as he waits to see if I'll respond, but I choose not to. Not easily discouraged, he changes tactics, trying a more direct approach. "Tell me about your parents—were you close to your mother?"

I don't like to think about her, but realizing that he's not going to back off, I force my mind to reach back, scrolling through long-forgotten memories. "For years I was raised by her, if you can call it that. Passed from sitter to sitter, and sometimes left alone for days."

His brow arches and he lays his pad down. "That must have been really hard; what would you do during those times when you were left alone?"

"I would stare at the TV when it worked, or I would sleep. I taught myself to read early so I could get lost in books—I could pretend to be someone I wasn't. We moved from one apartment to another, never staying more than a few months, and had little in the way of furniture. The electricity was off more than it was on. Sometimes I survived on canned peaches and tap water for days, and wondered if she would ever come back."

"How would you get to school?"

"I didn't attend school until I was eight, when my dad finally got custody of me."

Dr. Bradley stares out the window for a long beat. I'm sure he hears worse in his line of work, so his silence takes me aback. *I must be a bigger mess than I thought.* Finally, he speaks again, and I exhale. "Do you miss your mother?" he asks.

"She was the uterus that held me for nine months, and for that I am grateful. But it's not as if I stood in heaven with my finger on a button saying yeah, I'll take that one, the narcissist who chases losers for sport. We don't get to choose our parents, right? I don't blame her for the difficult parts of my childhood, nor do I give her props for my successes. I simply don't think of her at all."

"You have a remarkable attitude. What about your father, can you tell me about him?"

My arms stiffen and I push back in my chair; *this one's a bit more complex.* For some reason I find myself choosing my words carefully. "He's a good father; always showed me love. When my parents were married, my mother secretly opened equity lines on our home and took out credit cards, sending my father into a spiral of unimaginable debt. By the time he figured it out, he was on the verge of losing everything he worked so hard for, his world spinning off its axis. He tried to shield me from his despair—but eventually he had to walk away from her, and she won custody of me. He told me that he would pull himself out of his financial quicksand and would never stop fighting to get me back. For years she kept me away from him out of spite, always ignoring visitation orders, spending child support on the men in her life. But he never gave up."

"Do you want to talk about that?"

"No, not really."

"I'd like to revisit that relationship during our next session. Any other relatives that you were close to?"

"My father's parents were the most important people in my life. They were older when they had him, and have both now passed on."

"Sounds as if they were a very healthy influence in your life."

"They were. Gramps tutored me every weekend, so I caught up in school quickly, and he taught me that self-indulgent pity parties or the blame game neither healed nor advanced a person's place in life. Hard work and kindness would propel me forward. That's what he instilled in me."

Dr. Bradley smiles, then changes the topic. "On the phone you said that you were very close to both of the victims that brought you here today. I'd like to talk about your relationship with Mr. Wolfe, and how you're managing those feelings now."

At the mention of his name my chest bounces. He doesn't wait for an answer.

"Tell me about him."

"I'd never met a man who was so genuinely selfless. He had a way of making me feel important, as if I mattered."

"You do matter, Emma."

"Yes—well, since it happened, I've learned some things about Dean that make me question the man I thought I knew," I say, my eyes welling up.

"Sometimes people have a persona on the outside that they want us to see, but a darkness on the inside that they've worked their entire life to keep hidden."

I know this is Dr. Bradley's job—he's analyzing me, and the information available about the crime. And maybe he's right, but every word that just spilled from his mouth makes me want to rip that pen from his educated fist and jab it into his carotid simply for implying that Dean was responsible for what happened. I don't, of course—preferring to leave the way I came in, rather than in restraints. Instead, I grip the edge of the chair a little tighter and smile in acknowledgment. *Whatever it takes to get out of here.*

Dr. Bradley moves toward the window and looks out. "I'm gonna ask you a question, and if it's too difficult, you don't have to respond. How much do you remember about that night?"

My leg rattles, the heel of my boot ticking on the oak planks. "Only what I discussed with you over the phone, my brain pretty much remains a blank canvas."

Dr. Bradley seems to recognize that I've reached my limit. "Okay, we've covered enough for today, Emma. How about we meet again next week? Wednesday or Thursday at two o'clock?"

I slide my phone screen and check my calendar. "Thursday works," I say, standing and reaching for my coat. I swing my tote over my shoulder, and just as I'm about to cross from his office to the waiting room, I notice his notepad now resting on his chair. On the top, four words are written and underlined twice. *She has no memory.* I'm struck by his words—what an odd note. Obviously I can't remember everything about that night, but it's not as if I'm empty on every detail. Anxious to leave, I let the thought pass and cross through the doorway.

Dr. Bradley walks me out, and this time I grip the railing and take the steps a little slower, knowing the wet streets made their way into this corridor when I arrived.

I step out into the cool air; my foot catches a lip in the concrete and I nearly trip, but someone steadies me from behind and I spin around.

"Emma Gray?" the twenty-something asks, the shield of his helmet obscuring his face.

"Yes?" I respond.

"This is for you." He hands me an envelope before jumping back on his motorcycle and disappearing.

I tear off the corner and pull out the small note inside, my body quickly reacting with a clammy sweat. I read it twice.

Be careful who you trust.

CHAPTER TEN

Mason's call comes less than an hour after I leave Dr. Bradley's office, which is remarkable timing considering that I now have undeniable proof that someone out there *is* in fact watching me. He asked if I could come down to the Department for a formal interview, which I was under the impression we had already covered. I don't know if he needs to ask me more questions, or if he simply wants a convenient place to arrest me. So I agreed to meet but told him he would need to put on a heavy jacket and join me at one of my favorite thinking spots in the city.

North Point Park lies along the East Cambridge waterfront on the north shore of the Charles River. It's the perfect escape when you're in the mood to just sit and people-watch, or to take in the view of the Zakim Bridge—a spectacular sight even on those unpredictable, midwinter days when you don't know if you'll be treated to a refreshing cool breeze or taunted by a blistery chill.

It's unusually quiet as I sit and wait—layered up against the biting air, relieved when a ribbon of sunlight peers through the stodgy gray sky. I hear the bark of a dog in the distance and turn to my right; a couple is walking nearby, and as they pass along the bend in the path, I see him in the distance, a silky black shepherd by his side.

I want to be irritated with this guy and the accusatory tone of his questions. *But holy hell, why is this man so damn good-looking?* I haven't seen Mason dressed this casually before, and my eyes can't help but notice how nicely his jeans hug his toned thighs. I watch him adjust the dark beanie covering his chestnut hair and slide his hands into his pockets. As he approaches, the breeze carries his clean scent ahead of him, and it takes a few seconds before I'm reminded of why he's here. *He's the guy that very well might want to put me in jail—snap out of it, Emma.*

"You sure know how to pick a place to meet," he says, putting on a pair of leather gloves, the dog obediently sitting by his side.

"Who's this?" I ask, bending down. I remove a glove to pet his smooth black fur, his tail swaying back and forth as he licks my hand.

"This is Jet. Hey, boy, say hi to Emma," Mason says, watching Jet nudge his nose into my leg.

"Sit here for a while and I guarantee it'll clear your mind."

Mason smiles. "If I sit here too long, I'll crack in half. Mind if we take a walk?"

"Aw, the cold a little much for your girlish figure?" I ask playfully.

Mason arches a brow. "I mountain-bike whenever I can, and I just finished restoring an old Harley. It's the sitting outside in the frigid cold when a perfectly warm coffee shop is just down the street that I don't get."

"Well, then, I guess I should be flattered you made the sacrifice."

"I'm just looking for answers," he says.

"Okay, Detective, what is it you need from me this time?"

We walk up the path along the river. Jet scampers ahead to fetch sticks, trotting back with them dangling from his mouth. He does this nonstop, back and forth on an endless loop.

"We're having trouble getting in touch with Ms. Ryan's relatives. No one has come forward to claim her remains or to collect her possessions. Gotta say, I'm shocked at how little attention the family is paying to this young girl."

"Her family hasn't been all that present since I've known her. My impression was that their way of loving her was through sizable bank deposits."

Mason's finger massages his lower lip, and I can't help but notice that it's absent of a ring, or even a circular tan line where one may have once lived. His eyes are fixed on a tiny notepad; mine are trying not to stare at his perfectly imperfect face. He flips the pages back and forth, reading his previous entries. "You mentioned that two friends visited her shortly before the incident. When we first met, you said you didn't have any contact information for them; I'm wondering if by chance they've attempted to make contact with you since."

"No, not that I know of."

"How about their full names, can you give me those?"

"She referred to them as Jessie and Allie; I don't know their last names. We do have some mutual college friends, though; maybe they'll know more. I sent their contact info to Detective Foley."

"That's right, we've been able to interview them all; they had nothing but positive things to say about Claire. And you, by the way."

I sigh and manage a thin smile. "Actually, there's something I'd like to talk to you about as well."

"What's that?" he asks.

"I think … no, I'm almost certain that someone was in my home again while I was sleeping last week."

"Tell me you called 9 1 1?"

"No, I didn't at the time because I was confused. I woke up to a loud noise, but then I noticed that the back door was cracked open and the wind was howling. When I looked out the window I saw an overgrown branch striking the glass, so I explained it away in my head."

"And now you've changed your mind?"

"Well, there's more. Someone has been leaving me notes."

"What do you mean leaving you notes? What did they say?"

"I found an envelope under my door at home, and another was given to me by a man who was waiting for me when I left an appointment. He asked me if my name was Emma, and when I said yes, he handed it to me."

"So someone is actually searching you out. What did the notes say?"

"I brought them with me," I reply, reaching into my pocket and pulling them out.

"Can I get a description of the guy?"

"He was riding a motorcycle and had a helmet on; I didn't see his face, but he appeared to be young, maybe late twenties."

Mason reaches over and takes the card and the piece of paper from me. I watch for his reaction as he reads both, first the business card and then those five words that have haunted the past twenty-four hours of my life. His forehead creases. "Why didn't you call us immediately?"

"I don't know. The first time I was stunned, but the second time spooked me."

"This is confirmation that you're not safe and you should mix up your routine, or stay somewhere else for a while."

"The thing is, I think someone knows what happened and is trying to help me."

"I know you deal with the legal world every day and think you understand the bad side of people, but that's not in the same league as the moral rot that I encounter on a regular basis. These people don't care if you're a good person or not. Believe me, I've seen it all."

"I'm not as sheltered as you might think; I've dealt with more than my share of evil filtering through which pro bono cases to accept. But now that I know someone might be lurking, I feel better prepared to defend myself. That, and my neighbor is watching out for me."

Mason brings his arms in tight. "That's the type of confidence that gets people killed."

I don't want to be more afraid than I already am, so I don't respond. Jet runs to my side, and I drop to a knee, snuggling into his smooth fur.

Mason sighs. "I'd like to send a team in to print your place again so we can compare them to the previous prints. Then maybe we can confirm whether you're right about all of this. I can arrange to have someone outside your house tonight."

I draw in a calming breath. "Do what you need to do."

Mason clamps his hands together with his thumbs pressed below his chin and appears to consider his next words carefully.

"I don't usually do this, but I'm gonna text you my home address. If anything like this happens again, come to my condo and I'll help you find a safe place to stay."

My phone dings and I look down. His message has arrived and I save it into my contacts. "Thanks," I say, studying his address.

"I should get going, I need to get Jet back home. Foley and I have a meeting in an hour. I'll talk to him about the message you received, and I might want to get surveillance on your place. In the meantime, please contact me right away if you hear anything else. It's probably useless, but I'm gonna say it one more time—if you won't go stay with a friend or at a hotel for a while, then at least scramble your daily routine, and make sure you're aware of your surroundings," he says, reaching over and tapping my shoulder; his hand lingers for a few beats. "Promise me?" he asks.

The feeling of his touch works its way through me, the air between us charged with a hypnotic pull, and I want to return the gesture. *What am I thinking? Oh God, I can't let myself feel these things.* I snap out of it and respond, "I promise."

He smiles, his scar stretching upward, and I realize he might be the most attractive man I've ever come this close to. I watch him walk away, Jet trotting at his side; and as he leaves, a sensation curls through me that I don't quite recognize. *Could this be what it feels like?*

CHAPTER ELEVEN

I'm late!

A turbulent gust tumbles and swirls, whisking away everything in its path. I fight against the frigid wind, pushing aside strands of hair whipping at my face, small clumps sticking to my lips. Some people complain about the city—the unpleasant concoction of urban smells curdling their stomachs, or the endless noise that robs them of the peaceful moments they so badly crave. But I disagree—to me the city is imperfectly beautiful, even on days like this—no, *especially* on days like this—and I love it like a friend.

The new security clerk scrutinizes me as I wave my pass card but, apparently satisfied, motions for me to keep going. I *tap, tap, tap* on the elevator button as if the mechanics of the massive metal contraption will detect the urgency and somehow move just a little faster for me this morning. I pace nervously, the position indicator scowling at me from above—the bright light pausing at every floor. *Of course it does.* The bell finally chimes, and the doors glide open—I'm the only passenger for the ride up.

Rushing by the front desk, I notice Ronni look up, her mouth agape, eager to say something. I catch a glimpse of the new mix of lavender and silver highlights framing her thick brunette shoulder-length hair. She's wearing a black skirt suit with a bright purple blouse and large silver hoop earrings. She started at the firm last summer, and at nearly twice my age she is the most kick-ass receptionist a lawyer could ever hope for. She does more than the legal assistants in this office, and even some of the attorneys if I'm being perfectly honest. I hear her sharp Jersey accent trail off behind me.

"Emma, I confirmed your calendar," she calls out.

I wave and smile. "Thank you so much," I reply, scurrying into my office.

Empty vases line the credenza where the flowers were once displayed; the shade has been lifted, and my favorite oversized blue mug has been washed and placed on my desk. *Ronni has been here.* Tossing my bag onto the guest chair, I fumble for my charger, knowing I let the computer battery drain completely last night. In the distance, I hear the boom of Logan's voice— it's 8:55, and my hope of grabbing a morning coffee quickly dissipates. I sense someone in my doorway and fear that when I look up, Logan will be standing there. But instead, it's Kyle filling the doorframe, and I blow out a whoosh of relief. Kyle would be an intimidating figure if I didn't know him as I do. He left college for the Air Force, then finished his degree before joining our IT Department. He's in his late twenties, might actually be thirty now—tall with an athletic build, and is wearing slim-fitting khakis and a white button-up shirt that doesn't entirely hide his sleeves of tattoos. His dark hair is neatly parted, emphasizing his smoky brown eyes.

"I'm rushing to a meeting. Do you need something?" I ask, rising to my feet.

"I'm just dropping off some bills for approval," he says, laying clumps of clipped invoices over my in-box. "Another problem with your laptop?" he asks.

"No, it's fine," I say, noticing my cell flash. *I'm out of time.*

"All right, then, let me know if you need any help," Kyle says, turning to leave.

I stare back at my phone and see a new call coming in. It's from Robert Iaconis, the lawyer who runs the Innocence League. I answer.

"Hey Bobby, what's up?"

"Good morning Em. Did I catch you at a bad time?"

"Running into a meeting, as usual," I say with a light laugh.

"Right … ummm, maybe you should call me when you're done."

"It's fine, I have a couple minutes. Something I can help you with?"

"Well, I don't know how else to say this so I'm just gonna come out with it. I received a call from someone claiming to be a family member related to the Christian Wilkes case."

"Why would the victim's family call you?"

"Emma, she was threatening to file a complaint with the State Bar, accusing you of withholding evidence in the case."

I drop back into the chair, my temperature rising. "You know me better than that," I demand.

"I do, and I don't believe it. But someone is making it look bad for you. Apparently there was a prior incident that wasn't disclosed."

"It wasn't related to the charges, and I didn't learn about it until after the ruling."

"I believe you, Emma. Why don't we talk about this later, the next time you're in the office," Bobby says.

"I'll contact you later today and we can schedule a time to meet. Right now I need to get to my meeting."

"Sounds good, I'll talk to you later," he says.

After we hang up, I reel in the nausea and rage building inside me, and compose myself. I rehearse the discussion I'm about to have as I hurry down the hall. Logan is severely protective of the clients he's cultivated over the years and would explode if I were to contact Silverstone without talking to him first—about Dean's claims, that is. Standing outside his office, I see him sitting at a small round table near the window staring at his screen. I tap on the door. "Morning, Logan."

"Come in, Emma," he says, waving me over.

"Sorry I'm a few minutes late."

"You're fine. I'm sure your new position is putting a strain on your time. How's it going, by the way?"

"Well, if the earth would spin just a little slower, I might be able to catch up."

Logan smiles and gestures for me to take a seat. I slide into a chair across the table.

"So, what is it you needed to talk to me about?" he asks, still tapping on his computer.

"It's Silverstone Development."

Logan looks up and sits back. "What about them?"

I clear my throat. "I wanted to talk to you about this when I first got back, but you told me about Claire's claims and I thought it might be bad timing to add this to the pile. So I've been looking into it myself, to be sure there's something there before I bothered you."

"Looking into what?"

"The night before Dean passed, he talked to me about a problem he had uncovered while reviewing their files."

"What kind of problem?" Logan asks.

"He didn't say, but it troubled him enough to contact the client, and I know he planned on addressing it with the partners once the facts were confirmed."

"I assume we're talking about a contract he wasn't comfortable with? We both know Dean had a sharp eye for loopholes."

"Possibly. I've been combing through his cases, but what's really strange is that his notes are missing on every Silverstone file I've reviewed up to this point."

"You're not accusing one of our most important clients of doing something illegal?" he asks.

"Oh no, of course not. But you know Dean, he wouldn't just throw baseless accusations out there."

Logan curls his finger below his chin and presses in. *He's thinking.* "We have enough problems with all the media attention. The last thing I want to do is rile up a client as critical as Silverstone."

"I promise to be careful. I just want to talk to our client contact."

"Remind me who that is."

"I believe it's Alex Ford, he's one of their in-house attorneys."

Logan clasps his hands behind his neck and leans back. "If the client perceives that we're digging around, especially with our current mess, we could lose their business. And I hate to think of how that might spook other clients who get wind of it. Jobs would be lost."

"Just one meeting, and I'll be discreet."

"I can reach out to Miles Fisher myself, and get to the bottom of this."

"Let me talk to Alex first; if there's nothing to it, then we'll avoid stirring the pot."

"Fair enough. But here's the thing, Emma—if what Claire said was true, then Dean must have had a very difficult time focusing, so maybe he was wrong about his suspicions."

"I won't bill the firm for my time, or for reviewing the files for that matter. I could tell this was important to Dean, and I just want to finish whatever he started."

Logan sighs. "I'm gonna miss that man's bullshit detector."

"What do you mean?"

"Dean once stopped us from taking on a very lucrative client. And to be candid, I thought he was dead wrong, and I was all in with this one. He recognized something in our very first meeting that ticked at that part of his brain that told him something was amiss. He won the internal battle and the client went on to hire Smith & Crane. Six months later the owner was arrested for insider trading and copyright infringement, and the company collapsed inside of three weeks."

"You just made my case for seeing this through."

"You remember what I told you about the client who Claire claimed witnessed Dean's behavior toward her?"

"You're not saying it was someone from Silverstone?"

"I don't know, but you need to proceed as if it was."

"I won't overstep, but I need answers."

Logan removes his glasses and pinches between his brows. "Go ahead and schedule a meeting, but be careful. I don't want to come across as insensitive, but Silverstone is very important to the firm—and right now more than ever, we need to make the companies we represent feel as if we're on stable ground. But I want the same answers you do, so do what you need to, and let me know what you learn. And, Emma, this is sensitive, so be sure you work alone, and report only to me on this. If you need my help, I'll jump in."

When you get the answer you want, you end the conversation. "Understood," I say, rising and then quickly sliding my chair back in place.

Logan replaces his glasses and leans back. "Hey, Emma."

"Yes?"

"Dean would be proud of you."

"Thank you," I say, forcing a smile and turning to leave. I'm on the phone waiting to be connected to Alex even before I close the door to my office.

CHAPTER TWELVE

Silverstone Development is located in the financial district in a cloud-reaching high-rise on the twenty-sixth floor. Outside, the building is a mix of polished and unpolished gray granite and large black-framed glass doors stretching across the exterior. A uniformed doorman greets me, swinging open one of the hefty plates of glass, inviting me to enter. Inside, the voluminous lobby is lined with marbled travertine walls. An impressive silver chandelier looms overhead, shimmering off the midday sun.

The elevator zips me up and deposits me into the Silverstone lobby. The space is brightly lit with white walls and floor-to-ceiling windows, the clean scent of citrus and ammonia so prominent that my eyes begin to water before I take three steps onto the shiny stone floor. A beautiful man—possibly gay, because he's just that good-looking—sits behind the white quartz reception desk, tapping on a laptop. I wait for him to acknowledge me; it takes a few seconds.

"Good morning," he says.

"Hello, I'm Emma Gray—here to see Alex Ford. He's expecting me," I say, slipping a mint onto my tongue.

"Okay, hold on just a sec," he says, reverting his attention to his computer screen. He picks up the phone and punches in a number, then hangs up again when there appears to be no answer. His brows knit together with a quizzical look. "My calendar indicates that Mr. Ford is out today, and his phone went straight to voicemail. You sure you have the right day?"

"I am. I confirmed this meeting personally with Alex yesterday. Would you mind checking again?"

"Sure, of course—let me take a walk down the hall."

"I'd appreciate that," I say, grabbing my phone and calling Alex myself, but I too go straight to voicemail. Mr. Good-looking steps aside, modeling his tapered black pants and formfitting cashmere sweater as he disappears down the hall. I take a seat on the leather couch near the window and browse messages. I've responded to a handful of emails before I hear the squeak of rubber soles returning.

"Ms. Gray?"

I stand up. "Yes?"

"I'm very sorry, but there must be some mistake—I've confirmed that Mr. Ford will not be in today. Is there someone else who can help you?"

"No, I really need to speak to Alex." Before he can respond, another voice crawls from behind my neck.

"Ms. Gray?"

I pivot to see a woman that I don't recognize. She looks to be about my age, has a sharp auburn bob, and is wearing a black cap-sleeve dress with blush-colored pumps.

"Yes?"

"I'm Kristie—Mr. Fisher's assistant. Would you mind coming with me?"

Miles Fisher is the current owner of Silverstone Development, having inherited the business from his late father. I've met with him many times over the years while working on Silverstone matters, but it's been a long while since I've had any personal interaction with him.

"Of course," I say.

She escorts me down the hall, and we enter a large corner office beaming with natural sunlight. The wall on the left displays his impressive credentials—a pair of diplomas—one, a bachelor's degree from Syracuse; the other, an MBA from Columbia. To the right is a wall covered in framed photos of several projects in various stages of development, presumably built by Silverstone. A golf bag is propped in the far corner, and a bottle of seltzer water sits on a black desk pad. Miles Fisher enters the room dressed in a slimming navy suit and a white shirt unbuttoned at the neck. His caramel hair is tightly cut, complemented by a neatly trimmed goatee.

"Emma, it's been a long time," he says in an enthusiastic tone, extending his hand.

Confused, I return his gesture. *Why am I standing in the owner's office when Alex is clearly expecting me?* "It's good to see you, Miles."

"I understand you're here to see Alex."

"That's right. We have a meeting scheduled for this after-noon," I respond.

"Can I ask what the meeting is about?"

"I'm trying to catch up on a project Alex and Dean Wolfe had been working on. Today we had planned on going over some of the open contracts and lease agreements he had pulled together for us." It's not exactly a lie—there's at least a small grain of truth buried in that statement. But there's no need in alerting Miles at this point—at least not until I have a better idea of what's going on. What I really need is to confront Alex about what he and Dean were digging into, and that means getting out of this discussion without raising any red flags.

"Excuse me for a second, Emma," Miles says, typing a message into his cell, then watching the screen. When he raises his head back up, I don't know what I'm looking at, but it's some-thing—*concern perhaps?*

"Emma, I asked Kristie to bring you back here because I have some news that I wanted to deliver to you personally. Why don't we take a seat?"

I move to the table in the corner of the room and slip into a large black chair. Something about his demeanor tells me I'm not going like what I'm about to hear.

Miles sits across from me, his hands folded. "Emma, Alex no longer works for Silverstone; he gave notice yesterday, effective immediately."

I slip from the smooth leather, catching myself by the palm of my hand, pushing back into the chair. "Excuse me?"

"He had a family emergency, that's all I can tell you."

"I don't understand—I just spoke with him yesterday. Where is he?"

"I can't discuss employee information, but I'm more than familiar with the work your firm is doing on our behalf, and I can review those documents with you."

"Of course you can—I mean, you're right, but Alex and I were preparing to discuss some specific matters he had been working on with Dean Wolfe. You're aware of what happened, I take it?"

"Yes. We learned like most others, by hearing it on the news. Such a tragedy. I can't begin to express how sorry I am."

I adjust in my seat. "It's been an unimaginable loss to me personally, and to the firm generally."

Miles removes his glasses, rubs his eyes, then sits back. "Tell me how I can help you, Emma."

Tell him how he can help me? How is this man not getting how strange this all seems? I consider how much to share, deciding to keep it simple. "Dean and Alex had apparently been looking into a problem they discovered while working together, and that issue remains unresolved. I'd like to discuss this with Alex personally."

"What kind of problem are we talking about?"

"That's just it, Miles, I'm not exactly sure. Now that Dean is gone, I need Alex to fill me in."

He taps his phone. "Sorry, I should take this." He stands and walks to his desk, talking quietly. *I want to swipe that damn phone from his hand so I can figure out what's really going on here.*

A moment later he returns and sits down again. "I'm sorry, but I have something urgent I need to deal with, and I have a conference call coming up shortly. I'd like to dig into Alex's files so that this meeting can be more productive. Would it be okay with you if I take some time next week to do that, and then I'll arrange to meet with you at your office?"

"No … I mean yes, of course."

"Good, I'll ask Kristie to make arrangements." Miles gets up, slides his chair back in, and smiles thoughtfully.

"Sure … right, that'll be perfect," I say, lifting myself from the chair with a wild pang of unease. "I can show myself out," I say, turning toward the door.

"Oh, Emma?"

I look back. "Yes?"

"If a fund has been set up for the families of Dean and Claire, please have your office reach out. We would be happy to contribute."

I stare back at him with a weedy smile. "I'll pass that message along, thank you," I say, wetness pooling below my sweater.

Before I finish speaking, he's already plugged in his earbuds and resumed barking into the phone, apparently having forgotten all about me. I turn and make my way out of his office and down the hall. The receptionist tells me to have a great afternoon, and I tell him to do the same before retreating into the elevator.

Miles's words creep through me as I burst through the glass doors. Leaning into the side of the building, I breathe in a lungful of fresh air and look up toward the sinking daylight, an uncomfortable twist in my gut. This development is so bizarre that the only way I can make sense of it is that either Miles isn't telling me everything, or Alex didn't want to meet with me. But why would he change his mind in less than twenty-four hours without telling me? Maybe he *is* the person who witnessed Dean's behavior toward Claire at lunch, and now he's feeling guilty for not speaking up. Could he be so shaken by what happened that he wants to distance himself from this place altogether? *Or is it worse?*

CHAPTER THIRTEEN

A steady but muffled pulse of music emanates from the other side of the door. The soothing melody is familiar, and I find myself trying to figure out what song is playing while I wait patiently on the porch, gripping a bag in one hand. I shift the canvas tote to the other arm and try again, rapping my knuckles on one of the large black doors, a little harder this time, but again, no one answers. Looking down at my watch, I notice that seven minutes have passed and I begin to wonder if I have the wrong night. I tap one more time and then twist at the knob, surprised when the heavy wood swings inward. Right away I recognize Taylor Swift's "long story short," and I feel like I could be standing in my own home. I hum the lyrics under my breath and step inside. "Amy? I'm here," I call out.

The music volume lowers. "Sorry, Emma, I didn't hear you. I'm in the kitchen."

It occurs to me that I've never been inside Dean's house before. After one quick look around, though, it's so *him* that I half expect to see him materialize and greet me with a warm smile and a hug. The walls are a creamy white … simple and classy. I step down into an expansive living room and look to my right—a wall-mounted TV hangs over an impressive fireplace with a marble hearth. There's a taupe sectional with oversize cushions and a tufted ottoman in the center—a round table toward the back next to a row of thick-framed white French doors. The home is decorated with modern elegance, but at the same time it's homey and comfortable.

I glance down at the sofa table, lined with framed photos, and my chest heaves in rebellion—stung by the loving faces of Amy and Dean peering back at me. I guess I knew this wouldn't be easy, but being here immediately begins to stir up memories of the man I knew so well, and I ache for Amy.

I imagine the laughter erupting while Michigan football games played in here on Saturday afternoons. There's a box of poker chips and a deck of cards sitting in the middle of the table next to the back window—he offered to teach me many times, and now I regret not letting him. Then there's the empty corner where a Christmas tree might have stood, its branches stretched wide and twinkling with strands of warm white lights.

The irresistible scent of garlic and lemon butter lures me into the kitchen, where I find Amy dressed in dark jeans and a pale blue tee, busily stirring a pan. She glances toward me, offering a quick smile before turning her attention back to the stove. "It's chicken piccata. Hope you're hungry."

I drop onto one of the barstools at the island and watch as she fidgets with the burner. "You look really good, Amy. I think I'd be melting into the ground if I were you."

"Don't be fooled by my ability to put a meal together—I've been a complete disaster. In fact, I haven't even been able to do my laundry in weeks. Two days ago, I ran out of panties, and rather than washing a load, I bought thirty new pairs."

I spit out a laugh. "Well, you're resourceful, I'll give you that."

She chops asparagus into thirds, tossing them into a pan with olive oil and spices. "Do you mind handing me the Parmesan from the top shelf of the fridge?" she asks, sprinkling slivered almonds into the pan.

I find the plastic container, set it on the counter, then take a seat at the table. Place mats have been set, and candles lit. A glass filled with seltzer water and trimmed with a crescent of lime is next to each place setting. Amy serves the browned chicken breasts smothered in creamy lemon sauce, scooping vegetables on either side, and sits down across from me.

"This smells amazing," I say.

"I used to be a total wreck whenever I got near a stove, but my brother is a great chef, so he started coming by to teach me. Originally I just wanted to cook for my husband; now I do it so I can forget."

I swallow her sadness and slice through a piece of citrus-infused chicken and take a bite, then lean back. "I went to Silverstone Development today."

Amy looks up. "The client Dean was concerned about?"

"That's right. I requested a meeting with our firm's contact, and he agreed to see me today."

Amy sits up straighter. "What did he say?"

"He didn't. When I showed up at their office, I was told that Alex quit his job yesterday—the same day I confirmed the meeting with him."

Amy sets down her fork and swipes the corner of her mouth with her napkin. "Did you say his name is Alex?"

"Yeah, he's the in-house attorney at Silverstone who was apparently looking into Dean's suspicions."

Amy gets to her feet and looks down at me. "I need to show you something; I'll be right back." She disappears through the hallway, and I sit back, more curious than hungry now. When she returns, she's holding something in her hand. She sits down, then slides a piece of notepaper across the table.

"What is this?" I ask.

"It's a message that was left on our voicemail the night before Dean passed. The call came into our landline, which was already strange because we literally never use that phone. I had no idea why Dean would have given that number to anyone. He never had before."

I unfold the small note and read, my eyes widening.

Dean, this is Alex Ford. You were right, and now we need to figure out how to proceed. I'd prefer you not call me at the office. I can be reached on my cell tonight.

"Oh … my … God. Alex didn't say anything about what he learned, but this must be why he agreed to meet with me right away."

"Did they tell you how to get hold of him?" she asks.

"No, they've been unable to reach him. At least that's what they told me."

"Well, that's a load of crap. Seriously, Emma—Dean tells you he's looking into a problem that he uncovered, and now the only other person who knows what he found has gone dark? Not a chance."

"You don't think Alex had something to do with what happened at the Charles, do you?"

"How would I know? I've never met the guy. When I heard

the message I thought it was just another work call. I don't know if Alex lured Dean into a dangerous situation, or if something more sinister was going on. But someone needs to talk to this guy."

"Logan was on fire when I told him; you can imagine he lost out on my billable hours while I wasted my time going to a meeting that was never going to happen. He assured me that he'd reach out to the owner of Silverstone directly. Hopefully he'll get more out of him than I did."

"Look, I love Logan; after Dean passed he and his wife were thoughtful enough to drop meals by and offer their help. But let's face it—he's all business. You need to make sure he follows through while he's still heated. I'm giving you my professional advice here—Alex is holding the answers that could solve this case or at least provide a path to figuring it out. Find him."

"I'm just worried that the detectives are spending too much time looking in the wrong direction—at me, for example."

"And me," Amy says. "Some guy was hovering in the neighborhood the other day talking to my neighbors. I was sitting on the porch and could see the gossip-hungry nellies leering in my direction. I wanted to jump up and snip some of their stupid roses or throw an egg, but I just sat and waved like a good little widow."

Amy leans back and stares off for a second. Then she perks up and slaps the table. "I know exactly what we need." She stands and walks into the pantry and returns with a container of chocolate frosting, then grabs two spoons from the drawer. She reaches for her cell and turns on "last great american dynasty," then signals for me to stand and hands me a spoon. I rise and begin swaying, and we dance—and we keep dancing, and at least for tonight, sadness doesn't win.

PART TWO

CHAPTER FOURTEEN

Alex

A metallic *clank* reverberates inside my brain as I toss from side to side, nausea puddling in the depth of my gut. The hiss of a whistle startles me, and my eyes sweep open. I stare up for a moment, confused by the unfamiliar yellow stain hovering from the tiled ceiling. Lurching upright, I spin my head to look around, but a hand grenade explodes inside my skull, sending waves of pain pulsing down my spine. Disoriented, I try to make sense of what's happening here, but then it clicks and I gasp. My first impulse is to run. Standing is no easy task, but I manage to get to my feet, barely supported by unsteady legs. Halfway into my first step, my ankle snaps back, nearly sending me tumbling, a sting slicing at my flesh. *What the hell?* My eyes sink; I reach down and slide my fingers over smears of dirt swiped across the jeans hanging from my waist—*are these even my pants?* More alarming is the iron band protruding just below my right cuff, attached to what appears to be a chain winding across the floor. *Oh God, oh God.* I tug at the silver links, using every pound of muscle to free myself, but one leg slips, sending me to the floor with a hard thud.

Hunching to my knees, I wrench to the left. A thick film obscures my vision, but I can make out a split log wall and an oversized painting of what looks like a lake, framed in gold-painted wood. A long rectangular window sits up high, a dusting of daylight peeking through a layer of grit. Fighting the panic welling up inside, I force my lungs to expand, gulping in a breath. I get to my feet again and shuffle toward the closed door, my body once again jerked back by the thick chain snaking from my ankle. My eyes follow it to a hefty silver eyebolt fastened in the middle of the wood-plank floor. The musty scent of damp oak and cheap laundry detergent irritates my senses as I scan the cramped room. A tweed recliner sits in the far left corner, a basket filled with books and magazines resting beside it. Straight ahead is an alcove with a freestanding sink, and a toilet, exposed hinges where a door probably once hung. Finding my voice, I call out.

"*Hello!*" Remaining motionless, I listen for a response, but none comes. Growing more wary, I try one more time.

"*Who's out there?*"

Again, nothing but an unsettling silence. The steel leash is about ten feet long, affording just enough leeway to reach the small cubby serving as a bathroom. Dragging it behind me, I twist one of the sink handles, thankful when cool water pours out. I splash some on my face, then hinge upward to look into the mirror, noticing the top right corner is cracked off. The pale image reflecting back at me is not one I recognize—wings of matted brown hair sweeping wildly, the whites of my eyes striped red. A coarse shadow has sprouted in place of my typical clean shave.

A faint sound jolts my head to the right, and I notice the knob slowly rotating. The door swings inward, and an unfamiliar figure steps into the room. I instinctively move backward but the chain yanks my leg and I nearly trip again. It's a tall man, nearly the same height as me. He's wearing jeans and a black jacket over a form-fitted tee, a dark cap and a mask concealing his face. I pull away as far as my constraints will allow, maximizing the distance between us. "Who are you?"

"Sit," the figure commands, walking toward the side of the bed. He places a tray with a plate of scrambled eggs, a slice of toast, and a cup of what appears to be tea on the side table next to the glass lamp. I rotate to my right, tracking his movements.

"Where the hell am I?" I howl, trying to feign more courage than I feel.

The man pulls back his shirt, exposing the handle of a revolver tucked into his pants. "I said sit down."

He removes the weapon, an audible click as he cocks the hammer. He doesn't say another word, but the point is made. This time I obey, inching backward toward the twin bed, my bare feet cold and sore. My brain still foggy, I ease down onto the rumpled blue-and-white quilt without taking my eyes off the weapon. The light from the window is directly behind him, so I can scarcely make out his silhouette even at this close distance. Only his eyes and mouth are visible from behind the mask.

"I need you to understand the rules here," he says, reaching for a folded chair and dropping it open. He takes a seat and if not for the material obscuring his face, we'd be eye to eye. "If you try to touch me, I'll eliminate any chance you have of leaving this place alive. If you attempt to remove my face covering, there will be no reason for me to protect you. Nod if you understand me."

I raise, then lower my head, my right leg bouncing in sync with the beats in my chest.

"You are fifty miles from the next house on this mountain, so don't bother screaming. If you try to escape, I'll bolt you to that twin bed and you'll be spending the rest of your days here in your own waste. Are we clear on the basics?" the stranger asks.

I claw at my scalp, the lines in my forehead constricting together.

"I asked you if we're clear," he says, more firmly this time.

"What do you want from me?" I demand.

"Answer my question!"

"Yes, I get it," I say.

He tips back until his shoulders are pressed against the wall. "Good. Now, I'd like you to pay close attention to what I'm about to say. Messages were sent from your iPhone to your superiors at Silverstone resigning from your position effective immediately, due to a family emergency. Additional messages were sent to friends and family members with plausible stories to keep them from questioning your whereabouts. It was then turned off before you began your journey here; no one will be missing you, and your phone can't be tracked using cell towers," he says, unzipping his jacket before continuing. "As for why you're here—you will serve a purpose, which will become clear in time. As long as this mask stays secure, and you don't try to escape, you will go home when your job is done. For now, I've tried to make you as comfortable as possible, and I'll keep you safe unless you make a foolish move."

"*Oh my God, what's happening ...?*" I murmur to myself, standing to pace, but the shackles follow me, and their weight is too heavy to fight against.

"I see you found the toilet; there's a stack of towels on the floor to clean yourself up," he says. "You should eat something."

"I can't, I feel sick."

"For the past few days, you've been given something to help you sleep. It'll make its way through your system soon. There's some ginger in that tea. That'll help," he says. He reaches down, pulls on the chain to confirm that it's still firmly fastened, then turns to leave.

"Wait," I say, and he pivots back. "Why are my feet bleeding?"

"You tried to run when I pulled you from my vehicle; the gravel chewed you up pretty good before I got to you," he says. And then he turns again and I watch in horror as the door shuts, followed by the sound of a latch snapping into place and the click of a key securing a lock. I fall back on the bed, my watery eyes aching.

I'm just about to drift off when the grind of an engine fires outside. Leaping back up, I lose my balance and drop to the floor. The crunch of tires rolling through gravel is loud at first, then softens, and I realize that my captor is leaving. Crawling back toward the window, I try to look outside, but it's beyond my reach, and too high. Spotting the eyebolt, I lunge forward, stretching and tugging with every muscle in my body, but it won't budge. Sitting up against the chair, I search the room for a way out. I squint beneath the bed and scoot closer, lifting the mattress to reveal an old frame made of rusty springs. Tugging, I try to pry one loose, but I'm too weak. And then I hear something else, a noise coming from inside. Sliding back, I lean against the bed, listening. The sound of water rushing through pipes is unmistakable, and I know what that means.

Someone else is here.

CHAPTER FIFTEEN

Emma

Sometimes you need to turn to a professional for help. *Even if that person happens to be a criminal.* It's been almost three weeks and the answers I've been seeking have been trumped by a new question—*where the hell is Alex Ford, and what does he know?*

We depart South Station right on time. The murmur of passengers chatting softly and ticking away on keyboards reverberates through the cabin, blended with the tranquil sway of the vessel gliding along the steel tracks. But all I hear is the silence of the obstinate file staring back at me from my laptop—clinging to its secrets, a mystery to be unraveled.

For weeks I'd spent countless hours at the office reading through Dean's work, sometimes nights too, scouring every page that had passed through his talented legal mind—my attention planted squarely on Silverstone. The electronic files were perfectly organized, but he had a habit of keeping a skeleton hard copy—typed pages fastened old-school style with tiny brass clips for each client, with the exception of one. *This one.* I needed to know everything he knew, but as of now I have nothing more than tiny clues like splashes of color on an indiscernible canvas, a picture he never had the chance to complete. Normally I'd ask the associate working on the file to fill me in, but this client had been assigned to Claire.

I reflect on my last conversation with Dean and swallow a pang of regret, wishing I'd pressed him harder to tell me what he found. I may never know what happened at the Charles that night, but for some reason I'm driven to finish what he had started, as though it might bring some kind of closure to the abrupt and violent way his life came to an end.

Adjusting in my seat, I snap my computer shut and lean back, resting my head and closing my eyes. Just then I hear a soft melody drifting through the cabin. I look around to find the source, intrigued to discover it's coming from an elderly couple sitting a few rows ahead and facing me, nudged up against each other. The man—maybe in his eighties—is leaning into his wife, smoothing her beautiful wrinkles with the back of his hand, and quietly singing to her … *"You are my sunshine, my only sunshine …"* She stares off into the distance, as if her mind has fluttered away, but he continues to stroke her arm and comfort her. I watch and listen, absorbing the warmth of what I'm witnessing until I'm interrupted once again, this time by a voice echoing from the speaker overhead, announcing my stop.

—∞—

There's an oppressive loudness in the Massachusetts Correctional Institute, which is hard to describe to someone that's never heard it before. It squeezes at my head as soon as I pass through security—the clank of hardened steel bars ramming shut, a myriad of voices both calm and inconsolable. Desolate echoes of a forlorn world where freedom isn't on the menu. I've heard it all before, going back many years—but recognizing something is far different from getting used to it. As always, I march quickly down the wide corridor with my eyes cast straight ahead, trying to avoid seeing the abandonment of hope on the faces of other visitors. For many who call this place home, it's justified, necessary even; but for a handful of others, it's the unfortunate consequence of circumstance, and they deserve better.

Today is not a typical visit with one of my pro bono clients—no, it's not that. This time I'm in Norfolk, after a two-hour train ride that I take the second and last Wednesday of every month. I find a seat at an empty table near the window, bands of metal partially obscuring the afternoon sun. Moments later Barrett is escorted in; even in his late fifties, his tall frame appears strong and intimidating. He's wearing khaki pants and a white tee that fits snug against his thick arms. The guard exchanges a greeting with him—his charm apparently as endearing on this side of the bars as it once was on the other. Approaching the table, a grin spreads across his face as he takes a seat across from me.

"I was surprised when you asked me to add you to the visitor log today," he says.

"I needed to speak with you and couldn't wait two weeks."

"You look tired."

"I haven't been sleeping. You look good, though—have you been exercising?"

"The guys in here encourage me to push myself pretty hard—sounds strange but I feel better now than I did ten years ago."

"You sound oddly at ease with your circumstances these days."

"Still living in a cage; that never gets lost on me. But I accepted this fate long ago, and as odd as it sounds, I feel as if I'm doing some good in here; my mind's in a better place. Now, tell me what brings you out here for an unplanned visit?"

"I need your help," I say.

Barrett adjusts in his seat. "You're in trouble?"

I lace my fingers together and press beneath my chin. "I don't know ... maybe."

"I saw the news reports. Does this have something to do with the media circus around your co-workers?"

"Yes, in a way."

"You know I'd love to help you, but I don't see how I have anything to offer."

"I think you might," I say. "Before Dean died, he'd been working on a problem he uncovered with one particular client, but he didn't share the specifics. Now I've taken over his files, and I'm trying to spot the issue."

"You made partner?" Barrett asks. The corners of his mouth curl upward.

I can feel my lips quiver, yet I manage to get the words out. "Yes. But it's only because I replaced Dean; you remember meeting him, don't you?"

Barrett sighs and leans back. "I do. The reports made this thing look pretty bad for Mr. Wolfe—perhaps your mentor wasn't the man you thought he was."

"You of all people know you can't believe everything you read."

"Oh, I do. Now, let me see if I have this right—you think I'll be able to help identify a possible crime, because of my past?"

"Something like that, yes."

Barrett swipes his hands on his thighs toward his knees, then rests his elbows on the table. "How much do you know?"

"Not much. The client is a commercial real estate developer—we handle their contracts, leases, things like that. The last time Dean and I spoke he mentioned that he identified some inconsistencies that were troubling, and that if his suspicions proved to be correct, we would have a much larger problem on our hands."

"Have you been through the files?"

"Yep, but nothing seems out of the ordinary. I was hoping you might be able to identify something I'm missing, or at least point me in the right direction."

"I can't look at your files, you know that."

"Right—but you can tell me what to look for, and I can relay what I see."

"I'll help if I can. But I imagine there had to be other attorneys working on the files?"

"Besides Dean, the only other attorney working on these cases was Claire."

"Hold on, Emma—are you trying to say that what happened to your colleagues had something to do with what Dean uncovered? Is that what you think?"

My eyes water and I can't seem to choke out an answer.

Barrett leans in closer. "You need to go to the FBI, Emma."

"*You're* telling *me* to go to the FBI?"

"They were able to catch me, and I was pretty damn good. I could pretend to be angry and cheated—believe me, I can play that game all day long. But we both know that what happened to me was deserved, and I'm paying the price."

"Your sentence wasn't fair."

Barrett lifts his thumb and index finger, smoothing them along his chin. "My advice would be to stay in your lane and let the Feds deal with it."

I talk just above a whisper. "The same people who believe Dean murdered Claire and then took his own life?"

"Maybe that's exactly what happened."

My praying hands rest below my chin as I consider what he's saying, because he's right. But why would Dean give up everything for a girl who would never have given up anything for him. "I know you're right, but it doesn't sound like the Dean I know."

"Talk to the person at Silverstone, find out if he was able to substantiate what was discovered."

"I tried. I confirmed a meeting with him, but when I arrived at his office, I was told he had quit his job without any notice and couldn't be reached."

"Christ, kid, you need to share this with the people who can take action."

"That's just it, I don't have any proof of what Dean shared with me; I don't even know what he found at this point."

"I told you how I feel. But if you're hard-pressed to dig in, then without knowing specifics, this is where I'd start. Verify the legitimacy of Silverstone's vendors, look into the entities on the other side of the contracts you're working on. Look for names that are similar—even one letter that may differ from one name to another. It's gonna be tedious work, and you may even need a forensic accountant to sort through it. But if Dean was able to identify the problem, then you can too."

I sit back hard and billow out a breath. "I'll do whatever it takes. This man gave so much of his time to help others. He was a good man, and he left a heartbroken widow behind. I'm just so fucking furious."

"I don't like any of this ... not one bit," Barrett says.

"Me either," I say, looking up at the wall clock and noticing the time. "It's getting late. The last train leaves in forty-five minutes. I should get going."

Barrett sighs, then reaches his hand across the table, tapping mine. "Do what I told you; be as detailed as you can. When you come back, tell me what you find."

I smile. "I promise."

"It's good to see you, kid."

"You too. I love you, *Dad*."

"Love you back, Emma girl."

CHAPTER SIXTEEN

Visiting Dad is never easy, but it's next-level hard when the purpose is to learn how to think like a felon. I'm not sure I'll ever be able to completely forgive him; he's a good man who did a bad thing, and he'll never get a pass for that. But after seeing him, it's always the same—I can't wait until the day I can hug him any time I want. For now, though, I pull the crank on the mental Ferris wheel that never seems to stop spinning, and allow myself to breathe.

I begin my illuminating ritual, moving from lamp to lamp—then stream music at a mellow volume and fill a pot with water. Tossing in some coarse salt, I twist the knob and watch as the flame on the gas stove top sparks. While I wait for the water to boil, I wash the vegetables and begin a rough chop, then grab a pan, drizzle olive oil, and wait for just the right moment to drop onions into the hot skillet.

The water rolls and the heat rises. But just as I'm about to slip the pasta into the pot, I hear something—a faint rustling coming from somewhere outside. My chest squeezes as I spin the knobs to the off position. I kill the music and peer through the kitchen window toward Frankie's house, barely a glimmer of moonlight cutting through the blackness. There's movement—at least I think there is. *But he wouldn't be on the side yard this time of night.* I creep from one window to the next, listening and peering outside while checking the latches to make certain they're secure.

It happens again—a flicker in the dark—but the night air is stagnant, and this time I'm sure that what I'm seeing can't be explained away by a flurry of wind. *Someone is out there.* Tension crawls, and my heart pinballs against my rib cage. I rush to the hall closet, crouch down, and tug at the concealed door in the back—the one Gramps built decades ago to hide his valuables. Reaching inside, I feel the cold steel of his revolver. I retrieve it along with a small ammo bag, and slide a round into each of the six chambers. Slipping outside, I lock the door behind me, careful to not make a sound. I slink around the house, my bare feet finding every sharp rock and twig, wincing in silence, wishing I had taken the extra few seconds to pull on my UGG boots. A figure passes by the side window and I stifle a gasp, relieved when he doesn't hear me and spin around. As I come up behind him, my thumb instinctively pulls back the hammer, cocking the weapon. The unmistakable *click* that follows says more than words possibly could, and he immediately freezes, his hands rising slowly over his head.

"Take off your hood, and turn toward me," I say.

The figure steps back and I follow, pressing the muzzle into his back, surprised by the tone of the words that come next.

"Please! I'm not here to hurt you."

It's a female voice, warbling with fear. She obeys and turns to face me, dropping the hood.

I release the hammer but keep it pointed at her belly. "Who are you?"

"My name is Jessie—I'm a friend of Claire's. You may have heard her refer to me as J-Jess," she stutters, her voice unsteady.

I lower the gun, my other hand clenching at my chest. "Why were you sneaking around my house?"

"I knocked, but you didn't answer. The lights were on, so I tried to peek in, just to see if you might be home."

"You're lucky my neighbor didn't spot you—he would have pulled the trigger first, then asked why you're here."

"I didn't mean to scare you."

I release the long-overdue breath I'd been holding. "Tell me what you're doing here."

"I heard you were close to Claire, and didn't know who else to go to," she says. Her body sags, and her expression wilts.

"If it's about the murder, you should be talking to the police."

"I tried—that was my first stop when I arrived, but because I'm not related or next of kin, they wouldn't give me any information," she says, shivering, with her arms clenched over her chest.

"The detectives on the case have been looking for you."

"No one was willing to talk to me today. Besides, the media is portraying this thing as if it's a murder-suicide, case closed. I'm guessing the investigation isn't going anywhere fast."

Winter's chill bites at the balls of my feet and I adjust uncomfortably. "If you have information that points in another direction you need to share it with them."

"Claire was preoccupied while I was staying with her, and I worry now that I missed something."

"Why would you think that?"

"I overheard a couple conversations between her and Dean.

One time she called him while we were in an Uber. From what I could hear, it seemed as though they were clashing on how to handle a client—she didn't appear nervous or upset. The second time we were at the sushi bar when he called and they talked for a few minutes about another work issue. Maybe she was covering for his behavior so I wouldn't react or get involved, I'm not sure. But now I want to know for myself what exactly happened that night."

I'd like to tell this trespasser to leave, but the points she's making have been filtering through my brain as well. I ask her how she knew where I lived, and she goes on to tell me that while visiting with Claire, they passed by my place on their way home from dinner one night, and Claire pointed it out. *Plausible I suppose.*

I hear the squeal of hinges and see Frankie coming from his backyard, moving slowly toward us. "You okay out here, Emma?" he asks, lowering his Remington as he approaches, a shotgun I know he can operate with deadly precision. He looks over at the stranger, and then back at me, assessing the perceived threat.

"I'm fine," I reply, my fingers still gripping my own weapon.

He peers down at my hand and sees what I'm holding. "Okay, then—I'm awake in case you need anything." His eyes narrow and he shoots a menacing look at Jessie, then turns to leave.

"Thanks, Frankie," I call out, watching him retreat back into his house. As soon as the door clacks shut his silhouette appears in the kitchen window, observing from a distance. Now, I'm not one to toss caution to the wind lightly—but it's clear she's been sufficiently spooked by Frankie, so I do something I normally wouldn't. "It's cold out here; come inside," I say. I motion for her to walk ahead of me, then steer her toward the kitchen. She takes a seat at the nook, her dark brown hair pulled into a side braid. I feel the weight of her stare, hazel green eyes flecked with gold, following each step I take. She's wearing dark skinny jeans with black lace-up boots, a white tee, and a black puffer coat. She's pretty, maybe a couple years younger than me. I'm wary, but also curious. Losing Claire seems to have affected her deeply and she's not handling it well—*I understand her pain.*

"Have you lived here long?" she asks.

"It was my grandparents' home, so I've been around here since I was a child. I moved in three years ago."

She continues to watch me as I finish making dinner, but my appetite has waned. "Are you hungry?" I ask.

"I'm not, but thank you."

I put the pasta in storage containers, then fill the teakettle and light the burner. "Would you like a cup?"

"Do you have anything stronger?" she asks, her fingers twisting at the silver necklace dangling from her neck. When she stops, I notice a pendant with the cursive letter *J* hanging from the chain, and I feel a small measure of relief—thinking there's a good chance she is who she claims to be.

I snap off the stove and slide back the kettle, then grab two tumblers and pour us a generous splash of vodka. I top them off with seltzer, dropping a wedge of lime in each. She wraps her long fingers around the glass and takes a slow sip—her eyes momentarily closing in what appears to be an expression of relief.

Scooping my glass, I guide her into the living room, offering her the choice of seats. She selects the couch, so I drop into the chair facing her. An awkward silence drags by while she stares into the fire and thaws.

"What is it you want from me?" I ask.

"I'm here for answers, and I think you can help me," she says. "If you can't, I'll find them another way."

"Why me? You could have gone to one of her other friends—at least Allie lives in your area."

"Who's Allie?"

"She's one of Claire's closest childhood friends; I just assumed you two would know each other. You're from her hometown, aren't you?"

"I was born in South Carolina not far from where she grew up. My family still lives there. I moved to North Carolina to attend UNC, and ended up staying. Claire told me that she worked at a small photography studio where we used to get our Christmas photos done every year. Small world, right?"

"How did you meet Claire, then?"

"I was working at a tech company near campus, and she ended up doing an internship in our legal department during her first summer break from law school. We met and became instant friends."

"Have you talked to her mother?"

"Her *mom*? You're kidding, right?" She lets the thought dangle, as though I should know what that means. She doesn't elaborate, so I let it go. She stands and walks to the window, her finger gently swiping along the wood molding. When she turns back her expression is pleading. "I didn't know Dean Wolfe, but I knew Claire very well, just like you did. If someone in a position of power had been harassing her, don't you think she would have told one of us?"

I curl my legs onto the couch and sit up straight. "Claire wanted to move up in our firm. Surely you knew how ambitious she was. Maybe in the beginning she was flattered, and then things took a bad turn and she wasn't ready to talk about it."

Jessie coils her hands together and raises them pointing two fingers below her chin. "I want to get a look at Claire's personal laptop—there might be evidence of what was happening between them. Then we'll have the answers we need, and we can both move on with our lives."

I stand to toss another log into the fire, then turn back and fix my eyes on hers. "The detective told me they served a search warrant on her place to obtain personal items so they could do DNA comparisons; her toothbrush, hair brush, those types of things. I'm not sure if they also took her computer as evidence, but I imagine they did."

"How can you be so sure? I'm guessing they took her work laptop, but have you ever seen her personal computer? The cover is so bedazzled I practically needed sunglasses to pick it up. She used it to visit social websites and kept local restaurant apps on it. While I was there, she asked me to order dinner, so she gave me the password, and I remembered it."

"I don't think removing potential evidence sounds like the sanest of ideas."

"Well, if we go there and it's still in her apartment, then apparently the warrant didn't cover it. So technically, it wouldn't be evidence then—right?"

There's no playbook for how to digest what I'm hearing right now. I certainly can't flick a switch and know this girl's true intentions. I'd like to think I have a keen eye for BS—God knows I've had to wade through enough of it while doing my volunteer work. But something about her rings true, and I keep listening—clinging to a sliver of hope that's started to bloom, knowing that someone else is searching for the truth. But then the more measured, practical side of my brain asserts itself. "I'm still not comfortable with the idea of going to her apartment after all that's happened."

"What do *you* think happened? You must have a theory at least," she asks.

I grab a throw and wrap myself in it. It's difficult to explain why I do what I do next, but I begin to share what I know, how Dean confided in me that night. I tell her what I've learned about Silverstone, but I also tell her just how bad the evidence is against Dean. I sugarcoat nothing. When I stop talking, she clears her throat, then drops down to the couch and leans back, burrowing into the overstuffed cushions.

"You think someone may have targeted Dean because of what he uncovered, and Claire was just the cover story—don't you?"

"Honestly, I'm just not sure. My first thought was that Dean was too secure to behave the way they're portraying him—but Claire wouldn't lie about something as serious as a sexual harassment claim, so that doesn't make sense either."

"Then help me. I can recover deleted emails and follow her digital path. It's what I do, and I'm very good at it."

Nervous fingers tap against my thigh as I think about what she's asking. Claire gave me a key—so sure, I might be able to get into her place and find this mysterious electronic device—providing it's still *her* apartment, and the locks haven't been changed. But the thought of entering a home that Claire left without realizing what waited for her that night makes my stomach spin.

Jessie appears to sense my growing apprehension and chimes in. "Listen, I'm staying at an Airbnb nearby. I can go with you, or you can go alone—but please, let's do this," she says.

A thought sparks, and I lean in on my elbows. "How do I know *you* didn't have something to do with what happened?"

"Oh, that's rich. How do I know *you* weren't involved?" she fires back.

My right brow jumps as I sit straight again and pour the remainder of my cocktail down my throat. "I need some time to think; leave me your number and I'll get in contact with you."

She slides a card out of her phone case and lays it on the ottoman. "My cell is on the back. I'll let myself out," she says.

We don't say another word, both of us a little edgy. I close the door behind her and return Gramps' gun to the closet. As I step back into the living room, a new thought plays in my head. *If Jessie can recover messages between Dean and Claire, maybe something in them will hint at what Dean was digging into at Silverstone since they were both working on those files.* I lean into the wall next to the bay window and look down at the chessboard, my finger sliding along the smooth wood. When I look up again, I stare over at the sofa table where I know the key to Claire's apartment is tucked away, arguing with myself about how crazy an idea this is. But then I gently tip over the white king, watching the glossy marble figurine drop to its side, resigned to the fact that this argument with myself is not one I can win. I walk over, slide the drawer open, and remove the key.

`

CHAPTER SEVENTEEN

My thighs burn, ribbons of sweat slipping down my cheeks as I pound out six miles. For just a few fleeting seconds I imagine what life would be like if I kept running—if I were to leave the city I love so much and start somewhere new. But then I think about Dad and Frankie and trade those thoughts for a stop at the local market, grabbing a spinach salad and a water.

I drag myself through the city, now eight pounds lighter—the murdered friends diet is remarkably effective. Forty-five minutes later I reach the bottom step of my townhome and lug myself up to the door. My key is inches away from the brass lock when a voice booms from behind me, bouncing from one eardrum to the other.

"Hello, Emma."

I cast my eyes down at the berry-red welcome mat I bought for the holidays but forgot to put away, still resting on the weathered brick porch. My body rotates slowly to the right until our eyes connect.

Oh, this just keeps getting better. Finally a man who makes me want to take a second look and he just might think that I'm a criminal. "Detective Mason—you startled me."

"Sorry about that. I was wondering if we could talk for a few minutes?"

I circle back, my hand juddering as I dig the tip of the metal into the lock, rotating the knob and nudging the door inward. He follows me in, not waiting for a response. His demeanor is thoughtful, but I'm guessing he's not here out of the kindness of his heart.

"The first time I was here I was so preoccupied I didn't get the chance to take it in. It really is quite the place for a young lawyer," he says, removing his coat, a long-sleeved black button-up taut against his athletic arms.

"Don't be too impressed—I didn't earn it. It belonged to my grandfather. He passed away three years ago. I had no idea he would leave his home to me."

"That's a very generous gift."

"It was. It's also a lot to keep up with, taxes and maintenance, I mean. But he was very important to me, and somehow, living here makes me feel close to him. To both of my grandparents actually."

"Sounds like you had a tight bond."

"I spent a lot of time here growing up. After my Nana passed and Gramps was alone, I'd bring him lunch several days a week, and he would read to me. During the winter months we would sit over there by the fireplace, and he would bring fictional worlds to life with his gentle voice and love for the magic of books. He was more interesting to me than anyone my age could ever be."

"You play?" he asks, pointing to the chessboard sitting on a side table by the bay window.

I walk over and slide my finger along the glossy walnut. "This was his ... he played with our neighbor every week. He taught me the game—when they played, I would study his moves," I say with a heavy sigh.

"Are you close with all of your family?"

I consider how to respond; the truth is my typical go-to, but it's almost never the sexy answer. "My mom is no longer in my life—unfortunately, she loved every bottle of wine she met more than her daughter, and had a sharp eye for unemployed narcissists with powerful left hooks. She followed one particularly heinous loser to the West Coast, never to be seen again. And my dad—well, that would be a long story. I don't have any siblings. How about you? Close to your family?"

"I am," he says. "My folks are in North Attleboro, so I see them pretty often. I have a sister who's married and living in Seekonk with her husband and two daughters, and twin brothers not far from the city. My first nephew will arrive this summer."

"I'm not prone to envy, but that sounds really nice."

The corner of his mouth turns up. "Oh, we're plenty screwed up, believe me. One of my brothers is so broken that we constantly have to find new ways of jigsawing him back together. But we support each other no matter what."

This man is obviously good-looking, but why does he have to be so damn likable? The way he takes pride in his not-so-perfect family hits home, but full lips and a ridiculously sexy physique aren't going to get me to let my guard down. "Can I get you something to drink?" I ask, tossing logs into the fireplace; I strike a match and watch as the flame grows.

"I'm okay for now, but we do need to talk," he says, motioning for me to sit.

His tone has transformed into something more serious and suddenly he's not as likable as he was a moment ago. Anxiety bristles inside me, slowly inching its way from the soles of my feet to the nape of my neck. I crumble into the chair across from him. He adjusts in his seat and I know that whatever's on his mind can't be good for me.

"Emma, we show that a Beretta nine-millimeter is registered to you. Is that right?" he asks. The question hits me like knuckles to the jaw.

"Yes—I've had it for five, no … six years last month."

"Do you mind if I take a look at it?"

"Why would you need to see it?"

"Can you take me to see the firearm?" he asks again.

"I guess this is the point where I ask you if you have a warrant?"

"I'm afraid I do," he says, standing.

I stare at him for a few seconds. The invasion of my privacy feels so wrong, and yet I understand this part of his job well. I lift myself up, heat branching through each of my limbs. Mason follows me upstairs where I open the hall closet, revealing a small gun safe tucked away on the top shelf next to a stack of sheets and blankets. I punch in the combination on the keypad, grip the lever, and pull it open. Inside are two folders with personal documents and a plastic box. I instinctively snap a photo of the contents with my cell to preserve what we're looking at; Detective Mason stands to my side and takes his own photos. I remove the weapon and watch as he snaps latex gloves over his hands.

"Do you mind?" he asks, his hands open, palms up.

"I want to know what this is about," I insist.

"Please," he says, stretching his arm out toward me.

A zip of tension spirals up my spine as I reluctantly hand over the case. Detective Mason moves toward the built-in cabinet next to my bedroom, and gently places the container on the shelf. His thumb flips the latch, raising the cover. He lifts my gun from the foam padding, releasing the magazine. He cycles the slide, confirming that the chamber is empty, then sets the gun down. He then proceeds to empty the magazine, and I count as nine shells drop into his hand. My brain struggles to process what I'm seeing. *It's a twelve-round magazine.*

"Can I ask what made you get a gun?"

"I come from a family of gun owners. My grandfather worried that when he was gone I would be alone in the city and vulnerable, so he made sure I was trained properly and visited the range with me regularly. It's a safety thing."

"Do you make it a practice of keeping your weapon loaded?"

"No, usually I store it in the safe empty, along with a couple full mags. But I went shooting with my neighbor a few months back, and he told me about an assault that occurred not far from here a week earlier. So I left the mag in the last time I put it away."

"Let's go back downstairs and talk," he says.

I follow him, taking slow deliberate steps as I process what's happening. We enter the kitchen and sit down, right where we sat several weeks ago with Detective Foley. Mason glances down at the gun case, then back up at me. "Both Dean and Claire died from wounds caused by a nine-millimeter."

Stifling a scream, I stand up. Feeling unsteady, I take a step toward the counter, but don't make it before the painful reality is absorbed and my body slinks to the floor.

Detective Mason leaps from his seat and drops to a knee. He extends his hand toward mine, his brown eyes appearing more comforting than accusatory. I take his hand and lift myself up. After the initial shock of learning how they died wears off, my mind connects the dots about the caliber of the weapon that was used. "You think it was my gun that was used to kill them—that's what this is about, isn't it?"

"I'm conducting an investigation, Emma."

"You know that a nine-millimeter is the most common handgun caliber in use today."

"That's true. But three bullets were used in the crime. And as it happens, there are three rounds missing from your gun."

"I don't want this to come across as disrespectful, and I'm not trying to get arrested for speaking up loud and hard—but if you're trying to link me to the deaths of two of the most important people in my life, you're out of your fucking mind."

"My job is to follow every lead, and every piece of evidence. I don't know if you did anything wrong, but if you didn't, someone may be trying to make it appear like you did. You have no alibi for the hours from midnight until nine the next morning."

"Because I was *sleeping*. Can you honestly imagine me hatching some sadistic plan that would involve kidnapping two grown-ass adults, shooting them both, and dumping them in the Charles?"

"You don't even remember how you got home that night—how can you be sure of what you've blocked from your memory?" He slides the gun case into a plastic bag and seals it, then removes his gloves. "I'm gonna need to take your gun in for ballistic testing."

"Go for it," I say, my eyes welling up.

"So here's the thing—either you're involved in what happened to your friend, or you're in danger. I don't know which it is yet, but I'll find out," he says.

Typically I'm unflappable, but these revelations whip up and grip my throat. "Are we done here?" I choke out.

"For now we are," he says, his right hand raking through his hair.

I move toward the door, letting him walk ahead of me. As he reaches for the pewter handle, he hesitates and turns back my way, his gaze hanging on mine a little longer than it should. It occurs to me that this must be that elusive feeling everyone searches for, and here I am feeling it for the one guy who might put me in jail. *I wonder if he feels it too.* For some reason I want to convince him—the man, not the detective—that he can believe me, *that he can trust me.* But his job is to not trust me until he can. So I walk him out. "Watch your hand on the railing outside. It's the original wrought iron, so it's unsteady."

Mason looks back and smiles.

"I often wonder about all the people it has seen come and go through the years, imagining the stories it could tell," I say.

"If only it could share those stories," he says, his fingers gently skimming the rusted edge of the deep black metal.

"If only," I respond. The clean scent of his cologne lingers as he descends, his hand fanning a placid wave. He ambles away with deliberate steps until his shadow blends into the asphalt and I manage to peel my eyes away from him.

Back inside I sink into the couch, the warmth of the fire touching my skin. My pupils jig and jag with the sway of each tiny flame and I can feel my cheeks flush, wondering to myself why I didn't tell him that there's a *second* gun hidden in the house—Grandpa's Smith & Wesson.

CHAPTER EIGHTEEN

Meandering through Cambridge used to make me happy. Claire and I would often spend time here after class—mornings at the museum, afternoons at the theater; boutiques for her, cultural restaurants for me. We would walk through the city observing the rowing teams at Harvard in the spring, and eat warm pretzels while watching the Regatta, a two-day sailing race in October. Claire had always wanted to live here, and last fall it finally happened.

She found her place in Kendall Square on a rainy Saturday afternoon, a renovated building conveniently located near the best cafés, bars, and trendy restaurants. She called me from the empty apartment and gave me a FaceTime tour. It was perfectly *Claire* in every way, with its massive windows and soaring ceilings. Not long before the accident I visited her new place. I had brought her a basket that I spent weeks putting together—two large white mugs and a bag of organic coffee, a citrus candle, a cream cashmere throw, and a small turquoise box with a silver beaded bracelet that I knew she had her eye on.

As I approach the building, my chest thuds in an unnatural rhythm. After Jessie showed up the other night, her request stirred in my brain until I finally decided her intentions were good, and that I could trust her. *God, I hope I'm right.* I rationalized that if the apartment was not taped off as a crime scene, and if my key still worked, I would look for the laptop. I know how critical the tiniest of clues are in a case, and if there's even the slimmest of chances that some uncovered secret is lying in that little device, I want to find it.

I take the elevator to the fifth floor. The doors slide open and I make my way down the familiar hallway, my skin clammy. From here I can see apartment 506—the mere sight of the door so haunting that I nearly change my mind. But that silent voice inside that demands answers propels me forward.

The dreaded yellow tape that I expected to encounter is not there, so I work to settle my nerves and move closer. The key slides effortlessly into the lock, and with one short twist the door snaps open almost as if it's inviting me in. I'm not sure why, but I guess I'm a little surprised to see that the furniture is all still in its place. Even though I have a key, I still feel like an intruder as I close the door behind me. Almost immediately, I detect the faint scent of Claire's signature Flowerbomb perfume—and a ghostly chill tickles at my neck. The living area is just as it was the last time I was here. Clusters of candles spread throughout the room, a basket of throws, and the six new oversize white pillows she showed me during my last visit, now resting neatly on the sofa.

Everything between these walls triggers fond memories—the thick-framed gold mirror above the mantel that I helped her hang on a rainy Sunday in October, the pearl-gray sectional we picked out at West Elm last fall, and the four stacked photos of the coastline off Maine that I gave her for Christmas.

I maneuver around the ottoman into the kitchen. A wineglass sits on the counter, half-filled with clear liquid, a bottle of Rombauer chardonnay nearby. I choke back a stream of sadness as I imagine her getting ready for our night out, sipping as she danced to our favorite country music tunes, just as we both did so many times back in our college days—blissfully unaware that she would never do this again.

I look around, trying to decide where to start. *Where in the hell does one begin to look for a rhinestone-laden computer in a spotless apartment that Claire left without knowing it would be her last time?* I walk to the end of the hall to her room. The bed is beautifully made with a fluffy white duvet and pale blue pillows. Stepping into the walk-in closet, I see her clothes lined up neatly on hangers, and an eerie feeling wrenches my insides. Resisting a powerful urge to turn and backtrack out the door, I notice the shelf overhead and see the row of dust bags covering Claire's high-end purse collection, all perfectly in place. And then I see a blue box nudged up against the last bag. There's a footstool under a row of coats. I grab it and step up, reaching for the box, and pull it down. I take it to the bed and remove the lid, but a laptop definitely does not live in this little array of treasures.

Inside is a copy of the notice showing that she passed the bar exam. There are ticket stubs from the Bieber concert we attended last fall, and a stack of random photographs. I spot one of the two of us at our law school graduation. When I lift it, something else draws my attention—a small coin purse with the initial *L* formed in silver glitter, something a child might cling on to. I smile, thinking of a young Claire flitting around in sparkles and frills. Just then a loud bang startles me. I put everything back in the box and slip it onto the shelf, then rush back into the living room. I look through the peephole and see the maintenance man wheeling a dolly down the corridor. I grab my chest and wait for my pulse to slow down. *No one is here, no one is here, no one is here. Breathe.*

I examine the room a little more carefully, but again, nothing stands out. I consider washing the used wineglass and straightening the couch, but it seems better just feeling her presence, exactly as she left it on her last night.

I'm about to give up and leave, but then I spot the basket of blankets and another memory creeps in of all the nights we huddled on the couch watching old rom-coms while eating bags of candied nuts. I reach down and grab a soft gray throw, then fall back onto the couch and wrap it around me, breathing in her scent. A tear forms and I brush it away. But then I notice something peeking from inside the basket. I stand and move closer, then drop to one knee. My fingers reach in and flip another blanket, then a second, and then I see it—a thin Dell I've never seen before tilted on its side, the edge resting on the bottom. I lift it and smooth my fingers along the edges, feeling both guilty and transfixed by the information it might hold. I fold and replace the three blankets and stack them neatly into place. I hesitate for a long while, but then I slip the laptop into my tote and dial Jessie' cell. She answers before the phone even rings.

"Hello," she says.

"Jessie, it's Emma."

I hear her sigh. "Hello, Emma."

"I was wondering if I could come see you," I say.

"More questions? Still can't decide if you can trust me?"

I interrupt. "I found it." I hear a gasp.

"Oh, thank God."

"Where can I find you?" I ask.

"I'll text you the address where I'm staying, but there's a bar at the corner, which might be better. Should we meet there?"

"Send me your address just in case, and the name of the bar. I'll head over there now."

"I'll be there," she says.

Jessie is sitting on a barstool at the end of the smooth mahogany counter when I arrive. I drop onto the stool next to her.

"How long have you been staying over here?"

"Only since the night you put a gun to the back of my head." She looks at me and realizes I'm unamused. "I've been here a few days."

A stout man with gray hair and a wide smile appears, armed with paper coasters. "What can I get you two?" he asks.

"Vodka and seltzer," I say.

Jessie chimes in. "I'll have a Blue Moon."

"You got it," he says, turning and kneeling down to the beer fridge, rising again with a bottle in his hand. He pops the cap and sets it in front of Jessie, then places a lowball next to it on the counter. He pours the vodka, then squeezes the soda gun to fill the glass, tossing in a wedge of lime.

"Here you go," he says. I smile and take a long draw.

"So, where was it?" Jessie asks.

"In the basket of throws she keeps by the sectional," I say, pulling the computer from my tote and laying it on the bar.

"That's the one," she says, sitting up just a little straighter.

I take another long sip from my glass, then pull my cell out and snap a photo of Jessie holding the computer.

"Why did you do that?" she asks.

"Well, if it turns out that you're playing me in an effort to find and destroy evidence of your own crime, then that photo is now sitting in the cloud. So if something happens to me, it will lead directly to you."

"I've already missed a week of work, I haven't slept, my head is throbbing, and my good friend was murdered. I say this with the utmost respect—drop the fuckin' attitude. *Please.*"

I smile. "Fair enough. But what makes you think you'll find anything, anyway? Don't you think most correspondence would have gone through her work email?"

"Not if the person she was communicating with wanted to keep it out of the work sphere."

"Seems like you cared an awful lot about her to go through all of this."

"I'm guessing I could say the same about you."

"I cared about them both—very much. I just want the truth to come out."

"To the truth, then," Jessie says, raising her bottle toward me.

"To the truth," I respond, clinking my glass against it.

———

It's nine o'clock when we leave the bar—Jessie walking toward her Airbnb, and me in the opposite direction toward the subway. I check my cell and see a missed message—it's from Mason.

Mason: *I got your message. I can meet you tomorrow.*

Emma: *Do you know Murphy's on Newbury?*

Mason: *Can you meet at six o'clock?*

Emma: *I'll be there.*

CHAPTER NINETEEN
Alex

Peering up at the web in the far corner of the window, a tiny creature has spun its net of sticky silk strands, intricately designing something so beautiful that the unsuspecting prey will be powerless against it. I can't help but wonder about the trap that I fell into, or the type of evil who set it. Attempting to judge time by the height of the sun, I see only the daylight and evening stars through one narrow band of dusty glass exposing me to the outside world.

The stranger holding me captive hasn't spoken in what feels like a week, although I have no real way of knowing how long I've been here. I leave the empty food tray against the wall, and several times a day the door cracks open, just wide enough to exchange it with another unpalatable meal, a cheap plastic spoon, and a paper cup filled with water. Initially I tried to use the arrival of food as a calendar, but the drugs made me sleep away large chunks of time, lasting for what seemed like days, and I quickly lost track of any meaningful measure. At first I refused to eat, fearful that with each bite I might also be swallowing more sedatives. But as one day blended into the next, I began to realize that if I was going to find a way out of this log prison, I would need my strength.

To pass the time, and in an effort to maintain a grip on my sanity, I exercise in the small area within range of my shackles. Push-ups before breakfast, planks and squats throughout the day, sit-ups after dark. I read the books that have been left for me, but I never stop thinking of a way out—terrorized by the walls closing in around me, dreading the thought that I might die right here in this dingy room before anyone realizes I'm missing.

My clothes reek of sweat and itch against my dry skin, my heels carved with cracks so deep that specks of blood lace the sheets. Playing by the rules simply to stay alive, I hold in the screams that my lungs are aching to release; but the pain and discomfort have stretched beyond my tolerance level, so when the second meal arrives, I call out. "Please, I can't wear these filthy clothes another day, and my feet are bleeding—they might be infected."

The excruciating silence that follows is the only response to my desperate pleas as the door is pulled tightly shut, and once again firmly secured.

Soaking a small towel in hot water, I gingerly dampen my raw feet, then wipe down my body—my stomach queasy as I put on the same rancid clothing. Dropping to my knees, I repeat my daily routine of feeling each floor plank, hoping against hope that one will finally break loose, and might be used as a weapon. But just like every other day, or night, or whatever moment in time I'm living through, nothing gives, and I have no way of prying them free.

Sitting back in the chair, I fish through the basket and pull out another book. I'm only one chapter into a fictional tale about a diamond collector who crashes a small plane into a remote island when I hear steps approaching. Leaping from the chair, I watch as the wedge of light beneath the door is eclipsed by movement on the other side. The knob turns and the door moves inward, the glow of a soft lamp seeping in, growing larger as it swings wide-open this time. The mysterious stranger has returned, carrying a bag. His black pants are clean, and his gray button-down shirt has a tailored-looking fit, the way expensive fabric might hang on a body. His shoes are black leather with stark white soles, not the type you would wear on a gravel road; or, for that matter, in an outdated cabin lacking the basic comforts of a real home.

"I brought you fresh clothes and some new books," the faceless man says, removing objects from the brown paper tote and laying them on the bed, the smoky scent of his cologne lingering in the room. I hide my expression, now crimson with fury at the thought that this creature might be living a privileged life, while I'm slowly going mad inside a wooden cage. "Thank you," I respond, my disgust disguised as gratitude.

The man examines the room, tugging on the eyebolt to make sure it's still secure, looking intently for the slightest sign that I might be attempting to escape. Apparently satisfied that his hostage is behaving, he moves toward the door to leave—but then stops. Turning back, he leans against the wall, ankles crossed; he adjusts the mask covering his face. "I'm sorry you're going through this—I really am. But unfortunately, we have no choice."

"What do you mean, *we* have no choice?" I ask.

Catching his mistake, he attempts to correct himself; but once spoken, the words are impossible to take back—*I know someone else has been here.*

"I meant that I have no other options; I need your help to get out of a complicated jam I find myself in."

"How can I possibly be your answer? Is it Silverstone you're after? You should know that I'm just one of many attorneys at the company, and I'm the youngest by about fifteen years—there are literally dozens of people that outrank me," I say emphatically.

"In time you'll understand," he says, uncrossing his legs and moving toward the door again.

"No, please don't leave yet—talk to me, just for a while longer," I beg. Having the enemy for a companion is better than talking to myself. I'm surprised when he stops.

"Tell me your name, or what I can call you," I urge, my instincts telling me that establishing even the slightest relationship with my captor may be my only chance at surviving this ordeal.

"Call me whatever you want," he says quietly.

"Okay, then, what do I have to do to get out of here, Mr. Whatever You Want?"

The stranger dips his head, as if to acknowledge that his prisoner deserves better. "You can call me Beau."

"Thank you, Beau," I say, carefully considering my next words, knowing how time stretches between our interactions, and even one more minute of solitude is a terrifying thought. "If you truly are sorry for what you're doing to me, then take me outside, just for a few minutes. You can cuff me, rope me to a tree, whatever you need to do. I need to breathe in some fresh air before my skull explodes."

He leans into the wall, his large hands pressing into the logs until the tips of his fingers turn white.

"Here's the thing, Beau. If you need me to be lucid for whatever fucked-up plan you've concocted, then you'll need to do something to keep me from losing my goddamn mind."

Seeming to realize that he's said too much, Beau spins around, responding as if his prisoner's voice has been put on mute. "There's a pair of socks, some antiseptic, and foot healing cream on the bed," he says, his eyes darting to the splotches of blood on the oak floor.

I shudder, moisture dampening my swollen lids. Falling back onto the chair, I peer at the brooding eyes looking back at me, hidden behind the black mask. Beau leaves without another word, yanking the door shut. Dejected, I sink to the floor, coiling into the fetal position, my cheek flat against the wooden planks, splintered from years of neglect. The weight of my reality hits me again and hopelessness sinks in, eradicating any will to move. I've nearly drifted off to sleep when I manage to open my eyes just enough to see below the chair, noticing the swivel base made of what appears to be spokes of wrought iron.

Lurching to my knees, I crawl closer. I inspect each piece of the old metal, and notice a crack where the spokes meet the circular base. Sweat first pools and then spills from my matted hairline as I wrench and tug at the rusty stand in a hushed silence. I drive my feet into the back of the chair to get more leverage, and pull with as much force as my thinning body will exude. My eyes widen as I feel it rattle, believing that with time, I may be able to pry it just hard enough to get a piece to snap off. An idea forms in my head, and for the first time in days, I allow myself something I had abandoned days ago. *Hope.*

CHAPTER TWENTY

Emma

Murphy's is wedged between the Java House and a small antique store on a quaint street lined with historic nineteenth-century brownstones that house popular restaurants and boutiques. Narrow concrete steps take you from the sidewalk down a level, obscuring the entry from the street. The only clue to its existence is a painted wooden sign hanging high above the door, suspended by chains from a flat iron bracket mounted perpendicular to the distressed brick facade. It blows gently back and forth in the breeze, making the name of the restaurant hard to miss. On a warm airy afternoon, I'll sit outside with my laptop, listening to the delicate jangle of metal links, soothed by the harmonic chime.

Inside, one wall is covered in the same red brick that makes up the exterior; the others are adorned in light wooden molding from top to bottom. The mahogany bar was recently updated with a white marble counter and black leather-back stools. On any other night the wall of accordion glass doors might be swept open, allowing laughter and conversations to spill out. But this evening the cool air has left the pub nearly empty. Two older men sit at the bar eating chowder and sipping whiskey. Another couple is enjoying burgers at a table near the window, and three college-aged men have their laptops out, occasionally gulping from mugs of beer.

Mason isn't here yet, so I visit the ladies' room, run a comb through my hair, and brush my teeth—another one of Nana's reminders stored away in my mind like a spark of wisdom that goes off at random times—*we only get one set of teeth, young lady, so take care of them.* When she left this earth she still had a beautiful smile, youthful skin, and knowledge that could have filled a thousand journals. I miss her, just like I miss Gramps, who managed to outlive the love of his life by another seventeen years. He used to tell me that loving her was his greatest gift; that he saw her in me, and knew that I too would do great things with my life. And that is how I know what real love looks like, and why I will never settle for less.

When I amble back through the hallway, Mason has arrived and is sitting at a booth near the side wall. He notices me and stands, slipping his black quilted jacket over a small hook on the wall. He's wearing faded Levi's and a dark long-sleeve crew-neck sweater. I slide into the table.

"Thanks for meeting me," I say, breathing in his woodsy scent, my chest pitter-pattering.

"It sounded important," he replies.

A thud echoes from behind the bar, and I flinch. Already on edge, I throw a look toward the server, who's busy delivering a platter of potato skins to the college kids. He sees me and gives me a sheepish grin.

"Hungry?" Mason asks.

"Not very."

"Mind if I order something? I skipped lunch, and I'm starved."

"Be my guest," I reply.

The server stops by to take our order. Mason chooses the fish and chips and a Harpoon. I change my mind and decide on a cup of soup and a vodka tonic with lime. After the man walks away, Mason leans back against the cushioned vinyl with his arms wrapped behind his head. "So, tell me, what's on your mind, Emma."

My fists squeeze, then spread wide, but just as I'm about to speak the server returns with a beer and my drink. I lift my glass and take a large swallow of cocktail courage.

"There's something I didn't tell you about that night," I finally manage.

Mason sits up straighter and sets his bottle down.

I gaze down, skimming the rim of the sleek tumbler with the tip of my finger, and then I begin to spill it all—from Dean's concerns about Silverstone, to the envelope that was left under my door, to what I've done since then to uncover the truth.

"Why didn't you tell me any of this before?"

"Because at the time I thought it was just a work-related issue. Besides, if the two things were somehow linked, I assumed the investigation would have led you to Silverstone."

"Did Dean give you any specifics?"

"No, not that night. I reached out to Alex Ford—he's one of the attorneys who worked for Silverstone—and it was his name that was left under my door. I asked for a meeting so we could continue the conversation Dean started with him before his death."

"What did he have to say?" Mason asks.

"When I showed up for the meeting, I was told that he had resigned the day prior—the same day that we scheduled the meeting. Judging by our conversation, there is literally no chance that he had planned to quit later that day."

"Have you considered that Dean may have been wrong? You said it yourself, he never got the chance to verify his concerns."

"That's why I went to meet with the client myself."

The server stops by with the deep-fried cod and my soup. "Can I get you some malt vinegar or tartar sauce?"

"Vinegar would be great," Mason says, turning back toward me.

I lean into the table and lower my voice. "Both Dean and Claire were working on the Silverstone cases, and now both end up dead after one, maybe both of them really, notices an irregularity that bothered Dean enough to investigate? And now their contact leaves the company without any notice—surely you must see the possible connection?"

Mason finishes his beer. "How much do you know about the company?"

"It's family owned—very successful. They have several offices on the East Coast and continue to expand. Our firm has represented them for decades."

Mason sprinkles the burgundy liquid over his battered fish, then takes a bite. He lifts his napkin and smooths it across his face. "There's something I wanted to share with you too," he says, with a somber tone.

"Answers I hope."

"We got the DNA results back on the items recovered from Claire's apartment. They were a match with our female victim."

I stare toward the window as my eyes fill. I've believed for a while that this confirmation would be coming, but hearing it is altogether different. I swipe at my cheek and work to compose myself, unsure if I should add to the pile and tell him about Jessie. Something about my demeanor must clue him in to my dilemma because he props himself on his elbows and gives me his undivided attention. "Is there anything else you haven't told me?"

I don't want to lie, but I choose to keep it vague. "One of Claire's friends showed up at my house the other night."

"Who?"

"Jessie—I told you about her. She visited Claire shortly before the incident."

"You said you didn't know her. Why would she go to you?"

I don't tell him everything, like how she asked for my help, and how I gave it to her. I keep it simple. "She's struggling; and evidently when she stopped at the Department, she was shut down since she wasn't related to the victims. I was next on her list; she came to me for answers, but I didn't have any to give. I think she's worried that I might be in danger as well."

"Why would she think that?"

"Because she saw the way Claire was behaving while she was visiting, and what seemed innocuous at the time, now has her concerned."

"Her behavior could have been consistent with workplace harassment."

"Maybe," I say, stirring my soup mindlessly.

"This is why we need to interview Jessie in person," he says.

I look at my nearly empty glass and consider ordering

another, the guilt of breaking Jessie's confidence heavy on my mind. What was I supposed to do? I don't want anyone else to get hurt.

Mason pushes his plate toward the edge of the table and grabs on to his beer with both hands. "I need to ask you a very personal question, and I don't want you to be offended by it. Can I do that?" Mason asks.

I press back in my seat and brace myself.

"Were you and Dean involved? Intimately, I mean."

My head dips and I focus on the small drops of water pooling near the bottom of my glass. So many emotions stir—anger at the thought that he would suspect I could cheat with another woman's husband, acceptance because I know this is his job, and most of all sadness because the answer to that question is complicated. "No, we were not. I did care about him, though, and maybe in another life if we had both been single, perhaps there could have been something. But Dean loved his wife, and I loved that about him. We had a very close friendship, but our relationship had always been professional."

Mason watches me, searching my expression, as though deciding whether to believe me. "How well do you know Amy Wolfe?"

"Why would you ask that?"

"You of all people know how this works. We have to investigate everyone, especially those closest to the victims."

Mason's words surprise me, but of course he's right. "Amy loved her husband very much, and he loved her right back."

He smiles at the sentiment, then stretches back and puffs out a breath. I'm about to stand when I see his hand reach out, startled when he lays it on top of mine. I pull back. His mocha eyes stare and I'm not sure what I see in them. *Concern?* The moment passes, but the idea of his touch lingers.

He gets to his feet and looks down at me. "Why don't we get out of here? I can give you a ride home," he says, reaching over to snatch the check. He pays the bill, and I thank him, then grab my coat; he takes his off the hook and follows me out the door.

Twenty-five minutes later I'm standing in front of my door and Mason is on the step below me, insisting that he check my place. I disable the alarm and let him walk in first. While he begins his hunt for possible intruders, I start my nightly ritual of turning on every light in the house, with the exception of the living room.

I hear the pad of his slow steps shifting from room to room on the second floor—closets sliding, hinges curling open, the twist of window locks being secured. The thump of his shoes on the staircase lets me know he's coming downstairs, and I wish I could think of a reason to have him stay a little longer.

"Everything looks good upstairs. I'll just check the back door and closets; then I'll let you get some rest," Mason says, ambling down the hallway.

"Do you want something to drink? Coffee?"

"Thanks, but Jet is probably wondering where I am," he says.

"Oh God, right, you have to get home to him. Sorry I kept you out so late."

Mason smiles. "My neighbor walks him for me—and spoils him with bones she gets from the butcher. He'll be fine. He does get a little pissy when I'm not there to watch the Sox with him, though."

"Jet and I have something in common," I say, leaning against the wall with my legs crossed.

"A Sox fan?"

"I'm a Boston girl. I kinda have to be, right?"

Mason comes so close that I can smell the mint on his breath, then leans in and whispers, "Lock the door behind me so I know you're safe." He walks outside and pulls the door closed behind him. I secure the lock and set the alarm, then stand in my entry biting at my knuckle. *Why is it that every time this guy walks away from me, I wish he were walking toward me instead?*

CHAPTER TWENTY-ONE

Jessie

The Airbnb I rented is a single room basement apartment located one block off of Boston's famous Freedom Trail. The place is barely the size of a modest living room. The smell of fish sauce and garlic from the Chinese restaurant two doors down permeates the paneled walls, but at least it's warm, and the plumbing works. There's a comfortable twin bed nudged up against the wall with plain white bedding and a navy-blue decorative pillow. A street-level window sits overhead, smeared with remnants of winter's harsh weather, and underneath is a weathered oak desk with a chair, which suits my needs just fine.

I wake just before six o'clock for the fourth day and squeeze into the tiny shower, washing my long hair and allowing a stream of hot water to penetrate the fatigue clutching my shoulders. I tug on a pair of dark skinny jeans and a gray sweater, then twist my hair into a braid and smooth moisturizer on my face.

The Keurig rumbles as hot liquid drips into a ceramic mug. I grab a vanilla yogurt and a plastic spoon, then take my place at the desk *again*. Daylight sneaks through the tiny window as I tap on my keyboard—time is a blur, the task at hand demanding every skill in my wheelhouse to put the last pieces of this mysterious puzzle into place. I shove a memory stick into my laptop, saving my work as I go along.

I've been holed up in this obscure refuge since I arrived in the city, allowing myself only a few breaks. First, to find Emma; then, the occasional walk to fill my lungs with fresh air, and when necessary, to grab a quick meal. I've been sifting through the hard drive reassembling snippets of files, methodically drilling down to recover deleted emails and text messages. I follow the electronic trail to social networking sites that Claire had visited, and carefully track each new piece of information as it emerges. What began as a blank canvas the night Emma gave me the computer has been painstakingly reconstructed bit by bit and is nearly a fully formed image now.

Time passes quickly in this tiny space; the half-eaten turkey sandwich I forgot to finish still sits on the corner of the desk. I stand to stretch and am about to close my laptop when I notice something. I lean in on the palms of my hands, staring at the screen—and then I gasp. Sitting back down, I bring up a split view to compare the documents side by side, taking another look at the email chains and where each one originated. I check and cross-check my work, my hands sweeping to my face. *This can't be right.*

I pace the room until I'm convinced that what I'm looking at is real. Falling back onto the small bed, I stare at the ceiling as streams of anger and sadness comingle into a flood of exhaustion and tears. My bleary eyes feel heavy, and if not for my racing pulse and pissed-off desire to see someone pay a price for what I now know to be true, I'd do what I haven't done in days—*sleep*. But that will have to wait just a little bit longer—right now I have to let Emma know what I've found and contact the detectives working on the case.

I call Boston PD and ask for the detectives handling the Charles River murders. The officer who takes the call transfers it, and a moment later, a deep voice answers.

"This is Detective Foley."

"Hello, Detective. I have important information about what happened at the Charles in January."

"Who am I speaking with?"

"My name is Jessie Lynch; I was a friend of Claire Ryan's."

"We've been trying to get in contact with you, Ms. Lynch; tell me where you are and I'll meet you now," he says anxiously.

"I have somewhere to be, but I can come to you in the morning. I found your address online."

"Is nine o'clock good?" he asks.

"That's fine. I'll meet you then," I say, ending the call without waiting for his response.

I click the lever on the desk lamp and flip the switch next to the sink, brightening up the room. I tug on my boots, lacing them tightly against my ankles, then grab my jacket from the closet. Below the desk, my backpack is slouched on its side. I raise it to the chair and drop in both laptops, followed by my journal, and a memory stick. I don't imagine an apartment on the Freedom Trail is a target for theft, but I feel better keeping the critical stuff with me. I double-check the lock on the way out, then climb the concrete steps until I reach the street level.

Outside, a brisk breeze skims my cheeks; I tug the zipper on my jacket and blow into my palms. A couple blocks later I pass a shivering, middle-aged man crouching next to a small white dog, his tangled fingers so thick with dirt it's hard to know where the flesh ends and the nail begins. I reach into my backpack and dig for any cash I might have on hand, which is typically none, surprised when I locate a five-dollar bill. I slip it into the plastic cup next to his sleeping bag, then grab my cell and dial Emma's number. She doesn't answer, so I continue walking and leave a message.

"Emma, this is Jessie—I'm pretty sure I found the answers we've been looking for, some of them, anyway. I'm meeting with the detectives tomorrow morning, and then I'm heading home. I really need to talk to you first. Please call me as soon as you get this."

City life is still so foreign to me, but I don't mind it. Churches on every corner, museums, history at my fingertips, and a public transportation system that will take me anywhere I need to go on a whim. I wish I could take the time to soak it all in, but right now I can't stop checking my phone to see if Emma has called me back. *Nothing.* Knowing I won't be in town much longer, I finally decide I can't take a chance, and change direction.

Emma's home is dark when I arrive. I tap on the front door, although as expected, there's no answer. I take a seat on the cold stone porch, and after what feels like an hour, a blue Toyota Prius pulls up and I jump to my feet. The car door swings open, but it's a man that exits, turning back to hand the driver a tip before he quickly pulls away. I recognize him from the other night—it's Emma's neighbor. Only this time, thankfully, he's not carrying a gun.

He steps closer. "It's awfully cold to be sitting by yourself out here in the dark. If you're waiting for Emma to come home, she keeps late hours sometimes. I could give her a call if you like."

"I already left her a message, but thanks. I was just hoping to catch her before I leave town tomorrow afternoon."

"Anything I can help you with?"

"Don't you live next door?"

"Twenty-five years. Name's Francis Conley, but everyone calls me Frankie. I was close to Emma's grandparents."

"I think we met the other night; I was on the side yard with Emma and you came out to check on her."

"I thought you looked familiar," he says.

"I'm Jessie, by the way, and you're right—it's cold out here. Maybe … if it's not too much trouble, you'd be willing to do me a favor?"

"What is it you need?" Frankie asks, his US Navy cap the same color as his thick jacket.

"Would you mind giving this to Emma? It's important."

He smiles. "Sure thing."

I hand over the envelope, releasing it into his solid grip, an uneasy tinge pinging at my neck. "You'll make sure she gets it?" I ask.

"I'll deliver it to her personally."

"I'd appreciate that."

"You might want to call a car; it's a safe neighborhood, but a young girl like you shouldn't be walking the streets alone this late at night."

"I'm heading to the subway; it's not a very long walk. Besides, the fresh air feels good."

"All right, then, it was good to meet you. I'll reach out to Emma first thing in the morning."

I give him a warm smile, watching as he hoists himself up the steps. He stabs his key into the lock, then disappears into the house. I linger a moment, observing as the lights flick on, watching him move from one room to another. I wait another ten minutes, hoping Emma will return—but the fatigue of the past few days has taken its toll, so I turn away and head back toward the subway station, the chilly air biting through my jacket.

A sudden blast of warm air pushes through the tunnel ahead of the oncoming train; I take a step back, the headlight now visible. It squeals to a stop, and there's a *woosh* as the doors slide open. I step in and drop onto a side bench facing a university poster. A slender man with a grizzly beard is sitting toward the rear; he's talking to himself. I slide over to give myself a little more distance from him. A youngish guy is several rows over with a guitar between his thighs, and a cluster of giggling college girls wearing Northeastern sweatshirts occupy four rows of seats. Just before the doors close, a tall man wearing black running joggers, a gray zip-up, and a Sox cap pushes through and takes a seat a few rows back. I look over at him, and for just a second our eyes connect, but I politely look away.

My stop is announced; I slip the backpack over my shoulders and exit onto the platform, followed by other commuters, then climb up two flights of steps. It's late now, and each restaurant I pass appears to be closed. I notice the light on at a small pizzeria and tug at the metal handle, disappointed when it doesn't budge. I start to walk farther down the block, but then I hear something and stop. Seeing nothing, I keep walking, but I sense a second set of footsteps matching my stride from behind. I turn to look, but the street is desolate. Accelerating my pace, I keep moving, slipping my hand into my pocket, reaching for my keys. Then I hear it again—*I'm not alone.*

Chest hammering, I hold my breath and stop, then spin around again. This time there's a flash of movement and I catch a glimpse of a figure obscured by the dark; he quickly disappears into an alcove, but I know he's there. I press forward, hearing his movements mimic mine. My cell is in my backpack, but I can't stop—I need to move faster. It's only one more block until I'll reach the alley that cuts behind the building where I'm staying.

I slither between two parked cars and cross the street, the thump of his pace alerting me that he's moving faster now. I push forward until I reach the mouth of the alley and slip through, charging toward the safety of my rental. My backpack feels so heavy now, and my body is wet—I'm surviving on the kind of adrenaline that only terror can spark. But then I realize something, and it's even more frightening—*I don't hear him anymore.* I look from side to side; *where is he?* The brick building is now only feet away, but just as quickly as relief sets in, I hear him again. *He's back.* But it's too dark—he doesn't see me yet. I drop behind a metal trash bin, waiting for my eyes to adjust to the blackness, then peer below it, watching his thick soles inch closer.

A glint of moonlight illuminates a shiny object in his hand—I swallow a gasp. He's methodically searching—his movements smooth and deliberate. I press my body into the wall, growing more panicked with each step he takes. He's right in front of me now, close enough to hear me breathe. I clench my mouth and stifle a scream, but then he turns away. I peer down low again and watch—*he's leaving!* My body quakes violently, but I manage to discreetly let go of the air lodged in my chest. And then he's gone, and I collapse in an exhausted heap onto the filthy cold ground—the frigid air searing my lungs.

I crawl out from behind the bin, mentally preparing to make my move, the key juddering in my hand. I count to three, then hurtle upright and sprint to the stairwell, skipping steps until I'm at the door. *Oh God, the light above the door might as well be a target on my head.* I fumble with the key, jabbing it into the lock, but then I freeze—a shadow appears on the wall, slowly rising. I spin to the left and open my mouth, but he buries my scream with his bare hands, and I collapse.

CHAPTER TWENTY-TWO

Emma

The stainless-steel container careens off the first step, its loosely fitted lid unable to contain the liquid as it catapults down the stairs. It comes to rest at the bottom, settling in a pool of the hot coffee I had just poured. *Crap!*

A middle-aged woman walking a silver-and-black Australian shepherd approaches before I can reach the sidewalk. The puppy trots over, prodding its nose into the brown wetness, lapping it up. Appearing annoyed, its owner tugs at the leash, goading her little fur-baby to come along. I apologize, hunching down to pick up the mug, then set it on the porch, my fingers sticky from the vanilla creamer oozing between them. I rifle through my bag for a pack of tissues and swipe the moisture away. A voice calls out my name from behind me and I pivot to see Frankie standing outside his door, waving feverishly in my direction.

Knowing I won't be able to finish any conversation I start now, I'm forced to keep moving. Raising my hand high, I wave as my legs continue to propel me forward, but he keeps calling my name, his right arm sweeping in a high, slow arc. I glance back again, without slowing down. He stops waving, his arms sinking to his sides. My entire body sighs as I hurry up the street, trying to make up some time.

Passing the reception desk, I notice Miles Fisher sitting on the lobby couch with his earbuds in, talking on his cell. I slip by, hoping not to draw his attention. My office is warm, so I toss my coat over the chair and adjust the thermostat, then quickly print my notes. My cell pings and I look down—*Mason*. I ignore the text. When I look up, Logan is standing in my doorway. "Let's meet in the small conference room in five," he says.

"I'll be there," I respond. I look back down at my phone and notice a voicemail that came in last night. I recognize the number—*Jessie*. As I listen to the message, my pulse quickens; I want desperately to call her back right now, but I can't. I close my laptop and charge up the hall.

Curling my fingers into a fist, I tap lightly on the door and push it inward. The two men are sitting with their backs to the wall, staring out the window and chatting. The conference room is small, but even after all these years the panoramic view of Boston against the vivid blue sky still takes my breath away.

Mile stands, extending his arm. "Good to see you again, Emma."

I offer an obligatory smile and shake his hand.

We settle into the tan leather chairs, and I flip open my laptop to take notes. Logan powers up his iPad. "Emma, would you like to start?" he asks.

Suddenly the voices around me fade, while the one in my head rises. I can't stop hearing Jessie's message. But then Logan's voice booms and I snag a glance at his perplexed expression.

"Emma?"

"Sorry," I say, looking toward Miles. "As you know, we've lost two of our attorneys, both of whom were assigned to Silverstone. Prior to Dean's death, he had been reviewing documents for your company and noticed some irregularities—but unfortunately, he didn't share them with anyone else. We do know that he reached out to Alex Ford, and they planned to discuss their findings the same day that Dean was killed. I imagine you and Alex spoke about the matter prior to him departing your company, so we were hoping you can fill us in."

"This is the first I'm hearing about it. What type of problem are we talking about?" Miles asks.

"We're all a little in the dark right now," I respond.

Logan leans in, elbows resting on the table. "Miles, if I can be candid, one thing in particular has been bothering me. Emma confirmed a meeting with Alex the day before she arrived at your office to discuss this issue. How is it that he ended up leaving the company that very same day, and she wasn't notified?"

Miles sits back in his chair, his fingers raking through his hair. "I didn't know Emma was coming to the office that day. Alex was with us for seven years; he was very good at his job and would never have neglected a client. But he took us all by surprise with his resignation."

"If Dean suspected a problem, there's a good chance he was right. If so, we need to make sure it's corrected right away," I say.

"Silverstone was started by my family fifty years ago, and our reputation is everything to us. We have a team in place to make sure our operation is transparent, and we hire only the best lawyers, your firm included, to prevent mistakes from occurring," Miles says, a tinge of annoyance in his tone.

"You're right, of course—and believe me, it's a privilege to represent you. We want to make sure Silverstone is protected, and to do that we need to follow up on Dean's work," Logan says.

Miles rubs his forehead. "Okay, so tell me how I can help."

"Get in contact with Alex, and ask him to reach out to us," Logan responds.

I watch as Miles's face dips. *He's uncomfortable. Or is he nervous?*

"That might be complicated," he responds.

"Why is that?" Logan asks.

The tension in the room is thick as we wait for his answer.

"Because Alex isn't responding to me, or anyone at Silverstone."

Logan removes his glasses and sets them on the table. When he looks over at Miles, his expression is stern. "I think it's time that we alert the authorities."

"About what?" Miles asks. "We don't even know if there's a problem. And from what I've read about the incident, Dean wasn't in a good place mentally."

"He was a good man and a brilliant lawyer. More important though is that he wouldn't have compromised his work, no matter how strained his personal life might have been," Logan says.

Miles tries another tack. "Look, the marketing campaign for our new sports complex kicks off at the end of the month—we absolutely cannot have any negative publicity right now."

"How about this, then—when you get back to your office, try again to get hold of Alex. I'm sure in a few days, he'll turn up. Get back to us next week, and we'll decide how to move forward. In the meantime, we'll keep looking on our end for anything that might give us a clue as to what this is about. If we don't know any more by the end of next week, we'll make the call."

"I'll do what I can," Miles says.

Logan nods in acknowledgment. "I have another meeting in ten minutes, so I'm gonna need to wrap this up."

We all rise at once; Logan scoops his tablet and rushes out to his next meeting. Miles shoots me an awkward glance. "I'll be in touch, Emma," he says, stepping into the hall.

"Miles?" I say, and he turns back. "I've thought a lot about our meeting at your office the day I was supposed to meet with Alex, and nothing about my last conversation with him signaled that he was about to leave his job. I'm worried about him."

"You're an excellent lawyer, Emma. But unless your skills include mindreading, I don't think you're in a place to say why Alex left my company when he did," he says, before turning to leave.

As I watch him stride back toward the lobby, my cell vibrates and another message appears.

Mason: *Emma, you need to call me back right away. Something has happened.*

CHAPTER TWENTY-THREE

I turn the corner on my street, surprised to see lights flashing and whirling in the distance—it takes a second for my mind to register what I'm looking at. A brilliant display of reds and blues, so vibrant that if not for what they represent they might be beautiful, stunning even. The ambulance is positioned along the curb adjacent to the home next to mine. I edge closer, maneuvering around the police vehicles crissed and crossed in the middle of the street, the officers busy keeping bystanders at bay. The clank of wheels hitting concrete spins my head and I see a gurney dropping one step at a time, two paramedics on opposite sides gripping the metal handles.

My chest leaps when I see them hoist Frankie into the back of the vehicle, the bright white space filled with tubes and monitors. The female paramedic jumps in and crouches behind him, securing an oxygen mask to his face. A male responder kneels at his side, pumping his chest. I stop an officer to ask what happened, but he volunteers nothing, waving me on, ordering me to clear the street. That's when I see Jacob, Frankie's son, watching with a tortured expression as they work feverishly to stabilize his father. He notices me looking over at him, and charges through the crowd of onlookers.

"Jacob, what happened? Is he okay?"

"I don't know—he was fine when we talked this morning, and his physical was perfect last month," he says, his breathing so labored that I'm worried he too might drop, right here in front of me.

"Oh my God, I was going to stop by and see him tonight. He was trying to get my attention this morning, but I was in a rush to get to work. Now I feel terrible. What if he was feeling ill and looking for help?"

"He sent me a text just before ten o'clock this morning, asking if I wanted him to pick up tickets to a Sox game. I know he was good then."

I grab my chest and feel a tiny bit of relief. "Have you been able to talk to him?"

"He was unconscious when I got here. He called 911 himself, though, apparently right before he passed out. It must have come on so fast that he didn't have time to call anyone else."

"So scary," I mutter—the more meaningful thoughts trapped inside me. The ambulance doors swing shut and a siren wails, rising and lowering in pitch as it winds its way through the throng of vehicles and onlookers.

"I need to get to the hospital," Jacob says, his arms reaching out to wrap around me.

"You go. As soon as you know something, please text me."

"I will, Emma." He comes in close for another embrace, then waves and turns to leave.

Jacob's stride is long and swift just like his dad's; he squeezes into his blue truck, the screech of rubber howling as he pulls away. For a moment I'm caught up in the beauty of their relationship, an adult man almost childlike when it comes to the well-being of his father.

The spectacle over for now, each inquisitive mind quickly loses interest, and one by one the gawkers peel off and retreat to the homes from which they emerged. People are funny that way—eagerly welcoming any disruption to their insipid lives, regardless of how tragic it may be. I watch as the oscillating lights are extinguished, the police cars transitioning from emergency mode back to patrol as the block empties—and once again, it's just another forgettable night on a sleepy, tree-lined street in Boston.

※

Like most New England homes during the winter, there's a stubborn chill in this place that resides until spring—ignoring all futile attempts at eviction. I start a fire to keep it at bay, then fall back onto the couch and tap my cell, trying to reach Jessie again. But just as I stretch my finger toward the *call back* icon, the doorbell chimes. It's been a while since I've had an actual appetite—waiting for the delivery guy is oddly more thrilling than anticipating a first date. I look through the peephole, but there is no delivery person waiting for me on the other side. Instead, Detective Mason is standing on my porch. I open the door.

"Emma—sorry to stop by unannounced again; it seems I've been doing a lot of that lately. But I've been trying to get hold of you," he says.

"I'm the one who should be apologizing. I saw your messages—work has been hectic, and the night somehow managed to get worse."

"Everything okay?"

"Not sure. You just missed the commotion outside; my neighbor was taken away by ambulance, and I have no idea what happened to him. He's been a very close friend to my family for years."

"I'm sorry to hear about that. I wouldn't have come if it weren't important," he says.

I invite him in. "I don't suppose you're here to deliver good news for a change?" The clack of another knock at the door steals our attention. This time it's a kid holding out a bag. "Thank you," I say, handing him a tip and closing the door.

"I'm interrupting your dinner," Mason says.

"You're fine. Chinese," I say, lifting the bag toward him, then lowering it as I walk into the kitchen. He follows me. I pull two plates from the cabinet and set them on the kitchen table, then open the containers and slip serving utensils into each one. Mason slides onto the bench, and I take a seat across from him, trying to read his expression.

"Have you eaten?" I ask.

"We really need to talk, Emma."

His tone causes me to set down my fork. "What is it?"

"It's about Claire's friend—the one who you said showed up at your place," he says before looking back up.

"Jessie?"

"That's right."

"I was just about to return a call from her when you showed up tonight."

"When did she call you?" he asks, leaning forward.

"Last night, actually. She left a message, but I hadn't noticed until this afternoon."

Mason's gaze drops, his fingers fidgeting with his fork.

"You're making me nervous," I say.

"Something has happened, Emma."

Words feel thick in my mouth, but I push them out. "What is it?" I ask softly.

"Jessie Lynch was attacked last night."

His words ram through me like a club to the gut.

"She contacted the Department yesterday saying she had information about the murders. She was transferred to Detective Foley; they planned on meeting today. His number and the time of the meeting were found on a piece of paper in her pocket, so the detective at the scene contacted him."

Both hands whip toward my face, clasping over my mouth. "She's okay, though, right?"

Mason's eyes blink slowly, his hands twisting into each other. *I know exactly what he's not telling me.* It's strange how quickly a person can become important to you. I can't say that I really knew Jessie, we'd only just met—but I understood her, and she seemed to *get* me. And now I feel as if I've lost another friend. "You don't believe it was a random attack at all, do you? You think it's connected to Dean and Claire's case?"

"We don't know yet. But coincidences in a matter like this aren't my first thought."

I swipe at my forehead, then push my plate away.

"Do you mind if I listen to the message she left?" Mason asks.

I nod. Digging into my sweatshirt pocket, I fumble for the phone, and it drops to the floor. My hand judders as I dip down and grip the silicone cover. When I press *Play*, her voice rises from the tiny speakerphone. We look at each other and listen until the recording stops; then Mason plays it a second time, and by now I feel as low as a human can sink for not calling her back right away. "I should have answered last night. I should have *helped* her."

"What could you have done? Judging from the time of the call, she was probably just seconds away from her fate even as she dialed your number."

His sincere attempt at comforting me somehow makes it seem even worse.

"Do you get it now? Dean didn't do this to Claire. Whatever he learned made him a target, and I'm guessing Jessie too."

"We already knew that Dean didn't do this."

"What?"

"We have the autopsy report. The trajectory of the bullet in Dean's head established without a doubt that the wound could not have been self-inflicted. It appeared to the coroner that someone went to great lengths to try and make it look like a suicide, but that theory has been rejected."

"Why didn't you say anything?"

"This is an ongoing investigation; we have to be careful about what information we release. But it seems as though someone out there is willing to take lives to save their own, and that's as dangerous a human instinct as there is."

"Then do your fucking job!"

"Excuse me?" he retorts, a vein pulsing near his temple.

"Every law enforcement type who has touched this case considers Dean a diabolical criminal, rather than a victim. Meanwhile, the person who *really* did this is most likely blending into a crowd of innocent people with plenty of time to cover evidence of their crime."

Mason remains composed, but his eyes are punishing. "We

go where the evidence takes us. As we get more information, we reevaluate. In this case, the autopsy provided the facts that ruled Dean out. Until we had that, he was in play."

I stand up, my appetite having disappeared. "You're right … you're right. I'm sorry," I say, walking into the living room if only to alleviate the tension. *I can't help but notice that he didn't say he ruled me out.*

He follows me and we sit back on the couch without speaking, blankly staring into the fire. This is the part where I tell him what I've done—I know it's important, yet somehow the words stick in my throat. I begin, then stop, then try again, and once again I freeze. I don't know what I fear more, getting in trouble for what I've done, or disappointing him. Finally I say it. "There's something I need to tell you too."

Mason doesn't respond, but he's locked on, looking at me in such a way that I can physically feel the clutch of his attention.

"I went to Claire's apartment, specifically to look for her personal laptop."

His jaw clenches. "And?"

"And I found it. Then I gave it to Jessie to analyze."

He launches upward, gripping the back of his head while he begins pacing in front of the fireplace. "What were you thinking?"

"I don't know," I stammer. "She had spent time with Claire the week before the incident and didn't believe the story that was being told, and neither did I. She asked for my help and I agreed."

"You trespassed on my victim's property and removed potential evidence."

"I have a key—I told you that the first time we met at the station. And by the way, her place had already been searched, so that means your team missed it or didn't find it relevant."

That same vein flares up again. "So, where do you think it is now? Nothing was located near the body other than her phone, which had her ID and a confirmation for the room she rented. A search of the rental came up with only some clothing items. So whoever did this to her most likely has it now. Has it occurred to you that it may be the reason she was attacked—did you think about that?"

My chin sags under the weight of his rebuke.

Mason returns to the couch, only this time he takes a softer tone. "Look, I'm sorry. I didn't mean to raise my voice. Jessie put herself at risk by digging into this. What happened to her isn't your fault."

"No, you're right. I should never have given it to her."

The silent gaps between our words expand, both of us retreating into our own thoughts. Our arms are stretched toward each other on the couch; when I look over, I notice his fingers just inches from mine and I wish I could move just a little closer. I'm the one to finally break the silence, my voice a defeated whisper. "Why didn't you just call to tell me what happened?"

"I don't really know."

It takes a few seconds for his words to digest. "Don't you have anywhere to be? Isn't someone waiting for you?"

"Used to be."

"Sorry, it's not my business. I'm the last person who should ask about dating; I barely do it myself these days."

"Well, then, we're on the same page," he says, sitting up and looking directly at me again. "I should get going. I have an early day tomorrow."

"Right, of course." I lift myself from the couch and move toward the door. He follows me. And then he maneuvers around me, but rather than stepping outside this time, he leans in; we're separated by a breath of air, his lips so full I can feel them without touching him. Oh God, is he going to … I want him to … *please do it*. But he doesn't. He leaves without saying another word, and I shut the door behind him. Thoughts twist inside me and all I can think about is Claire, and how I wish so badly that I could talk to her right now. I want to tell her that for the first time *there is someone* who makes me want to look twice.

CHAPTER TWENTY-FOUR

My head is still lost in the rubble of Mason's revelation about Jessie last night, so I'm oddly thankful that my next therapy session just happens to be scheduled for today.

Dr. Bradley takes his seat across from me, just like every other session. He wastes no time revisiting the incident, again poking at my memory as if one more question might crack open the events of that night—illuminate the visions that remain a mystery. After I give him the same answer, he asks me about my dad again. He's persistent that way, despite many of what I thought were clever attempts at deflection.

Whenever the awkward subject of Barrett Gray rears its uncomfortable head, my mouth clamps up like a razor-sharp trap. I'm not sure what that says about me or how I manage that fragment of my complicated life—it's far easier to describe my mother, the words *selfish* and *neglectful* rolling off the tongue rather effortlessly, with a hard *the end* for dramatic effect. But expressing how I feel about my dad just isn't that simple. This time, though, I do it—every sordid detail left bare to dissect—the missing jigsaw pieces of my life revealed. I lean back and begin.

"When I think of my father, my thoughts are good ones." That's how I start, and it's true. I recall summer days at the beach as some of my happiest memories—long after the sun would fall asleep and the stars made their first appearance, Dad would light a firepit and we would roast marshmallows while he recounted stories of when he was a child. And I loved hearing them. He was a willing participant in my young life and taught me that with hard work I could do special things. *That was love.* Of course, none of that erases the images of that terrible night—a moment in time when I was forced to look at my father through a much different lens.

"Can we talk about what happened that night?" Dr. Bradley asks.

I continue as if my brain is relieved to unlock the grip this piece of my life has had on it.

"I was home from college for the summer, and Dad had taken me out to dinner at our favorite restaurant in the North End. We just happened to run into a group of friends I knew from high school who were there celebrating a birthday. We didn't notice the two men sitting at the table next to us—but then, why would we? Neither of us knew them. They blended into the background just like any other unremarkable customer might. But when we stood to leave, I could feel it—something was off.

When we walked toward the exit, I remember looking over at Jenny; she was waving at me from the table where the girls were seated. I turned back, and the two men who had been sitting beside us were now only steps behind me. My father pushed through the door first. Without warning, a flash of bodies rushed past, and I was stunned, but nothing could prepare me for what would happen next. I can still hear the shriek of voices shouting his name and forcing him to the ground, and the clack of cuffs being snapped around his wrists. I watched him rock and buck, an emotional pain so jarring that I fell to the ground and wailed like a child."

"You were left alone as they took your father away?" Dr. Bradley asks.

I swipe at the back of my neck, a nervous moisture pooling. "I remember a hand cupping my shoulder and a voice asking me if I was okay; it was the owner of the restaurant who knew my dad well. He guided me to my feet, and when I looked back, I could see my friends standing behind the glass peering—*judging*—anxious to regurgitate what they had witnessed that night. *And they did.*"

"Let me stop you there for a minute, Emma. When they took your father away, where did you go? Did you have a support system in place?" Dr. Bradley asks.

"I sat in a coffee shop three doors down until my grandfather arrived. Seeing him was like being wrapped in a soft blanket of hope. Over the following days and weeks, though, the FBI raided our home multiple times. Our house was eventually auctioned off, the pristine ice-blue '66 Impala that Dad loved so much and his brand-new SUV were hauled away. At twenty-one years old, I learned in some small way what it felt like to be orphaned."

"How is it you think your father was finally caught?"

I consider his question, and although I don't know how it's relevant, it does send me back to the trial, and I remember all those witnesses who showed up to testify against my father. "I suppose most people would say that he got greedy and rolled the dice one time too many. But the reality was that his partner knew about his financial mess and decided to dangle an opportunity that would require a financial expert to succeed. My dad never was the type to care about stuff; he enjoyed experiences and making sure I was taken care of. But he landed on temptation island with his cohort and soon his money problems, and my mother, were in his rearview. What he didn't plan on was that his partner was far more greedy than he was, and not nearly as bright—he left a trail that even a vision-challenged mule could follow."

Dr. Bradley stares for a few seconds digesting what I just said. I can't tell if he's disgusted or fascinated by my story. He finally speaks up and I realize he's simply adding another piece to the mind puzzle he's putting together about me. "Greed will do that to a person. I'm wondering how you handled life after your dad was incarcerated."

"My new reality barreled over me like a rogue train veering off the tracks, slicing through my little world. College tuition payments that had arrived early each semester abruptly stopped coming, and the twelve hundred dollars I had saved from my summer internship evaporated rapidly. It was right then that the secure place inside my brain where naive thoughts lived was extinguished, and in its wake a crippling anxiety began to grow. I headed straight to the financial aid department, praying that the news of my father's arrest would go unnoticed. I needed to find the resources to pay my own way through college now; a month later I had secured two grants and a loan that would allow me to finish the semester, and the following year I was awarded a partial scholarship and additional loans.

By the time I applied to law school I was completely independent and had learned the fine art of coupon-clipping and dinners consisting of Top Ramen and on-sale vegetables du jour. I knew that I would graduate with the kind of debt that might keep a person up at night, but I didn't care. I was determined to never have to rely on another person again, and it felt good."

Dr. Bradley lifts his left hand to his chin and gives me a quizzical look. "A lot of people would have folded and followed in their parents' footsteps, blaming the world for their problems. Where do you think you found your strength?"

"When it happened, Nana was already gone, and Grandpa lived alone in a town house at the South End of Boston. There was one thing I knew about my grandfather; aside from the fact that he wore pajama bottoms under his Dockers and that he would have a glass of scotch every night at exactly seven o'clock—Patrick Gray didn't believe in handouts for those capable of earning their own way, and for that reason, I never asked. But I did love him dearly, and I visited him every chance I got. Not because I felt sorry for him—he neither required nor wanted pity. I spent time with him because he was interesting and kind and made me realize that the blood sloshing through my veins wasn't only composed of the alcohol-craving, self-obsessed, loser-loving female called my mother, or the amiable thief otherwise known as my dad. Rather, he reminded me that I was capable of anything, and I was determined to make him proud."

When I finally stop talking, Dr. Bradley is still feverishly jotting down notes. He stops and looks over at me, an air of satisfaction as if he has just fractured the internal barrier hiding my mental wounds. But it's what he says next that makes my chest hitch.

"Emma, it's true; you can do anything you want to, but you have to understand something about your father first. He isn't in jail because he was a kind thief; he's in there because he didn't know when to stop."

"Well, I'd say he's behind bars because he took what wasn't his, but I understand what you're trying to say."

Dr. Bradley looks at his watch and closes his notebook. "Our time is up, Emma. I think we made a lot of progress today; why don't we meet up again next week. Wednesday at the same time work for you?"

"I'll see you Wednesday," I say.

When I leave I head toward the subway station with Dr. Bradley's words rumbling in my head; I wasn't sure why he said them to me or what purpose they served. It felt like a warning; *but for who?*

CHAPTER TWENTY-FIVE

Ronni taps on the glass outside my office, and as usual she's dressed with the kind of confidence people should pay money for. She's wearing a snug black dress with thick white stripes on the sides, and black pumps. I gesture for her to come in, and she enters with a cheerful smile, her large gold hoops peeking through her dark hair cut sharp along her shoulders. *She's always so damn happy; I want whatever it is that lady is taking.*

"I ordered the lunch you requested for Monday's team meeting and confirmed your ten o'clock for Tuesday. Is there anything else I can help you with?"

"No, that's perfect, thank you." She turns to leave and I call her back in. "Hey, Ronni?"

"Yes?" she says, stepping back in.

"Is this what you want to do? I mean are you happy at the receptionist desk? I was told that you're a paralegal."

"I am, but I don't mind the work. I'm just thankful to be working here; great benefits and the hours are good for me."

"So the work you're doing is satisfying then?"

Ronni smiles. "Emma, I'm a fifty-year-old girl from Jersey who decided to follow her dream of opening a bakery, and then seven months later my husband's heart had other plans for us. Suddenly I found myself alone and looking for work again, so I moved to Boston to be closer to my sister. I wasn't sure how many firms would be looking for someone with my years of experience. I'm just glad to have a job."

"You're wrong. Those years have given you the kind of wisdom and knowledge that makes you more valuable."

"You're a doll, but don't you worry about me. The attorneys here seem to trust me with special projects, which keeps me from getting bored up front," she says.

"What kind of projects?"

"Confirming case law or proofreading long documents, organizing projects, all different things."

"Oh, I'll bet you're in demand in this office."

Ronni taps her long purple nails on the doorframe and winks. "I should let you get back to work, then; you have a nice weekend, Emma."

"You too, Ronni," I say.

She turns to leave, but just as she steps out, she spins back. "I almost forgot—Dean asked me to help him with a project shortly before the incident, and to be honest, now I'm not sure who I should give it to. It doesn't involve a particular case; it was more like an organizing project. Since you've taken over his team, maybe I can give it to you? I would give it directly to Accounting, but he was pretty adamant that it go directly to him first—'For my eyes only, Ronni.' That's how he said it."

"What is it?"

"He asked me to match up internal invoices for one of our clients. He had me go back many years."

I sit up a little straighter and swallow hard. "Which client?"

It's almost as if I can see the words tumble out of her mouth, floating in my direction in such a slow deliberate path that I can reach out and grab them midair. "Silverstone Development," she says.

"When did he ask you to do this?"

"Two days before the ... well ... you know. Before it happened."

"Have you shown them to anyone else?"

"Not yet. I just finished it up this week and wasn't quite sure what to do with it. I planned on bringing it to one of the partners yesterday, but I was busy with the monthly staff lunch."

"Can I get it from you?" I ask, leaping out of my chair.

Ronni smiles. "Sure, but you just finish what you're doing. I'll bring it to you."

"Perfect," I say, filling my tote with the work I plan on doing over the weekend. While I wait I type a message to Jacob to check on Frankie. He's been keeping me updated, but as of now they have no idea what happened to him.

Ronni returns carrying an expanding folder secured by an elastic band, and places it on my desk. "I'm gonna shut down the kitchen, then head out if it's okay with you, Emma."

"Absolutely. You have a nice weekend," I say.

I slide the large folder into my bag and head to the elevator. The contents I'm holding on to right now might as well be a box of salted caramel cupcakes; I can practically feel the drool building near my lips as I'm thinking about the answers that might be buried in these documents.

CHAPTER TWENTY-SIX

A nxious to crack open the file, I peel off my jeans and sweater, and grab leggings and a tee from a pile on top of the washing machine. Twisting my hair into a loose braid, I call out to Google to start my playlist on low. I get to my knees and slip the elastic cord over the thick redwell and lift the flap, exposing its contents. Inside I find clumps of papers fastened together in small increments, each one with a spreadsheet on top. The significance of what I'm looking at isn't obvious at first glance, but Dean wouldn't have asked Ronni to keep this project guarded if it wasn't important.

I lift the first clipped section and examine page one. The heading *Summit Landing* is printed at the top right. I recognize the reference immediately—that was a Silverstone project our firm worked on some years back. Below it are rows of dates and numbers, which appear to be billable hour entries. I move on to the next clump of documents, and this one has the name Seventh Street Plaza, which I also recognize. I recall helping Dean with a lease agreement for this project. I scan through the attached pages—more columns filled with dates and numbers. I'm about to pick up a third set when a pounding thud seizes my attention. I freeze and sit motionless for a few long seconds. I hear it again, and my chest constricts.

Rising slowly, I slink into the hallway, glancing over my shoulder toward the back door. Another thump—it's coming from the front of the house. I creep forward with hesitant steps, peering through a bend in the shade, a flurry of taut nerves stretching behind my neck. *Detective Mason.* Relieved, I unlatch the lock and open the door.

Still gripping my chest, I attempt to ease the wild beats thumping inside me. "You're here again so soon, not sure if I should be nervous or terrified."

His expression is rigid, so I imagine it's the latter and immediately my pulse accelerates again. I wait for him to continue.

"Can I come in?" he asks.

I wave my hand, gesturing toward the living room. He walks in and removes his coat. I close the door and secure the dead bolt before following him.

"Do you mind?" he asks, motioning toward the sofa. Without responding, I walk past him and fall onto the couch, and he takes a seat next to the fireplace. His forehead pinches, and his chin drops. I watch as he digs his thumb into his palm, then slowly raises his eyes, looking back up at me.

"Emma, we got the results from the ballistics test on your gun."

"My God, I was afraid you were gonna tell me someone else had been hurt. So we're good, then?"

"No, we're not. The tests confirm that the shell casings found at the crime scene were fired from your pistol."

My eyes bug out and I hold my hand to my chest. "Excuse me?" I whisper.

"What I'm trying to tell you, Emma, is that your gun was used to kill Dean Wolfe and Claire Ryan."

I launch upward, tripping over the pile of blankets on the floor, catching myself just before vaulting into the brick hearth. The room whirls and shrinks, the walls squeezing in around me. I begin to pant, pacing in jagged motions, my fingers dragging through my hair. "Please tell me you're joking because I'm holding my breath for your punch line right now."

"I wish I were; I really do."

"Well, it's straight-up bullshit and you know it," I insist.

"I think you're too smart to leave a murder weapon locked in your own home—especially when you were the last person to see one of the victims alive. But this is a fact, Emma, and one that is really difficult to explain away."

"Someone took that gun without my knowledge—I've never pointed that thing at a human being in my life."

"I believe you, and so does Detective Foley. But I'm here to tell you that not everyone is convinced."

"Why isn't anyone listening to me? Someone was in my house that night. I told you I thought someone was in my house days later; I heard them. They must have been here to return the gun."

"But how did they get your weapon in the first place? Think, Emma ... I need you to think very carefully here. Who would know where you keep your gun safe, and who would have the combination to it?"

"I'm thinking."

"Could someone have observed you opening the safe?"

"No, I don't think so."

"Let's start with an easier question—who had a key to your house?"

"Only Claire—and I have hers as well. We kept one for each other, just in case. But I didn't give anyone access to my gun safe, and never would."

"What about your father?"

"What about him?"

"Well, for starters, you didn't tell me that he's serving twelve years in a federal prison for embezzling client funds."

"You didn't ask. Besides, it's not exactly the type of family history I like to share with strangers."

"Have you stopped to think that someone might be targeting you to get back at him?"

"My father may be a thief, but he never hurt anyone."

"He never *hurt* anyone? Stealing from a company always hurts people. Lives are affected in ways you may not think of—bonuses can't be paid, insurance is lost, leaving the sick vulnerable; it destroys relationships. The lust for revenge burns deep, and it doesn't just fade away for everyone."

What's begun to feel like an interrogation shrouds me in a layer of panic, bordering on mania. "You're right—of course you are. But he's paying the price for what he did. And I pay for his crime every time someone mentions his name. After his arrest, everything he owned was auctioned off, including the home we lived in. My understanding is that his victims were made whole. I can't believe anyone would go to this length to get back at him. Besides, if they were really trying to hurt him, they could have just killed me."

"Not if they wanted to prolong the suffering, forcing him

to watch from behind bars, helpless, knowing that his daughter would lose her freedom and every penny she earned from her highfalutin degrees, not to mention the home her grandfather handed her."

That last statement rocks me, and I shudder. "That's insane."

"There's something else, Emma."

My face drops to my lap, my hands clamped over my head. "What?" I whisper.

"The crime scene unit logged the evidence found in the SUV where Claire's body was recovered. We've gone through each piece, and one item can't be explained."

"What's that?"

"A small silver pill box with your name engraved on the bottom."

I lift my head, tears spilling to my chest. "That was a gift from my grandfather—I've been looking for it. After watching my dad's arrest I began suffering from anxiety, and I didn't want to take the medication that was prescribed. Gramps told me to fill the box and keep it close; he said just knowing it was near might be enough to quell my nerves. That's what I've done for years, and it works."

"Did you know it was missing?"

"Not until I returned to work—I felt an attack coming on; that's when I noticed it was gone."

"What did you think happened to it?"

"It was shortly after the murders; my head wasn't in a good place so I didn't spend much time thinking about it."

"Dean purchased his Range Rover in November. Have you ever been in that vehicle?"

"No, I didn't even know he had one. Why does that matter, and why isn't anyone listening to me? The person who was in my home uninvited and without my knowledge did this."

"I'm not the one you need to convince. The problem for you is this—not only has your gun been linked to the murders, and a personal item of yours found near one of the victims, but you were the last person to see Claire after leaving O'Malley's. After that, nobody can vouch for your whereabouts until the next day."

"Give me one logical reason why I would kill two people that I'm so close to."

"With Dean out of the way, you made partner."

I glare. "Fuck you."

"I'm trying to help you."

"You're accusing me." I turn away and walk into the kitchen. I reach for the bottle of Ketel One and unscrew the lid, filling a tumbler halfway. I can feel him standing behind me. "Want one?" I ask.

He declines and takes a seat at the table. My hands fidget and my leg taps uncomfortably. "Do you remember me telling you about the last conversation I had with Dean, and his concerns about one of our clients?" I ask.

"The real estate developer?"

"That's right. I worked with Dean for seven years, and I knew him long before that when he led our moot court team in law school. And in all that time, I never heard him express his concerns quite the way he did that night."

Mason stretches his long legs outward, then crosses one over the other. "We've interviewed several representatives of Silverstone and as of now we haven't found a link between what Dean discovered and the murders."

"This is one of the largest developers on the East Coast. Their projects are worth hundreds of millions of dollars—if an employee has gone rogue with their funds, that's a lot of incentive."

"I promise we're looking into it. In the meantime, I need you to know what's coming your way," he says, his eyes focused on my fingers as I attempt to stop them from trembling. He reaches across the table, his hand lands on mine, and I feel him press down. I want to curve my palm upward and grip his just to feel safe, but I retreat, finishing off my drink.

"I'm not trying to scare you, but if a warrant is issued—and I'm almost sure it will be—it can happen at any time."

My body buzzes with nerves. But then I force myself to think clearly, knowing all too well how easily mistakes can land a person on the wrong side of a long prison term. I peer toward the file Ronni gave me, and then back up at Mason. "Can you do something for me?" I ask.

"Anything," he says, his thumb swiping at my cheek.

"Dean asked a staff member to work on a file in confidence— she gave it to me today. I'm not entirely sure what it contains, but it may provide some insight into what Dean uncovered. If you're right and they come for me, I'm going to need someone else to look into it. If you can stay for just a half hour, I can scan the documents onto a flash drive and give it to you. I don't want you to do anything with it for now, please—just hold on to it, unless I'm arrested."

"If you share something with me that turns out to be illegal, I'll have to follow it to its conclusion."

"I'm counting on that."

"Okay then, if you're sure."

"I'll be right back," I say, padding over to the living room and grabbing the stack of documents. I carry them to my home office and begin pulling each packet apart and scanning them one by one. When I return to the living room, Mason is sitting with his elbows dug into his legs and his hands folded below his chin. He sees me and leaps up. I hand him the flash drive, then move toward the front door and open it. He steps out and turns back.

"Emma, if you're arrested, I'll contact an agent who I work with at the FBI. He's a good guy and he'll have a forensic analysis team look at it. If it's something, you should know that these documents will require turning this case over to the FBI; they have jurisdiction over white-collar crimes, which, considering this is a file filled with client invoices, I'm guessing it is."

"Do it," I say, and gently slide the door shut.

CHAPTER TWENTY-SEVEN

No one tells you how to feel, or what to do, on the day you're going to be arrested for a crime you didn't commit. I've tried my best to stay on the proverbial straight-and-narrow path my entire life, sucking up bad parenting, caring little about the finer things in life. I worked my ass off, graduating with honors from both undergrad and law school. *And I never complained.* But you don't survive parenting like I did and come out a weak gal; I've got the kind of edge that knows how to play with the worst of them. And now someone is trying their best to use me as a scapegoat, and I plan on holding a massive fucking grudge. No one wants to incur the wrath of the girl who climbed her way out of the trailer only to be in danger of losing the most precious gift of all—*freedom.*

It takes effort, but I compel my brain to think like a prisoner-to-be. I've spent my fair share of time meeting with incarcerated individuals, so I'm no stranger to the process—I've learned a thing or two.

First things first—after Mason left the other night, I fired off an email to the father of one of my law school friends. Paul Jennings has been a criminal lawyer in the Boston area for nearly twenty-five years and has a reputation as a take-it-to-the-mat type—*that's who I need.* Yesterday afternoon he called and said he would contact the district attorney's office to arrange for me to turn myself in, rather than deal with a public arrest.

I pay my utilities early and toss perishables from the fridge. I wash the sheets I haven't used in weeks, clean the bathrooms, and vacuum the house. I wash my hair with moisturizing shampoo and a leave-in conditioning treatment. Soon my only option will be to strip my hair with a bar of soap—my long mane will tangle into an angry nest so tight I'll have to shave my head bald even with one soapy application. Hopefully this will carry me until I'm released unless, God forbid, they don't grant me bail. I slather body oil from neck to ankle, until a thick film glistens under the bathroom lighting—naively hoping this will give my skin a little time before it leathers up. I transfer enough money from my savings to checking so that I'll have easy access to my finances.

Next, I slip into my most comfortable stretchy jeans and the camel cable-knit sweater I picked up at the Nordstrom holiday sale last year. These interviews can be long, and most stations are cold—I'm guessing I'll be spending a fair amount of time in one today before being processed, so warm clothing it is.

The one thing left to do is the most difficult, and I decide to let it wait. I can't face the partners with this news, and they probably won't want anything to do with me once they've learned it. It's ironic really—how long it takes to build a life, and how little it takes to destroy it.

When we arrive at the station, the interview is cut short—*my lawyer is good*. But even he can't save me from the harsh reality that's about to slam into me like a drunk driver. The arresting officer is round, with a serious expression and long lash extensions. She asks me to say my full name out loud, then lifts my wrist, my fingers hovering over the black pad. My hand trembles, and she stops to look at me. "Take a deep breath," she says as she rolls my thumb into the dark ink, pressing it firmly onto the paper. For a moment, I wonder if she can feel my innocence, or maybe she just wants to move the process along. She repeats the procedure with each finger until all ten have been printed. I swallow hard and force a weak smile—my shaky nerves no match for the anxiety now sizzling inside me. My photo is then taken and I'm patted down—a far better alternative to a cavity search, a thought that has haunted me the past two days.

I had mentally prepared myself for what was to come next, or so I thought, but there are simply no words to describe the horror of stepping into a cold, tiny cell for the unforeseeable future. My entire body spasms as the heavy metal rams shut, leaving me to dwell alone in the suffocating silence.

There's a stench of sewage rising from the exposed toilet burrowing through the bare concrete floor. The walls anchoring the claustrophobic space are the same drab gray stone as the interrogation room. A stained metal sink is attached to the wall, too small to hold even the most basic necessities. I look up, where a window that's barely three feet square sits close to the ceiling, obscuring all but a scant fragment of natural light oozing through. The only piece of furniture is a slat of wood resting on

four legs with a one-inch-thick pad and a thin blanket folded
into a large square.

Sitting down for the first time, I lean back and close my
eyes, demanding more from myself than I might be capable of—
straining to keep the tears from tumbling and my thoughts from
turning dark.

CHAPTER TWENTY-EIGHT

You have a visitor.

Those are the unexpected words that wake me from an afternoon grog. I try to close my eyes, hoping that when I open them this vile nightmare will finally stop prowling around my mind. I drag myself up, sliding into the rubber slippers that are far too large for my feet, then obediently turn around as the bars grind open. My wrists are secured; then the guard leads me to a room lined with small cubbies and chairs, divided by glass partitions, barricades that separate faces and emotions. I shuffle past a few other inmates, one woman sobbing, head buried in her hands; I feel a sudden impulse to wrap my arms around her, but fight against the urge—*you don't dare break a rule in this place.*

I drop into a hard plastic seat in a small cubicle, and wait. The room smells like antiseptic and window cleaner—the walls so close together, it's as if a vise has been clamped around my skull, threatening my sanity. Staring without purpose, I slouch my shoulders and lean into the table, but then I see him and my spine stiffens. Anxiety clutches my neck, followed by a swell of adrenaline—emotions flood in, ranging from relief to shame. I tuck a loose strand of hair behind my ear, nerves rattling as he takes a seat across from me. The edge of his mouth tips up as if he's trying to manage the right response—this situation doesn't warrant a full-on smile, but it would be strange to greet someone in my predicament with a frown.

"I expected to see my lawyer," I say.

"I'm not a lawyer, but I do have a law degree." He grins.

"Well, I have one too, and look where that got me," I respond, and this time I manage a smile.

"How are you doing?" he asks.

"I haven't tried to dig my way out yet; that's something."

"You will. Get out, I mean."

"I expected to bond out days ago; I hope my lawyer has good news for me soon."

"You've got to trust me; Foley and I are doing everything we can to get those charges dropped."

"I'm having a hard time trusting anyone these days—seeing how my own gun was used to murder two of my closest friends and all."

Mason tips his head down and clamps his hands together. "I need to ask you about Alex Ford."

"What about him?"

"How well do you know him?"

"Only professionally, why?"

"Because we can't find him. I went to Silverstone myself and I was given the same story you were. We've also done some internal searches and interviews. No one has been able to talk to him, and he's not using his credit cards, which might mean he doesn't want to be found."

"You mean he's actually gone? As in he fled?"

"I don't know what to think; I suppose he could have had a sudden epiphany and decided to travel the world alone, but he didn't pay his rent this month, which leads me to believe either he's in hiding or something has happened to him."

"Alex is a smart guy; I worked with him for years before Dean reassigned the clients. I don't think he would risk the career he worked so hard for, just to plan some master crime and then frame me—if that's what you're thinking."

"Could he and Dean have been concealing something—together, I mean?"

There was a time not so long ago when I could have answered that question without hesitation. But now my jaded brain lets the idea simmer before I respond. "No, I don't think so."

"That doesn't sound very convincing."

"Before January tenth, my answer would have been a definite no."

Mason slopes back in his chair, his palms stretching up his face. When he looks at me again, I know there's something he's not saying. "What is it?"

He leans forward, his elbows pinned into the table. "Do you remember anyone at the bar that night who tried to get close to you or Claire, or who walked out with you?"

I think back to the flicker of images my memory allows in. My skin pricks, the tiny hairs behind my neck rising. I can almost feel the air—sharp and chilled, as if it's happening now. I remember passing through those heavy doors, out onto the sidewalk. And that face in the SUV—my brain couldn't connect the image to a person, but he was somehow familiar to me. That face, that face … why can't I see it now?

"Are you okay?" Mason asks.

I shudder. "Sorry, I was just …"

"Did you remember something?"

"Someone was there that night when we left O'Malley's. There was a man in the car and I recall at the time feeling as if I recognized him, but it's all a blur now."

"Emma, you didn't take an Uber that night."

"You're wrong. Claire called an Uber. We left the bar because the car had arrived."

"Who was driving that vehicle, Emma?"

"I don't know … I just remember thinking I might have seen him before, but I couldn't quite place him—by that time even the buildings in the distance were swaying."

"Think, Emma."

"Nothing about that part of the night is very clear," I say, an ache forming near my temples.

Mason appears to sense my frustration, and sighs. "I'm sorry, I know this is difficult for you."

"No one wants to remember more than I do, but at some point that night just stops for me."

"I know you do," he says, standing. "I need to get going. Foley and I have a conference call at four thirty."

"All this excitement and you want to leave me now?" I muster a smile.

"I wish I didn't have to leave you," he says, pushing his chair in place and turning to leave.

I swallow his words, swiping at my cheek, then begin the long shuffle back to my cell.

CHAPTER TWENTY-NINE

I 'm escorted through a narrow hallway and into a small meeting room where inmates can meet privately with their counsel. Inside, my lawyer is already waiting. The guard unlocks the restraints and I immediately reach to my right wrist and soothe my chafed skin, then to the left, before taking a seat. My hair is pulled back in a braid, my face bereft of both makeup and joy. I've been on the other side of this table many times, but until now I never fully appreciated just how maddening it is—being incarcerated for another person's crime.

"How are you doing, Emma?" Paul asks. I can tell he's staring at my red-rimmed eyes. I curl my hand and drag my knuckles below my chin. A sarcastic "fabulous" is all I can manage.

"I have some news for you," he says.

"What is it?" I ask, sitting up straighter.

"I met with the detectives working the case this morning. The toxicology reports are in. Turns out Claire Ryan's blood alcohol level was at zero-point-two percent, which was expected, but what was surprising was that she also had high levels of flunitrazepam in her system."

"The date rape drug?"

"That's right. It's amazing she was even conscious when you two left the bar; she couldn't have fought if she tried."

"And Dean?"

"He had even higher levels of the same drug."

"So that means there's no way he would have been able to drive that night."

"Right, but there's more. The labs the detective ordered on you the morning you reported Claire missing showed moderate levels of the same drug. That would explain why you couldn't remember pieces of the previous night and why you were confused the next morning. With the amount of flunitrazepam in your system, they assumed it would have been administered toward the end of the previous night. You may have felt good at first, completely unaware that you had ingested it. But once it kicked in, you were probably disoriented, maybe your speech was becoming slurred, a little dizzy. Sound familiar?"

I grip my mouth. "Yes, I explained exactly that to the detective the next morning."

Paul flips through a binder of documents. "That's right, I see it right here in the report. There is one additional development that proved to be interesting."

"What's that?" I ask, more alert now.

"The video from O'Malley's."

"Tell me it didn't record over," I say.

"No, but the camera is angled so that you can only see the top of the bar and the register—you can't see faces or clothing details," Paul says.

I lean back, dejected. "So it's useless?"

"Not exactly. You see, they suspect the drugs were given sometime between midnight and one o'clock. They showed me the video footage during that time frame. At one point you walk away from the bar area and go down the hall presumably toward the restroom. A few seconds later, a male figure is standing next to Claire while she's talking to the bartender. You can make out his hand reaching into his pocket, and then it appears to hover over the space where your glasses were sitting. The video isn't clear enough to see exactly what he's doing, but immediately after, he heads toward the exit without so much as ordering one drink."

My hands whip toward my face. "What about the area where Dean was sitting?" I ask.

"Too limited a view from that camera, and the one on the other side of the room isn't working."

"That's why I can't remember the details of that night. I was right, whoever did this brought me home, undressed me, and put me in bed. But, more importantly, they stole my gun."

"And if you're right about the sound that woke you two weeks later, then chances are the same person was returning your weapon as you slept."

I drop forward, my face resting over my folded arms.

"It's gonna be okay," Paul says, his hand reaching to me. "The detectives brought everything to the district attorney this morning, and I'm just waiting for a call now so I can go meet with her."

I lift upright again. "You think they'll release me?"

"I'm almost sure of it."

"Oh my God," I say, my hands in the praying position, the tips of my fingers pressed into my chin.

"I should give you a cautionary warning here, though," he

says, causing me to jerk upright. "There's a chance the DA will interpret these new facts differently. She could say that the drugs in your system were self-administered after participating in the crime to make it look as if you too were a victim. We have to be ready for anything."

My chin sinks in disappointment and my head sways from side to side. "No, no, no, I can't let myself go there in my head."

"The detectives have been working around the clock for you—stay positive."

I used to say those exact same words to my clients; what a crock of shit. How does he expect me to muster optimistic feelings when every move I make is controlled by intimidating gun-carrying guards? I know his intentions are good, and he is using everything in his wheelhouse to keep me sane, so I pretend to smile and agree. "Okay, I'll try."

"I hate to leave you, but I have another meeting. I should receive a call about your case in the next couple hours. If it goes as I suspect it will, you'll be released shortly. I'll get a message to you as soon as I hear back."

"You know where to find me," I say with a hopeful heart. As I'm led back to my cell, anger erupts inside me as I think about who could have done this to me, and to my friends. The only thing that keeps me from snapping is knowing that karma will come to collect one day, and I'll be there to watch when it does.

CHAPTER THIRTY

I t took another three days, but finally *I'm out.*
Amy picked me up, and we made two stops on our way
back to my place. First, we had a drink to celebrate my return
to sanity. Then she took me to the local market to pick up a few
items so I could feel normal again. When she dropped me off, I
couldn't believe how amazing it felt to be home.

Freedom smells different—it's magical really. The delicate mix of spices and tea leaves drifting from the kitchen, the
aroma of chicken filled with lemon slices and garlic roasting in
the oven. Even something as simple as the scent of well-worn
leather against my cheek as I lie on the couch can never again
be overexaggerated. Since the moment I walked free from con-
finement, I've been breathing liberty with exuberant gratitude.

The house isn't warm, but it's not freezing either. Winter's
sharp edge has softened a bit, and it almost feels manageable. I
still feel the need to scrutinize every space—securing doors and
windows, double-checking under beds and in closets, assuring

myself that I am alone. And, of course, I leave most of the lights on as I have done for months now, making it more challenging for evil to return for uninvited playdates.

My cell chimes and I rush into the kitchen to retrieve it from the counter. "Hello," I answer.

There's a muffled sound like a distant rattling on the other side, and then nothing.

"Hello?" I say again.

This time a hushed silence fills the space—audible breathing as if someone is searching for words that fail to materialize. I tap the *End* button, then set the phone down and stare at it, trying to convince myself that it's nothing. Shaking off the uneasy feeling, I stick it in my pocket, then head upstairs to draw a bath.

My room remains spotless from my prearrest marathon cleaning session. Examining my bed, I still can't bring myself to spend the night in here. *Not yet, anyway—soon maybe.* The living room couch has become my sanctuary, my second gun now tucked safely beneath it. The cell rings again, and I glance at the screen this time—it's an unknown number. My palm is instantly moist as I pick it up, touching the green circle. "Hello?"

Once again, there's no response—so this time I hit *End,* then silence the phone.

I flip on the heat and set my cell on the small white table next to the linen cabinet. I twist the silver knobs, and water streams into the tub; then I drop in a scoop of jasmine-and-citrus bath salts, watching as the small crystals dissolve. Striking a match, I light two candles and dim the wall sconce. I strip down and toss my jeans and blazer over the hook on the back of the door. As I dip my foot into the water, the warmth calms me, and soon my entire body is immersed in tranquil stillness. I lie back and relax, gliding a loofah along my arms, taking in the fragrance of flowers and tangerine.

Just when I begin to relax, the intrusive buzz of my cell rattles again, and I tense up. From here I can see the glow of the screen and sense the vibration. I want to ignore it, but I can't, so I lean over and reach for the phone, water trickling to the floor as I answer.

"Hello?"

This time I hear him. "You're not safe, you need to know that."

Dread winds through me. "Who is this?"

"Be careful who you trust."

I hurtle upright and step out of the tub, puddles forming near my feet. Wrapping myself in a pink terry cloth robe, I grip the phone tightly against my ear. "You're the one who has been leaving notes for me?"

"I'm trying to warn you."

"About what?"

"It's not what I know, it's *who* I know," the voice says.

"Talk to me," I demand.

"I can't."

"Why are you calling if you can't give me any information?"

"Because I don't want to see anyone else get hurt," he says. I look down, watching as the screen goes dark; *he's gone.*

Hunching over the sink, I start to pant—my pulse going wild. I wipe a smear of condensation from the glass, taking in my reflection—my face flushed, a film of steam and sweat dripping down my neck. Pulling myself upright again, I hurry to my room and throw on a pair of yoga pants and an oversized sweatshirt.

Charging downstairs, I grasp the railing, skipping steps. I check again, but no new calls have come in. I try to call the number back, but it doesn't work. Falling onto the couch, tension ferments inside me and no matter how hard I try I can't let go of that voice. I heed the warning and dial Mason's cell, but it goes straight to voicemail. I didn't used to be the type that would scare easily, but these calls have me thoroughly spooked.

I think about calling Amy, but I know she was going to her brother's house for dinner. A thought pops into my head and I try to talk myself out of it—but then I give in, deciding to do something out of my comfort zone. I order an Uber and grab my coat. Stepping outside, I lock the door and drop a clump of new keys into my bag. It seems like forever, but the car arrives fifteen minutes later, exactly on time.

CHAPTER THIRTY-ONE

The door opens and Mason is standing on the other side in gray joggers and a white tee. His eyes appear sleepy. Jet lets out a stern bark but then retreats when he realizes I'm not a threat. "You're out," he says.

"I was released just this morning. I'm sorry to show up like this, but I tried to call you, and then well … you gave me your address and I'm just a little shaken."

"What happened?"

"I received another warning, but this time the caller had my cell number."

Mason's smile stalls, his lips curling into a frown. Jet sits next to his bare feet with a protective stare. I wonder if I should turn away and leave, but then Mason takes a step back. "Come in," he says, shutting the door behind me and twisting the lock. Jet nudges between my legs, his tail thrashing from side to side. "Hey, buddy," I say, stroking his silky fur.

The condo is everything you would *never* imagine in a bachelor's home—for one thing it's tidy, everything in its place. The walls are a light gray without visible scuffs. A lived-in blue sectional with cream throw pillows sits in the corner, and a moderate flat-screen hangs on the wall across from it—not the typical theater-sized behemoth you'd expect in a single guy's place. Wide-planked, light wooden floors stretch throughout the room, and paintings of watery landscapes hang on the walls. I detect the faint scent of soap lingering in the air, maybe from a recent shower. My angst now under control, I stop for a minute and think about what I've done. *What was I thinking coming here unannounced?*

"I woke you up?" I ask.

"Dozed off watching the game; it was time to pry myself up anyway. Can I get you a drink?"

"Thanks, but I'm good."

He smiles. "I have a feeling I'm gonna need one." Jet follows him into the kitchen, and I follow behind Jet. *This kitchen puts my OCD cleanliness to shame.* White stone countertops are clear of clutter, and there are no dishes in the sink. Two empty Harpoon bottles rest along the side counter next to a juicer, and a bag of ground beans sits against a glass coffeepot. He grabs a beer and walks to his couch, gesturing for me to join him. We take a seat on either side, and Jet lies on the carpet below Mason. "Tell me what's going on," he says.

"You told me I should say something if anything else happened."

"You finally listened to me," he says, tipping the bottle to his lips.

"I have a new security system, so you'd think I'd handle this a little better, but the guy's tone was severe; he wanted me to pay attention."

Mason's forehead creases. "I assume you don't know him."

"I wouldn't be here if I did."

"Touché," he replies. "So, what did he say exactly?"

"He told me that I'm not safe, and just like the note that was given to me outside my therapist's office, he reminded me to be careful with who I trust, or something like that."

"We can get the cell records and trace the call."

"It was from an unknown number."

"Technology is not crime-friendly these days; we have ways."

My shoulders drop and I lean back, my head resting on a cushy throw pillow. Even the worn-in fabric smells like him. I inhale a little deeper. "To be honest I'm not sure why I was so spooked that I thought bothering you at your place would be a good option. It's not as if the guy was threatening me."

"You're not bothering me," he responds, setting down his beer.

"Women often show up at your door at night?"

"You're only the second one tonight, but it's early," he says with a wink.

I smile. "Have you lived here long?"

"Bought it four years ago."

The light catches the side of his face, and he notices me looking at it. This time he doesn't lift his hand to shield the jagged scar. "It happened a long time ago," he says.

"It's not my business," I say, wishing I could tell him that there isn't a flaw that could possibly change how attractive he is. But I can see that he wants to elaborate so I lean back and listen.

"It was my last year of law school; I was at a sports bar with my roommates. Just an ordinary Thursday night—the place packed with students unwinding after midterms. My friends were shooting pool, and I was standing there watching, when the sound of shattering glass seized our attention. We all froze for a second, but then we saw him standing outside—his thin body wrapped in a rain-soaked jacket, the rifle aimed directly at the crowd inside the bar. He fired again, and bodies dropped to the floor, scrambling for cover. It was chaos—people running to the back, away from the gunshots, trampling over one another. But we were too close, so all we could do was duck down behind the table and scan the scene for a way out."

My lips move, but nothing intelligible comes out; so I just stare over at him, too stunned to speak.

Mason takes another long pull of his beer before continuing. "The guy disappeared for a second as he made a move for the front door, and then the firing began again. I could hear the shrill mix of screams as shot after shot rang in my head. But then just as quickly as it began, it stopped, and the room was still. I could see him turn back toward the window, reloading as he watched a group of students cowering below a booth. We all knew what was about to happen, so one of my buddies leaped to his feet and rushed the shooter, knocking him to the ground. I jumped up and ran toward him but smears of blood and spilled drinks covered the floor and I slipped, landing on my side, my face planted on a jagged shard of glass. I didn't feel anything as I rolled over, hoisting my body on top of him, using all of my weight to pin his flailing body to the floor. When the police finally arrived, they had to peel me away—he was cuffed with me still holding him down, and when they lifted him to his feet it was my blood that was dripping down his face."

"You just described my worst nightmare."

"Yeah well, it definitely changed my life. After I passed the bar exam I realized that law enforcement was my calling, so I entered the academy. Turns out my longtime girlfriend at the time wanted a lawyer, so I said goodbye to her without looking back, and here I am."

"You probably saved a lot of lives that night."

"Three were lost, and that was three too many. It took a lot of therapy to get my head straight over it," he says.

What do I do with a story like that? This man has experienced tragedy that mimics my own, and that explains why he just seems to get me. Jet trots over and rests his chin on my lap.

He flips the subject and I'm thankful. "Do you like to travel?"

"I'd like to, but student loans keep me planted."

"Where would you go?" he asks.

"That's an easy question. Japan."

"Why there?"

"There's a Japanese concept that I've always loved, it's referred to as wabi-sabi. It tells us to search for the beauty in imperfection, to accept what is flawed and incomplete in life. I'd love to visit the part of the world where a sentiment like that originated."

"I've never heard of it, but I agree with it completely."

Sitting here I suddenly realize how ridiculous it was for me to just show up at this guy's place. I get to my feet. "Okay—so, you'll check into my cell records to trace the caller?" I ask.

"First thing tomorrow morning."

"I should let you get some sleep, then," I say, tapping my phone, bringing up Uber.

He leaps up. "It's late. You can stay here."

My heart thumps. "Excuse me?"

"I have a second room—the sheets are clean. There are extra toothbrushes in the bathroom, second drawer. I have an early day tomorrow, but I can give you a ride home in the morning."

I imagine walking up the steps to my house alone this late at night without Frankie to look out for me, and shudder. "Okay, if it's really all right with you."

He gestures for me to follow him. Jet snaps upright and trails behind. The room has soft taupe carpet and a queen-size bed with a charcoal pintuck headboard. A tall black dresser stands against one wall, and a rack filled with weights and a spin bike sit on the other. He walks over to the window and lowers the shade, then tosses the throw pillows to the floor. Moving back toward the doorway, he brushes by me and our shoulders accidently touch. He looks up, and it practically requires an act of God to not pull him close.

"I'll see you in the morning," he says.

"Good night," I reply, lowering myself to the bed, my hands smoothing along the thick quilt. He turns toward the room directly across from this one, the door closing behind him.

I visit the bathroom and then fall back onto the bed, my eyes planted on the white ceiling. The sinister voice that frightened me earlier is now muted—I feel safe knowing Mason is nearby. Everything about this place is comfortable, but I can't sleep. I toss from side to side, curling the blankets over me and then kicking them off. Wide-awake, I stumble through the dark to the bathroom again and take a sip of water from the tap. Turning back toward my room, I stop, spin around, and look at Mason's door. I tread lightly on the balls of my feet, inching closer, laying my hand on the smooth wooden surface. Motionless for a moment, I think of him on the other side. I'm about to turn and go back to my room when his door swings open, and I gasp in a breath.

"I'm so sorry, I just …"

He takes another step closer and leans in toward me—my chest bouncing. His face tips toward me but then Jet barks and he pulls back. We hold each other's stare for a few seconds, our breathing in quick succession; but then I rebound to reality and spin around, returning to the guest room.

The smell of coffee stirs me awake. I stretch, then slink out of bed, hastily pulling the sheets taut, fluffing the pillows, and smoothing the quilt in place. I slip into the bathroom and run the water, a warm steam and the smell of shampoo from his morning shower filling the space. I brush my teeth and sweep my hair back into a loose ponytail, then study my face for a quick second, wiping away black smudge marks below my lashes.

Mason is sitting on a stool at the narrow counter that separates the living room from the kitchen. He sees me and stands.

"Good morning," he says.

"Thank you for letting me stay last night," I say.

He smiles. "I filled a Yeti with coffee for you, but I wasn't sure how you take it—you can help yourself."

Is this a thing? Did men suddenly become thoughtful since the last douchebag I dated? "Thank you," I say, pouring cream into the tall silver mug. "What about Jet?"

"He stays here. The neighbor walks him a few times a day— he's plenty spoiled." Mason walks over to the closet next to the front door. He shrugs on an overcoat and returns to the kitchen, twisting a lid onto his mug. I pull up the zipper on my jacket and follow him outside, the early chill nipping at my exposed fingers. Gripping the container with both hands, I'm thankful when we reach Mason's Jeep; the leather seats are icy cold, but the heater is up to the task and within minutes I'm enveloped in warmth.

The traffic is nonexistent this morning, and before long we're pulling over in front of my place. He switches off the engine and we sit for a second. I'm reaching for the door handle to get out when I feel Mason's hand rest on my thigh. I swivel toward him, but he pulls back. "I'll call you about those cell phone records," he says.

"Thank you," I reply, stepping out and onto the curb, gently pushing the door shut. I watch him pull away, wishing that he would come back and finish what he almost started last night.

CHAPTER THIRTY-TWO

THREE WEEKS LATER ... MARCH.

The sun fades into brilliant ribbons of purple and orange as Amy and I push through, our steps in sync. Wrapped in nylon tights, my legs burn as they churn faster, sweat sliding down my back. Amy pulls slightly ahead, charging up the last stretch of the path, sprinting toward the Chestnut Hill Reservoir with me right behind. Completing the loop, we exit at Comm Avenue, our bodies bowing over in exhaustion, both of us panting while searching for a steady breath. I curl over to stretch, my fingertips reaching toward the thin gravel, but then I hear the crunch of steps moving closer, and realize that we're not alone.

A familiar voice booms from behind—but it's not my name I hear him say. This time, it's Amy's.

Standing upright, I pivot to look at him. I haven't seen him since the night I stayed at his house, and now here he is. My face feels bloodless and my chest is wild. I turn to look at Amy, and she stiffens.

"What are you doing here?" I ask, praying like hell that I'm not headed back to jail, or her for that matter.

Amy retreats another couple steps, looking from me to Mason and back to me.

"I was hoping to speak with Ms. Wolfe," Mason says. "I didn't know you two were close."

"Call it a friendship born from tragedy," I respond.

Mason looks toward Amy.

"How did you know I'd be here?" she asks.

"You and Detective Foley apparently had a pretty involved conversation about your running habits—you might remember that he's also a marathon runner. You told him about Thursday afternoons at the park and it stuck with him because it was so specific, so he suggested I give it a shot, and here you are. Now, do you mind if we talk? We can do it here, or if you prefer, you can come back to the Department with me."

"Ms. Wolfe is my mother-in-law—please, call me Amy. Now, what is so urgent that you couldn't call to set up another meeting at the Department?"

"I tried—left three unanswered messages. Like I said, I only have a few more questions, and thought we could take care of it quickly if you're willing."

Amy lifts her tee and swipes at her neck, then pulls her leg from behind, tugging at her calf, stretching first her right, then her left leg muscles. "Emma, are you okay if we talk for a couple minutes? I don't mind if you listen in, as long as he's okay with it," she says, gesturing toward Mason.

He appears to think for a second. "No ... I mean it's not a problem, she can stay."

Amy spots a pair of wood-plank benches alongside the path and crosses the trail, taking a seat on one. Mason settles down next to her, sliding the zipper of his jacket toward his neck, his hands buried in his pockets. I sit on the next bench over feeling oddly out of place. Every word they say carries as if I'm sitting right between them.

"I'd like to talk about your life insurance policies," Mason says. My mental antennas rise and I'm actually interested in hearing her answer to this question.

I hear her exhale hard before she speaks. "I went over this with Detective Foley."

"Apparently there was a second policy you didn't mention during the interviews."

Oh God, where is he going with this ... it's cold out here, but I'm sweating more now than I was during the entire six-mile run.

"Yep, you're correct about that one. At the time, I hadn't even checked to see if the policy we discussed was valid, let alone looked for others. Dean paid the bills."

"And now?"

"Last week I called Genworth Life. I'm sure you already know that there was a million-dollar policy on Dean, and he had the same on me. The one you're referring to was taken out when we were first married and I had forgotten all about it—two hundred and fifty thousand on me, and the same for my husband. Those were still in effect but would have expired in a few years. Would you like to charge me for being too responsible?" she asks, swiping dampness from her forehead.

Mason smiles. "Let's move on. Why don't you tell me about Chris Murray?"

"What about him?"

"You've been spending a lot of time with him, now and before your husband passed. Can you tell me about that relationship?"

Amy's body rocks forward, her face falling to her lap as she puffs out an exhausted laugh, then sits straight up again. "*This* is what you need to clear up?" she asks.

"Were you in a relationship with Mr. Murray prior to the incident?" Mason asks.

"I was."

"For how long?"

"For years. He's married to my brother, and he's handled our taxes for at least a decade. He also happens to be a close friend of mine."

I let out a sigh of relief and watch as Mason sits back, his hands dragging along his thighs. "I realize this process is tedious and inconvenient, but it's necessary," he says.

"You're right—I know you're just doing your job, but Jesus …"

Mason taps notes into his cell. "Let's turn to Claire. How well did you know Ms. Ryan?"

"I met her a couple times at office functions, that's about it. If you're asking about my husband's apparent fixation on her, I knew nothing about it—that is, if it was true."

"Did you hurt Ms. Ryan?"

"Absolutely not. I only learned about the alleged incidents between Claire and my husband after his death."

"How about work? Are you employed?"

"I'm not. I started out in the district attorney's office, then worked for a general litigation firm for years. But Dean and I were trying to have a child, and the specialists thought that the stress of my job might be adding to my challenges with conceiving.

So we agreed that I would stop working temporarily to see if by some miracle my broken body might fix itself so we could get pregnant," she says, edging a tear from the corner of her eye.

"My sister had a similar experience. I'm sorry you had to go through that."

Amy adjusts in her seat and inhales deeply. "Is there anything else, Detective?"

"Just one more thing—did your husband ever talk to you about Silverstone Development?"

I sit up straighter, hanging on every word.

Amy rests her chin on her hand and appears to think back. "I wouldn't put it that way, but I did hear the name from time to time."

"He didn't generally discuss cases with you? With you both being attorneys, I thought maybe he would bounce issues off you from time to time."

Amy stands. "Detective Mason, my husband worked long hours, often late into the evening. When he got home at night we would share a glass of wine, maybe eat a late meal together—we liked to play cards on occasion. On Friday nights we would binge-watch Netflix shows and eat popcorn—sometimes we just sat and listened to music. What we *didn't* do was rehash his already stressful workday.

Mason nods, then slides his phone into his pocket. "Well, I think that's about it for now," he says, standing. Noticing that the foot traffic has dissipated, and the sky is now dark, he turns toward me, then glances back at Amy. "I can give you two a ride to your cars if you'd like."

Amy looks around, the path nearly barren. "Normally I might foolishly believe we could run faster than the creeps out here—but given recent events, maybe we should take you up on that," she says, looking toward me for approval.

"Yeah, sure. A ride would be helpful," I say.

Mason smiles. "Good—dark running trails are not the best venue for displays of bravery."

The walk to his black Jeep is quiet, and the drive to Amy's car equally silent until we reach the lot where she's parked.

"That's me over there," Amy says, pointing to a white Audi.

"Sorry I had to interrupt your run, but I do appreciate you being willing to talk," Mason says.

We step out of the Jeep, and then I watch Amy turn back and lean into the open window. "Is there a problem?" Mason asks.

"Was she ever able to have a child? Your sister, I mean," Amy asks.

He sighs. "Two daughters."

Amy smiles. "Good for her." She lifts her hand and gestures that she's leaving, then turns to walk to her car.

I step toward the window, and Mason looks up at me. "I'm going to wait until I know you two are safely in her vehicle," he says.

I bite at my lower lip, a coping mechanism when I want to do something I know I can't, or shouldn't, do. I want to stay and talk, but I keep it simple. "Good night."

Mason's lips curve upward and it practically takes an act of God not to lean in and try to kiss those things.

CHAPTER THIRTY-THREE

Alex

The dank odor between these walls has driven me to work through the night. I've pressed and tugged and rammed every pound of my thinning body into the ring of iron with no luck. But just as the orange glow of the morning appears, I hear a snap and the bar finally gives, thrusting my knee into the jagged edge of the broken stand. The metal tears at my flesh; I swallow the groan and pull myself from the gully of the battered recliner. The chair squeals as I tilt it back into place—mature wood and rusty parts declaring its age. The room is particularly cold this morning, but my body is dripping with moisture, and the bar feels slippery in my grip. Sliding it through the steel loop on the eyebolt, I try to pry it upward but can't get enough leverage to break it loose.

Looking around, I see the dirty heap of cloth strewn on the sink. Dragging the chain cuffed to my ankle, I reach for a towel, fold it into a small square, and place it on the floor. Using my good knee, I try dropping the entire weight of my body onto the end of the bar, but the bolt still won't dislodge, the tube of iron no match for the beastly contraption robbing me of my freedom.

I fall to my elbows and shriek silently, blood pooling beneath my injured leg. Tipping gingerly to one side, I roll over onto my back, the elation of my initial success replaced by crushing defeat, so devastating that it aches. Staring up at the ceiling, I'm overtaken by the persistent silence threatening my mental grip, terrified that before long, I'll be talking to the walls—or worse, they'll start talking to me.

The gravel outside stirs and I bolt upright, listening. There's nothing at first, but then I make out the faint whisper of an idling engine. A moment later it accelerates, the sound of tires crackling through rocks as it speeds away. *He's gone again!* Wasting no time, I get to my knees, absorbing the pain as I try again to break my ankle free, taking advantage of the brief few minutes when noise won't raise suspicion. But then the doorknob rattles—I fall off balance, skidding backward toward the chair.

The wood judders and I scramble to hide the evidence of my failed escape attempt under the bed. I listen carefully while my chest beats wildly. I recognize the jangle of keys on the other side, and then there's movement, and the door swings inward. I leap to my tender feet, receding as close to the wall as I can until the chain yanks me forward, my vision obscured by the ray of sunlight darting toward me.

"We need to hurry," the figure says, but the sun is too bright to see her clearly. My lips move, but my throat clutches tight. Her bare feet inch closer, causing me to flinch. She kneels, nervously flipping through the ring of keys, selecting one, and then I see her face.

"Claire?"

"Raise your leg toward me," she demands, stabbing one serrated edge after another into the lock. There's a sudden click, and the shackle unlatches. I reach down and rub the inflamed red ring just above my foot and begin to sob like a child.

"Let's go," she says. "Right now, before he comes back."

"I, uh ... don't understand."

"I've been held here for what feels like months—I'm getting the hell out of here. You can come with me, or you can stay," she says.

"I'm coming with you!"

"If we don't hurry, he'll come back and we won't get another chance."

"You were all over the news before they took me," I reply.

"And yet no one has come for me. I don't even know what day it is," she says.

"They think you're dead. They said it was a murder-suicide and that your body was pulled from the Charles River," I say, still unable to grasp what's happening. "How did you get here ... and how did you get those keys?"

Claire squats to the floor and grips her head. "I've been lying next to a subhuman night after night, pretending to care, forcing myself to touch him. I watched him closely and figured out that he keeps doses of what he's been feeding us in his jacket. I waited for the moment when I could slip into his pocket without disturbing him, and finally got my chance. There was only a single pill tucked into the threads, but I curled it into my fingers and waited. Every night he would pour a glass of red wine, and lately he's been bringing one to me. I broke the capsule and emptied the powder into his glass last night so he would fall asleep, and I could search for the key. I wasn't sure how long he'd be out and I wanted to try and free both of us, so I waited until I knew he'd be gone this morning."

"You must have seen his face," I say.

Claire leaps to her feet. "We don't have much time," she says, her blonde hair in a loose ponytail and her tee ripped at the neck.

"Where are we?" I ask.

"I don't know, but there's an old truck in the back, and I'm just praying one of these keys will get us out of here."

"How do you know about the truck?"

"I could see it from the window in my room."

"What is this place?"

"We're in an abandoned cabin, and we need to get the hell out of here *now*, before he returns."

Crossing over the threshold into the living area, I notice a door to my right and a large window above a blue plaid couch. Outside, the sky is a spectacular mixture of blue and gray. Claire grabs two waters from the fridge, edging me toward the door.

"Quick, look around—do you see any shoes?"

I scan the small space, peering beneath the couch, opening the tiny closet by the front door. A few empty clothes hangers swing from a wooden rod, and an old ironing board is leaning against the wall. "Nothing," I respond.

"Then let's go," she says.

Claire opens the door and pushes through the bent screen, with me trailing close behind. A conflicting wave of nausea and hope churns inside me as I taste fresh air for the first time in what seems like months. She runs to the side of the cabin, and I follow her, ignoring the gravel chewing into my heels. The faded blue Ford is sleeping beneath an old carport, a dented gas can leaning on its side nearby. It's a classic that appears to have been forgotten, the windows dirty and covered in cobwebs—but the tires look okay, and a light comes on when I open the passenger-side door. Jumping onto the bench seat, Claire slides behind the wheel. As she digs through her pockets, her expression grows panicked.

"What's wrong?"

"The keys, I can't find them—I must have dropped them in the house. I'll be right back," she says, pushing the door outward.

"No, I'll do it," I say, hurtling out of the truck and running back, wincing as I leap to the porch and tug the door open. I search frantically, my chest throttling as I inspect each inch of the room until I spot them on the edge of the rug below the couch. Scooping them up, I rush back outside, nearly tripping as I drop from the porch and round the corner—*but then I freeze.* Claire is standing in front of me, and her hand isn't empty.

"What the fuck is this?" I shriek, my eyes expanding. Stepping back, I turn to my left, and then to my right, searching for an answer that makes sense. The muzzle is pointed directly at me.

"There's nothing even remotely close to this shithole, and as you were told, no one will hear you scream, so don't bother."

"Why are you doing this?"

"The rehearsed version? I needed you to kidnap me so I could return to society a victim. The truth? Dean was feeding you his suspicions and you were about to confirm them. I worked for years to get to this point, and you were about to fuck it all up."

"So it was *you* who was padding the invoices for the last five years?"

Claire shoots a scraggy grin and cocks the gun, a gleam of sunlight catching the slick metal.

I hear it before I feel it. The explosive charge rings inside my brain in chorus with the thrust of lead punching through my gut, driving me backward—my body dropping to the ground with a thud. My distressed heart continues to pump, clinging to life as the blood spills out of me. I can feel my body working harder and harder. *Thump. Thump. Thump.* My pulse weakens, slowing as I begin to lose consciousness. In the distance I hear a door slam, and as I lie here, staring toward the cloud-streaked sky, the muffled sound of a truck grinding through gravel reaches my ears, growing softer as it puts more distance between us.

And then I hear … *nothing at all.*

CHAPTER THIRTY-FOUR

An unremarkable blue Ford slows to a stop in front of the Boston Police Department. No one inside the brick building can possibly anticipate what is about to happen—or know what to do—when moments later a dead girl walks in. The first officer to notice her blinks hard and takes a second look. Her blonde hair is disheveled, her feet dirty and bare. She's dressed in pink sweatpants and a long-sleeve T-shirt that's torn at the neck. Recognizing her face from the news coverage, an officer behind the desk turns to the female officer approaching the woman. "Do we know who at the Homicide Unit is handling the Charles River murders?"

"Mason, I think," she says.

The young officer dials the phone and waits a few beats until someone answers. "Um, yes, Detective Mason, this is Officer Stoles. Can you come down to District A-1 right away?"

"What do you need? I'm finishing up a report. I can come by later."

"Believe me, you're gonna want to see this now."

Mason exhales. "I'll be right there."

A half hour later the elevator slides open, and Mason steps out, walking toward the front desk. Officer Stoles spots him and gestures toward the side wall. Mason moves slowly, pivots, then stands immobile when he notices her sitting in a chair below a framed photo of the current police commissioner. "What the hell is this?" he asks, his eyes fastened on the face of the pretty, disheveled woman leaning back with her eyes nearly closed.

Officer Stoles comes around to his side. "She just walked in and sat down right there."

"Alone?" Mason asks.

"Appeared to be," he responds.

"How did she get here?"

"Seems she drove herself. There's an old pickup in front of the station, with the keys still in the ignition—one of the officers said he saw her get out of the driver's side."

"What did she say?"

"Nothing yet—might be in shock. We had one of our female officers try to talk to her, but so far she's nonresponsive."

"Have her taken to Mass General for a full medical workup, including a rape kit. And don't let anyone else try to talk to her until Foley and I speak with her first."

"Will do," Stoles responds.

Mason sticks his earbuds in and dials Foley.

Foley chuckles. "Damn, but you can't live without me for even a few minutes."

"You need to turn around," Mason says.

"What? I told you, Stevie has a game today."

"You're gonna want to get back here," he says.

"What happened?"

"Claire Ryan just walked into A-1."

"What did you just say?" Foley asks.

"You heard me. I'll meet you at Mass General."

"On my way," Foley responds.

Foley's feet barely hit the floor as he flies down the hall. When he arrives, Mason is sitting outside a room with his head tilted against the wall.

"You want to help me understand what the hell is going on here?" Foley asks.

"We don't have much yet. She walked into the Department around three fifteen and hasn't said much."

Foley marches to the end of the hall and back again, his hands clutching the sides of his head. "You can imagine my next question."

"Oh, I can. If Claire Ryan is lying in that bed, then who was the woman in the river with Dean Wolfe?"

"Exactly," Foley responds.

The door cracks open, and a petite dark-haired woman in blue scrubs slips out.

"Excuse me, when can we get in to see her?" Mason asks.

"And you are?"

"Detective Luke Mason," he says, revealing his badge.

"I'm Dr. Sanchez. The patient has been through a traumatic experience; the exam is complete, but we've ordered some additional lab work and will be keeping her overnight for observation."

"Is she talking?"

"She is."

"We don't mean to be insensitive, but in cases like this, it's critical that we get the information right away, while it's still fresh in the victim's mind."

Dr. Sanchez appears to think for a few minutes before responding, "You can go in, but just for a short while. She needs some rest."

"We won't be long," Foley says.

"Okay, then, I'll be back to check on her in about a half hour," she says, before turning toward the nurses' station.

When they enter the room, another nurse is busy removing a tourniquet, placing a small square of gauze over the puncture site, then stretching a piece of tape across the white material to secure it. She labels the tubes and drops them into a collection container, then looks toward Claire before leaving. "Are you hungry?"

"Just thirsty," she replies.

"I'll be back with some juice and I'll refill your water pitcher," the nurse says, picking up the blood work before walking out.

Mason moves closer to the bed and smiles. "How are you feeling?"

She looks up, her eyes glazed. "Who are you?"

"I'm Detective Mason, and this is my partner, Mike Foley. We'd like to ask you a few questions if you're up to it."

"I can try."

"That's all we can ask. First, can you confirm your full name for us?"

"My name … I mean … I'm Claire Ryan."

"It's good to meet you, Claire. I don't know how much you've been told, if anything, but we've been investigating an incident that occurred at the Charles River two months ago."

"I haven't had access to my phone or the news since the day I was taken. But what does that have to do with me?"

"Do you recall being out with Emma Gray the evening of January tenth?"

"Yes, we were together at O'Malley's for a work event."

"What is your last memory of that night?"

"Leaving the bar with Emma."

Mason slides a chair from the small table near the window and sits down close to the bed. "Claire, that next morning, two bodies were pulled from the Charles River. One of the victims was mistakenly identified as you."

"*What?*" she exclaims, both hands sweeping toward her face, her expression contorting into a look of distress. "Oh my God, is Emma okay?"

"Physically she's fine."

Claire lets go of a breath. "Then who was in the river?"

"The second victim was identified as Dean Wolfe."

Claire's face dips, her hands cupping her mouth.

"We took some personal items from your apartment and then performed DNA analysis using samples from the decedent. It was a match. How do you explain that?" Foley asks.

"I have no idea; maybe whoever took me switched out items they knew you would look for?"

Mason's eyes narrow. "That's a lot of trouble for someone to go through."

Claire adjusts in her bed, the tips of her fingers digging into her thighs. "I'm guessing there's some level of planning when committing a crime of this nature?"

Foley tosses out the next question. "Do you have any idea who took you, Ms. Ryan?"

Her chest rises and her eyes close, tears slipping down her cheeks. "Yes, I do," she says.

"Tell us his name."

Claire swallows and then whispers, "It was Alex Ford."

"Where did he take you?" Foley asks.

"I'm not entirely sure. It was a log cabin that felt abandoned, somewhere in the mountains."

Mason stands. "Are you saying that Mr. Ford kidnapped you, and he's been holding you at an unknown location until today?"

"I've been chained to the floor for weeks, or months I guess, I don't even know how much time has passed. He would leave for long periods of time, then return. There was no way for me to escape ... until today."

"And where is Mr. Ford now?"

"At the cabin. I think he may be dead."

Foley's forehead furrows. "How did that happen?"

"I shot him with his gun."

"Tell us how that happened," Mason says.

"I want to help you, I really do. But I've had God only knows how many drugs coursing through my veins, and now I have a massive migraine. I don't think I have it in me to revisit the past two months right now."

"We understand, and we'll keep this short, but there are some questions we need answered so that we can move forward with the investigation."

"I'll do my best."

"How did he manage to take you that night?" Foley asks.

"I can't remember anything other than waking up the next morning in a strange place with a splitting headache and a metal leash around my leg."

"You arrived at the police station in an old Ford. Where did you get it?"

"It was parked outside—I found a key that worked, so I took it."

"So where were you then? You drove home, so you must know where you were coming from."

"I just drove as fast as I could downhill, until I found my way out of the mountains."

The nurse returns with a tray of apple juice, a plastic container filled with water, and a sandwich, and places them on the adjustable table next to the bed.

"I realize this is important, but like I said, it's all a blur right now."

The nurse checks her blood pressure and heart rate. "She should probably get some rest now," she says, glaring at the two detectives.

Mason clears his throat. "Right, of course. We'll come back tomorrow."

"I'm sorry that my memory is so unclear. The drugs have taken a toll on me," Claire says.

Foley stands with his back at the door looking at Claire, his expression blank. Mason taps the edge of the bed and turns to leave, signaling to Foley to join him. Once outside, Mason stops, leaning against the wall.

"What do you think?" he asks.

"I think we need to find out exactly what was in this girl's blood. I'd like hair analysis as well."

"Oh, you don't believe her," Mason says.

"She didn't tell us how she got out of the restraints so she could get her hands on a gun; supposedly it happened this morning, so you'd think this would be clear in her head. I doubt she managed to drive herself down a mountain half-baked with a system full of drugs."

Mason smiles. "I love how your mind works."

PART THREE

CHAPTER THIRTY-FIVE

Emma

hat does one say to a ghost?

WThe lobby of the boutique hotel is midcentury modern—wide-open with expansive walls of glass, and geometric carpets resting on polished concrete floors. Gold-tufted couches surround oval fiberglass meeting tables, topped with simple black tripod lamps. I look up; sunburst chandeliers radiate a warm ambience. Near the check-in desk is a delicate table with a glass pitcher of water and a thermos with a card in front that reads *Help yourself to warm cider*. It smells magical— cinnamon and cloves drifting after me as I wander through the corridor, a rumble of unease in my gut.

The detectives handling the case convinced Claire not to return home just yet—apparently believing it better to surveil her place for a while first, to see if anyone else might be targeting her. I offered to let her stay at my place, but she was afraid that the local press might be lurking, aware that I was the last person with her the night it all happened.

We considered meeting in her room, but she thought the lounge was a better idea because of its remote location, a spot that should attract little traffic on a Wednesday night. The entry to the bar is pretty—the walls a deep teal, with cream-and-gray triangular-inlaid floors, the ensemble lit by several Edison bulb fixtures suspended from the ceiling. It's much darker than the rest of the hotel, and rather intimate. When I arrive, a small group is huddled at a round table in the middle, deep in what sounds like work-related conversations. I look over and notice a young couple sipping on chardonnay, eating from a plate of appetizers and talking quietly. Two middle-aged women are perched at stools chatting and slurping cocktails. The craft bartender is dressed in a white shirt with navy stripes, his cuffs rolled back, and a denim apron tied snuggly around his waist. As I step inside, he acknowledges me with a wide smile and a nod.

Having scanned the room twice, I begin to worry that she's changed her mind—but then I see her sitting in a dimly lit booth in the back corner and my chest swells. She looks as stunning as ever—buttery waves tumbling onto her gray turtleneck sweater. She stands when she sees me walking in her direction, and instantly I taste the saltiness of my tears. My legs start to move faster and soon our arms are wrapped around each other. Her familiar scent brings a sense of calm and I inhale deeply, an indescribable bliss at having her back. We both swipe at our cheeks, dropping into chairs, our hands stretched across the table for a long squeeze. There's a tense moment when neither of us says anything; then I break the silence, my body charged with nerves while I search my brain for just the right words.

"It's really you—I can't believe you're here. I thought about what I'd say when I saw you again for the first time, but I couldn't think of anything that would capture how thankful I am that you're okay."

"God, I've missed you, Emma."

I lower my voice. "I have to tell you that imagining what you went through, or what I thought happened to you and Dean, has been unimaginably painful."

"There's nothing as terrifying as examining your life, knowing it's about to end. Except the idea of spending the rest of it in a prison cell, which is what the last two months have felt like."

I lean in. "How are you really doing—now, I mean?"

"It's all very raw, and it feels as if everyone wants me to relive my story; sometimes I just want to curl up in a ball and scream."

I sigh and shift the subject. "I heard you plan to come back to the firm; I wasn't sure with all that … I mean … well, you know."

The bartender appears, breaking the thick emotional tension. He's bald, with a heavy black beard—tattoos winding around his wrists, exposing the art hidden beneath his sleeves. "Can I get you two a drink, or something to eat?"

"Anything with vodka," I say.

"Same for me." Claire smiles and folds her hands into each other on her lap.

"You got it," he says, turning to leave.

Claire's phone chimes and I watch as she digs through her bag and takes it out. It's wrapped in a glittery cover, and looks new. As she stares at the screen, her expression wilts.

"Do you need to get that?" I ask.

"No, it's fine … it's just the detective working on my case. I'll call him back later."

"Detective Mason?"

"That's right. He and his partner need to interview me again—it's fucking exhausting. He is kinda cute, though."

My spine stiffens. I think about the message I received just before coming here tonight, insisting that I go back to the Department tomorrow. I have no idea what Mason needs to talk to me about, but Claire has been through enough for now, so I leave that part out. "I've met with him several times, actually. He's why I'm no longer behind bars."

"Oh, Em, what's wrong with me? I didn't even stop to think about what you must have gone through. I should be asking how *you're* doing."

I smile. "As well as can be expected, I guess—a lot better now, of course."

The bartender returns with two craft cocktails so beautiful that I don't know if I should drink mine or put it on a shelf and pray to it. I choose the former and remove the orchid garnish, taking my first sip—the smooth vodka infused with fresh lime juice and passion fruit slipping easily down my throat.

"We're quite the pair, aren't we?" Claire says, holding her glass up to clink mine.

I smile in agreement, but my fingers fidget, and she notices.

"Are you okay?" she asks.

I hesitate. "There's something I want to talk to you about, if you can manage."

"Sure, anything," she responds.

"I know you had your reasons for not talking to me about what happened with Dean, and I want to respect that. But while you were gone ... I mean ... well, what I don't quite understand is how Alex Ford got involved. Did you know him well?"

"Of course—I was the associate assigned to work on all Silverstone matters, so we got to know each other very well. He called me often, actually."

"Right … right. I knew him too. But I'm having trouble understanding why he would abduct you—what reason could he have had? I mean, it was Dean that was making the advances, right?"

"I can't explain why monsters do what they do," Claire says.

"I hope this doesn't come across as insensitive, but you weren't secretly dating Alex, were you?"

Claire bristles, and her posture stiffens. "Why would you ask that?"

"You told the partners that one of our clients witnessed Dean's behavior toward you at a lunch meeting. That got me to thinking—if it was Alex you were referring to, and if you two *were* involved, then maybe jealousy could be an explanation for what happened."

"The answer is no—I never dated Alex, and I have no idea why he did what he did. I was kept in the dark, quite literally."

"Do you think there's a connection between your claim against Dean, and Alex Ford coming up with this elaborate plan to take you and to murder two innocent people?"

"I don't know what to tell you, counselor," Claire says, taking a sip from her cocktail.

"I'm sorry, you're right—I'm asking all the questions."

Claire sits back—*I know this look*—she's stirring, maybe a little agitated. "Alex never planned on letting me leave that cabin, but I did. I wish we could hear his story, but unfortunately, we'll never get the chance to ask him."

"So, why the other girl, then?"

"Who?"

"The girl that was mistakenly identified as you?"

"Em, *please.*"

"You're right—God, what am I doing? You see, I knew I wouldn't know how to handle this. It's just that there are so many unanswered questions."

Claire smooths her hand over mine. "Someday I'll tell you everything I went through. For now, let's just pretend the last two months never happened."

"Sounds like a plan," I say.

"Hey, I heard you made partner. That's amazing," she says.

"Not the way I wanted it to happen, obviously."

Claire grins. "You wanted it, and now you have it. It doesn't really matter how you got it, right?"

I offer a weak smile in return. "Thanks. But I always imagined that if I made partner, Dean would be there to steer me in the right direction, just as he's done my entire legal career."

Claire sighs, throwing me one of those *don't be so pathetic* looks. "He really meant a lot to you, didn't he?"

I adjust uncomfortably and fight a tear. "Of course he did."

Claire becomes preoccupied with her phone again.

"Are you sure you don't need to get that?"

Her expression constricts; this time she types out a quick message.

"Everything okay?" I ask.

"Yeah, just another local reporter asking me to tell my story. I should probably get back to my room now."

"Right … anything to avoid the circus. I really was happy to meet you in your room."

"I needed to get out. I picked this hotel for a reason, and so far, no one has figured out that I'm here. But I guess it's just a matter of time," she says.

"Well, if you need anything—clothes from your apartment, a chai latte—just let me know."

"I will. And, Em … thank you."

I start to lift out of my chair, but then I sit back down and gulp in a deep breath, looking at my friend. "Listen, Claire, I want you to know something. I never discounted what you claimed Dean did to you—when I learned, it shattered my heart. I just never saw that side of him, so it's been really hard for me to accept."

Claire swallows the last of her drink. "Sometimes we miss what's right in front of us."

CHAPTER THIRTY-SIX

My eyes linger on a small child with soft ginger curls, holding his mother's hand outside the Boston Police Department. He looks up at me—his freckled nose wrinkles when he flashes me a sweet smile. His tiny fingers clutch a toy airplane; he whirs the sound of the engine while his mother adjusts her grip, bringing him closer. An unusual ping of envy passes through me when I think of my own mom—I can't recall a single time when she chose to pull me in, rather than push me away.

Inside, the station is bustling with the crime-fighting types that make you think twice about playing with the law. One rather large uniformed cop is working to control a belligerent man scantily dressed in a dirty white tank top and sweatpants, while another talks delicately to an intoxicated gal with a nest of hair piled on top of her head. I recognize the officer at the front desk from the day I reported Claire missing—Officer Adams, or something like that. He looks me over with a quizzical eye, as if it might help spark a memory, but he can't seem to place me.

"Good morning, I'm here to meet with Detective Mason," I say, wondering what this is about.

"And you are?"

"Emma Gray."

The mention of my name induces another inquisitive look, but he still doesn't seem to make the connection.

"Why don't you have a seat and I'll let him know you're here." He presses the receiver to his ear and punches a number into the phone.

"Thanks," I say, turning and dropping into a blue chair. The walls are uninteresting, lacking in color, but my gaze stops on a photo of a fallen officer, a brass memorial plaque glistening below the thick black frame. My heart sinks and I drop my head, imagining the family he may have left behind.

The desk officer calls my name and I look back up. "He'll be right down."

"Great, thank you. Oh, and do you happen to have a bubbler?"

"I have some water bottles behind the desk. They're not cold, but you're welcome to one if you like," he says, sliding a plastic cylinder of clear liquid onto the counter.

Standing to take the water, I hear Mason's voice. He's talking to another officer when he enters through the back hallway. Noticing me, he ends the conversation and starts in my direction.

"Emma, thanks for coming in. We're gonna meet in a conference room on the second floor," he says, motioning for me to follow him. We pass through a long corridor and into the elevator.

"I suppose if another arrest was imminent, you'd have warned me," I say, only half kidding, hoping he'll give some hint of why I'm here. He doesn't say anything and my mind wanders as I wait for the elevator to open.

We step out and turn the corner into another hallway. After passing several open doors, we stop in front of one that's closed, with a frosted glass panel. Stepping inside, I'm surprised to discover that we're not alone. A man who appears to be in his late thirties with olive skin and dark hair, wearing a navy suit, is seated at the table typing into a laptop. When the door closes, he looks up, then rises from his chair and leans in, his arm reaching toward me. "Ms. Gray, I'm Special Agent Brian Riley with the FBI."

Confused, I shake his hand and sit down across from him. Detective Mason walks to the other side of the table and slips into a chair facing me. I look across at the two men and it strikes me that the purpose for this meeting can't possibly be good.

"Emma, while you were incarcerated, I took the flash drive you gave me to the FBI. Agent Riley here turned it over to Forensic Accounting for review. He did me a favor and expedited the process."

Riley takes over. "Ms. Gray, I imagine you're familiar with how we handle white-collar crimes. The special agents on these teams are very good at finding suspicious activities or transactions. The financial data you provided Detective Mason, and that he turned over to me, proved to be rather troubling."

"So, what does that mean exactly?" I ask, not sure where he's going with this.

"This is what we call a classic padding scheme. In short, one side overbills, and the other side overpays. The increments are kept small enough so that the overbilled party never notices the irregularities. But there are a lot of them, so over time it can amount to a large sum of money."

"Are you telling me that Silverstone Development was overcharging their contractors and pocketing the difference?"

"No, that's not what we have here."

"Then what is it?"

"What we're saying is that Parker, Hill & Lee seems to have been exaggerating the hours on their invoices, and someone in the firm is siphoning off the additional fees that are collected."

"Wait a minute—are you suggesting that Dean Wolfe was stealing from the firm?"

"No. We believe it's more likely that Mr. Wolfe uncovered the scam. The threat of losing the financial windfall, as well as facing jail time, may have been enough for someone to come after him. It's also possible that Silverstone Development was just one of the clients targeted. Our next step will be to expand the investigation to determine how widespread this crime is and who exactly is involved."

"I hope you don't think I had anything to do with this."

"In my experience, thieves rarely bring their crimes to the attention of the authorities, unless they're looking for some kind of deal. At this point we don't believe you had any knowledge of the crimes being committed. However, you did gain access to these documents, and we need to know exactly how that came about."

"I had taken over Dean's cases, and now I'm the one overseeing his team. One of our staff members was in my office confirming my calendar for the following week and happened to mention a special project Dean had given her, which she had just finished. With the other partners already gone for the day, she asked me what she should do with it. When she said it pertained to Silverstone, it sparked my attention. According to her, no one else knew that he had asked her to do the work. When I looked at the file it contained invoices and billing statements going back several years."

"What made you turn them over to Detective Mason?"

"I learned that I was going to be arrested, so I turned everything over."

"Who is the employee that provided them to you?"

"She's our receptionist—she's also a paralegal and has some experience with billing."

"Can you give me her full name?" Riley asks.

"Veronica Davies. But she goes by Ronni. Who is it you think is behind the fraud?" I ask.

"After reviewing the billing statements, we think there are many potential suspects. But in cases like this it's usually one or two rogue participants who are manipulating the numbers. We just need to find them."

"What is it you want from me?"

"We're in the process of preparing a search warrant for the firm now. However, if the person or people responsible are alerted to what we know, they may attempt to destroy evidence. We need you to act as if everything is normal—just continue reviewing invoices and doing your work as you normally would."

"Why don't we just ask Accounting, or IT even, to print the invoices for the past five years? Then I can review a sample to see if the hours billed make sense for the work."

"Because there's likely someone in one of those two departments with dirty hands."

"Right … that makes sense. You don't think that what happened at the Charles is connected to this financial crime, do you?"

"It's possible, yes."

My stomach rolls with nausea. I look toward the window, then down at my cell, and notice the time. "If you're done with me for now, it's getting dark, and I'd like to get home."

Mason stands and his voice rises just a bit. "I can give you a ride home."

I look up. "Are you sure it's not too much trouble?"

"None at all," he says with a blank expression.

"Okay, then, yes, I'd appreciate that."

Agent Riley snaps his tablet cover shut and drops it into his backpack. "Ms. Gray, I'm well aware of the events leading up to this meeting, and I'm sorry for everything you've been through. But I promise you this—we'll make sure the responsible parties pay for their crimes."

"I hope so," I say.

Agent Riley hikes up the hallway in one direction while Mason and I take the elevator down in silence. My mind swings wildly, scrutinizing everyone at the firm, knowing that someone I work with might be involved after all.

CHAPTER THIRTY-SEVEN

The scent of warm raspberry pastries rises from the pink Katie Kakes bag looped over my arm. Balancing two grande lattes on a paper tray in my other hand, I'm about to kick myself for not taking her spare key out of my purse, but then I remember she said the door would be unlocked. Nudging it in with my knee, I enter the apartment for the second time in a month. Only this time, I've been invited—the disconcerting silence replaced by the gritty wail of Luke Combs streaming from the overhead speakers. Everything in here feels different now; it's *alive* again, the fresh remnant of citrus shower gel wafting from the hallway.

It's been cleaned since I saw it last. Pillows fluffed and perched upright on each corner of the sectional, the throw blankets neatly folded into the wicker basket, and the area rug streaked with vacuum trails. Claire doesn't clean anything herself, so I smile to myself, realizing that she's quickly snapped back into her routine and brought in her favorite cleaning crew.

"Morning," her voice calls out from the bathroom.

"I come bearing coffee and your favorite sugar," I reply loudly.

"Raspberry scones?"

I chuckle. "Yes, ma'am."

"I'll be right out."

I set the breakfast on the counter and remove my jacket, folding it over the back of a stool. The white quartz countertops sparkle against the stream of sun slipping beneath the shades. A novel is open, it's pages spread facedown. I grab the bookmark and slip it in, closing the book and sliding it to the side, noticing the title. *Surviving the Lion's Den.* Oh God, maybe this is a self-help book? *Should I be doing more to help her reacclimate back into her regular life?* Claire appears, wearing torn black jeans and a camel turtleneck sweater, tendrils of blonde slipping over her shoulders.

"Smells amazing," she sings, wrapping her arms around me.

"They're still warm."

She opens the bag and breathes it in—then removes one of the scones and places it on a napkin. She drops onto a stool and tears a piece off—her eyes roll back as she devours the pastry. "My God, I missed these naughty little things."

I hand Claire a coffee, then take a sip of my chai. "How does it feel being back home?"

"I appreciate my bed a lot more now. And I have an appointment to get my highlights done this afternoon. Plus, I'm gonna get a poke right here," she says, pointing toward her already gorgeous mouth. "A little fullness will go a long way toward repairing my psyche," she says, smiling.

I sit for a minute and wonder how I might deal with the aftermath of what she's endured—somehow I doubt plumping my lips or lightening my hair would be top of my list. Although to be fair, I imagine if I were in her shoes, I might be bathing in a vat of alcohol right about now. I consider telling her what I learned from the FBI yesterday—of all people, she should be even more careful now—but I decide it's better not to add to the torment she's already suffered through.

"So, what do you have planned for this afternoon?" she asks.

"I'm going to see Amy Wolfe, actually."

Claire coughs, and for just a second, I think she might be choking.

"Are you okay?"

She clears her throat. "I'm fine—it went down the wrong pipe is all," she says, her eyes watery. "I had no idea you and Amy were that close."

"We weren't, but after Dean was killed, I met with her to see if there was anything I could do to help. As it turns out, she and I have a lot more in common than we thought."

"Oh yeah? Like what?" she asks.

"Well, we both loved Dean for starters."

Claire rises from her seat and walks around the counter, tossing her napkin into the trash and removing the lid of her cup to add a packet of Splenda. Her hands appear to tremble; I realize I may have struck an uncomfortable chord.

"I'm sorry, I didn't mean to upset you," I say.

"It's fine, really. Hearing his name is still just a little jarring, I guess. How is Amy doing?"

"Not well, but she's a strong girl."

"Right … of course she is," Claire says, then quickly changes the subject. "Hey, I have a couple hours until my appointment. Why don't we go shopping on Newbury?"

"Sure, sounds nice."

"Let me get my purse—I'll be right back," she says.

I clear the drink holder and bakery bag, then wipe down the counter and slide into my jacket. My tote catches on the barstool; I lift the strap and slip it over my shoulder, then pick up my tea and head toward the hallway so I can start to prod Claire. I know her well enough to realize that she's launching into her typical rituals of makeup-perfecting and outfit second-guessing, which if I let it can take another hour.

I enter her room, and as expected, she's in the bathroom leaning over the counter armed with an eye pencil in one hand, and a curling iron in the other. I fall back onto the bed, tilting on my arms, humming along to "Cold as You." But then the heater kicks on and with it a faint rattling begins. I sit up and look around the room, but nothing stands out. Claire's voice hums over the music, "Hey, Em, come, come. Tell me which one looks better—the hoops or the studs?"

I get to my feet and when I look down, I see it—the heater vent at the bottom of the wall is loose. "Hold on," I say, dropping to one knee and pressing the metal grate inward. But as I'm pushing, I see something behind the thin slats—I slide my finger behind it, trying to grab onto it, but it's out of reach. Claire calls out again and I press the metal plate back into place.

"Coming," I say.

She's holding two earrings, both shiny and glistening beneath the crystal sconces. "Which one?" she asks, the hoop against one lobe and a silver bar on the other.

Without really looking, I select one just to placate her. "I like the hoops."

"Hoops it is, then," she agrees.

The ticking continues, so I walk down the hall and plop onto the couch, waiting for Claire to finish up. A half hour later I hear her padding down the stretch of wood.

"I'm ready," she says, sauntering out into the living room.

Claire is second-look gorgeous in perfect blue skinny jeans, camel ankle boots, and a cream-and-tan blazer with a simple tee. Her hair is lying in soft twisty waves, and her makeup is layered with perfectly arched eyebrows and a bronzy glow cheek. I look down at my torn jeans and white Keds, and feel just a little under-dressed now. But this is how it goes with my fashionista friend, and I've never been one to worry about what others think—so I smile and give her the accolades she craves.

"You look amazing!" I say, lifting to my feet, tote in hand.

We walk out together; she swings her arm into mine and leans her head toward my shoulder. "Have I told you lately how much I love you?"

I smile. "You have, but it never hurts to hear it again."

CHAPTER THIRTY-EIGHT

I watch through the store window as pedestrians pass by with light jackets and wistful smiles—it's a perfect spring day, the sky outside a vibrant blue, the air unseasonably warm. The line in here, though, is long and windy as I wait for my drinks. Two snarky gals nearby are sniping quietly about a full-figured woman waiting in front of them, and I hear them hiss in disgust—judging from toe to brow. I feel the urge to grab a random stranger's coffee and hurl it toward their bony little bodies—confident that from here I'm bound to nail them both. As tempting as that is, though, I think better of the moment without even shooting an eye roll. My drinks are finally announced, prompting me to scoop them up and head outside.

Heading up Boylston toward the Old South Church, I hear the clang of the tower bell ringing. Amy is sitting on a bench next to the wrought-iron gate, reading her Kindle. Her blonde hair is pulled into a loose ponytail, and she's wearing a thin blue jacket, gray leggings, and sneakers. She notices me and rises with a wave. I reach out and wrap her with a tight hug.

Standing for a moment, we step back just to observe the spectacular structure. "It's something, right?" I say, looking around and taking in the splendor of the Venetian Gothic building, admiring the grand arches and walls coursed with beige-and-red sandstone.

Amy reclaims her seat and slides over, making room for me. "Dean loved this spot. We used to walk here on Sunday mornings—what I would give for just one more of those days with him. I would tell him all the things I didn't get to say that last morning before he left to work."

"The last thing I said to Dean was that I left a brief on his desk; my God, work seems so insignificant now."

Amy smiles and takes my hand. "At the time I'm sure it meant a lot to him. He could rely on you."

"So you said on the phone that you went back to work?"

"I did—a small securities litigation firm downtown. I've only been there for a week, but I like the people and it makes me feel as if I have a reason to get up each day."

"You have all the reasons in the world … your family … your friends … me. So many people that need you in their life."

A tiny black dog trots by, its black fur streaked with the same silver as its owner's shortly cropped hair. Amy smiles and curls down to pet the little creature. "Hey there," she says, tickling below its scrappy neck. "Boy or girl?" she asks.

"His name is Tank," the woman says proudly.

"He's a handsome guy," Amy says, and the woman thanks her before tugging at the leash and continuing on her walk. Amy is quiet for a minute, and then she asks the question I knew was coming.

"Have you seen her?"

"Who—Claire?"

"Who else?"

"Yep. I saw her this morning actually, and she's back at the office now. Well, I guess you can say she's back—when she does show up, it's even later than usual most days."

"Too busy sharpening her fangs to make it into the office on time?"

"What do you say we cut her a little slack, knowing what she's been through and all?"

"Gawd, you're naive, Emma. Unless that girl has undergone an exorcism, she's still the same wicked cow that destroyed my husband's reputation."

"You don't believe her story at all, do you?"

"Not a single word. Oh, she's good, all right—playing the helpless innocent victim—I give her props for her acting skills—*bravo, bitch*! But trust me, you need to go in with eyes wide-open when you're near her."

I peer down at the pebbled trail and take in a sip of my tea, my mind traveling back to my visit with Claire. I think about her calm demeanor and how her apartment is so perfectly in order as if life has just gone on without a hitch. And then I remember what I saw this morning and my curious brain begins to wonder exactly what was sitting behind that vent.

"Where'd you go?" Amy asks, pointing toward my forehead.

"Sorry, I just remembered something. The building Claire lives in is an old hotel that was renovated into a high-end apartment building a few years back. Today when I was there I noticed something behind the heater grill in her bedroom and it made me think about all the lives that may have lived there over the years."

"What did you see?"

"Not sure. There were a couple things in there, but only the top screw was loose, so I couldn't get a good view. A card maybe, a letter, I don't know."

Amy stretches out her long legs. "Why didn't you ask Claire?"

"And delay her makeup routine? Not a chance. Besides, she wouldn't be interested in the history of her place."

"Unless she's the one who put it there," Amy says.

I hesitate and stare at her for a moment. "Why would she do that?"

"To hide something that would expose her."

I massage my temples and lean back, the sun tickling my cheeks.

Amy sits straighter and curves toward me. "I know you care about her, but you need to get a look at what's behind that grate. If it's nothing, then fine, maybe you get to see a little piece of Boston history. But maybe it's more than that."

I toss my cup into the bin next to the bench, then turn sideways and face Amy. "How exactly do you propose I do that without her noticing?"

"You still have her key?"

I search the pockets in my bag and find the silver ring with Claire's apartment key, then hold it up, studying the tiny crystals channeled in the smooth metal. "I do."

"The next time she tells you she's going out, you slip in. She'll never know and if you find nothing, then no harm done," Amy says.

I think about my conversation with Claire this morning and how she has a two o'clock hair appointment to get her highlights touched up. With her hair, that will take at least a couple hours, maybe a little longer. I stand. "You know what, I think I have somewhere to be."

Amy smiles. "Let's talk later?" she says, standing and wrapping her arms around me.

I give her a squeeze, grab my bag, and head back to Claire's apartment.

———— ✿ ————

As soon as I'm inside, I lock the door and begin rummaging through the junk drawer next to the stove. There has to be something I can use to remove the screws. Finding nothing, I open the next one and settle upon a butter knife with a rounded tip—not ideal, but it should do the trick.

The apartment is quiet and thick with perfume. I kneel down and slip the blade of the knife into one of the screws, and twist. It slips, but I wrench it again and remove the first one. I do the same for the next one, and another one after that. And then one more time until all four are out. I carefully remove the large square of painted metal and stare inside the black void. Reaching in, I feel around until my fingers touch something dusty yet smooth, and pull out a small card. It's an employment ID for someone named Libby Reed from Roland Pharmacy. There's no photo, but it has a bar code, perhaps for entry to a secure office suite. I stick my hand in a little farther and pull out a plastic bag with a folded sheet of paper covered in a fine layer of dust. I open the bag and pull out the document, carefully unfolding it until the contents are revealed. There are groups of numbers in one column, with another corresponding group of numbers to the right. *What do these numbers mean, and who is Libby Reed?*

I take a photo of the ID card and the document, then slip the bag and the card back inside the wall. I refasten the grate and return the knife to the kitchen. And then, just as quickly as I crept in, I creep back out. The sky has darkened and soon the city will be covered in an early-spring downpour. I hurry toward the subway, only now with more questions than I had this morning.

CHAPTER THIRTY-NINE

Claire

A gentle pattering of rain falls against the windshield—wipers *click-clacking* from side to side, clearing a swath of visibility. She adjusts her rearview mirror and taps the heater, raising the temperature to a comfortable warmth. The road is narrow and dimly lit, but she's acutely familiar with the area, having made the drive several times prior. She listens to Billie Eilish's "bad guy," drumming her fingers along the steering wheel, mouthing the lyrics under her breath—the slight curl of a satisfied smile etched on her face.

A blast of thunder rattles the car, followed by a torrential downpour, and suddenly her vision is obscured. Slowing down, she maneuvers carefully until breaking free from the clutch of the dark mountains. In the distance she sees the glow of the rustic mountain resort, guiding her in—*inviting her in.*

Curving through the entry, she pulls the Audi SUV into the self-parking section. She unlatches the seat belt, then slips on her raincoat. The wind has picked up, so opening the door takes some effort, a flurry of showers whipping at her face. She rushes into the lobby and stops at the front desk.

"Good evening, welcome to the Shady Mountain Inn. Do you have a reservation?"

"I'm actually here to meet a guest—Mr. Johnson, bungalow eleven. He said there would be an envelope waiting for me."

"Oh yes. You are exactly right. Hold on just a sec," he says, pulling out a drawer. "Ms. Crane?"

"That's right," Claire says.

"If you would be kind enough to show me your ID, I can give it to you now and you can be on your way."

Claire grimaces. "My ID? For a package?"

"Sorry, that's right. It's the inn's policy. You'd be surprised at how many people try to sneak into rooms while guests are away, or try to buy items from the convenience counter and put it on a room that isn't theirs. So, if you can just show me your ID, Ms. Crane?"

"I'd be happy to, but I just realized I left my wallet in the car and … well … I mean, have you looked outside? It's pouring. Maybe you can just call Mr. Johnson and he can confirm that it's me?"

"Sure thing, hold just one more minute," he says, lifting the phone and punching in his number.

Claire fidgets with a travel brochure on the counter.

"Looks like he's not answering," the clerk says.

"I'll wait," Claire replies with a scowl.

"You know what … I guess I can make an exception this time, but keep it between us. Here you go, Ms. Crane," he says, handing her the envelope.

"I appreciate that, and I'm sure Mr. Johnson will thank you on his way out."

"Enjoy your stay. Breakfast is served from eight to eleven tomorrow," he responds.

Claire forces a smile, then flips the hood of her jacket back on and steps outside, dragging a small suitcase behind her.

She slips her finger below the flap of the envelope and removes the room card, waving it over the sensor, nudging the door inward. Her jacket drips on the tile entry as she slides it over a hanger and places it in the closet. The room is warmly lit—and in the corner she notices a tray of cheese and fresh strawberries sitting next to an open bottle of cabernet—the purr of classic piano playing from ceiling speakers. She pours herself a glass of wine and takes a long sip, savoring the woodsy essence of dark fruits and vanilla.

She senses movement outside and leaps up, looking out into the rain-soaked lot. She sees nothing out of the ordinary, just random vehicles with wipers fanning across their windshields. She takes another sip of wine and smiles when she hears the chime of the lock unlatching again. His shadow appears first until his wet hair and damp skin move into the light with the smug satisfaction of a cheating man.

"Well, hello, handsome," Claire says with a grin.

"God, I missed you," he responds, moving hungrily toward her.

Claire wraps her arms around him and buries her mouth in his, before pulling back and kissing his neck. "We're almost there," she whispers.

"You're soaked. Let's see what we can do about getting you out of those clothes," he says with a groan.

"By the way, nice motel choice. This place is creepy AF."

"It's discreet, which means it's safe. No one knows about it, and after what we've been through, now's not the time to take unnecessary chances."

"I guess so," Claire whimpers.

"Would you rather listen to the cries of your fellow inmates?"

"Would you stop fixating on prison? We're gonna be fine," Claire says.

"I don't do well in elevators; I sure as hell wouldn't last long in a cell."

"Then you're good, because you'll never be inside one."

"Everything okay with Emma? You don't think she suspects anything, do you?"

"She's fine. You gave her the partner position, which should be mine, by the way. But ... it was a clever move on your part. She's blissfully unaware that we're involved."

"It didn't help that Dean talked to her at O'Malley's; maybe you should have stepped in and stopped that conversation."

"How did I know he was going to bring that up at a work party? Besides, it would be awfully suspicious if I were to play nice with the man who was harassing me."

Logan nods, walks over to the table, and pours himself a glass. The cascade of heavy rain continues its assault on the large windows, the sound of waggling glass echoing throughout the room. Claire reaches out and takes his hand, guiding him toward the bed. Falling into their comfortable routine, they drink each other in, neither of them noticing the motion outside—a figure lurking—peering through the window. *Watching.*

CHAPTER FORTY

Emma

Books & Beans is an old store nestled among a cluster of brick buildings on Newbury. The first thing you notice is the enticing smell—not just the typical scent of old books and aged wood that you might find in a place like this—although there is that for sure. No, in here it's the aromatic harmony of homemade cinnamon cake and espresso that draws you in and makes you want to stay just a little longer than you should. The floors are unintentionally bucolic, and rustic shelves shroud the walls. The only other décor is a large menu board and a glossy antique oak counter. There's a loft on the second level where readers can go for solitude—I often claim one of the six small tables looking out onto the sea of fellow readers. Usually I come here seeking refuge, a way to escape being found by the world, if only for a short while. Tonight, though, I'm here to find a gift for Frankie.

The doors to this quaint little shop opened for the first time long before Kindles were a thing, and certainly before those of us who read for entertainment could order up alluring titles with the click of a finger. Still, there's nothing I enjoy more than spending time with Ray's three-legged, visually challenged Lab, Tully, while getting lost in a good book.

Ray is the owner, in his early seventies now. He walks slower than he did when I first found this little gem, but is incredibly charismatic, and on occasion, I catch him snapping a wink at his wife, Ellie, who spends her days searching for literary treasures. The regulars arrive right when the doors open at eight o'clock, and there are many—I prefer evenings after the rush has passed, when serious college kids come to study, planting themselves for hours with a silent focus, the way I did when I was in law school.

I left work a little early after getting Jacob's message, letting me know that his dad will be coming home today. I asked him what had happened to Frankie, but he said that his dad would explain when I dropped by, which sounded ominous. I browse through the latest selections of nonfiction, finding a tale of a daring escape during World War II—*it's perfect*. Ellie offers to wrap it for me in kraft paper and navy-blue ribbon, and I happily accept.

Tossing the gift in my bag, I leave the shop and head up Newbury; it's always lively on Friday nights, and tonight the temperature is unusually forgiving. I insert my earbuds and search my library of audibles, choosing a psychological thriller I started a few days ago, then begin my twenty-minute walk home.

Turning the last corner toward my place, I notice that the streetlamp next to Frankie's house is still broken, making it appear darker than usual. I'm relieved when I see a light glowing in his front window, hopeful that he's still awake.

I launch my first step up toward his door—but just as my foot skims the pebbled stone, a hand reaches out of the darkness and snatches me in midstride, yanking me backward. Seized with panic, I buck and squeal, trying to shriek through the tightly laced fingers but then another hand clamps over my mouth, preventing my scream from escaping.

"I'm not going to hurt you." It's a man's voice in a hushed tone, coming from behind my right ear.

I continue to fight, trying to stretch upward, but his grip is a vise that I'm not strong enough to break.

"Listen to me," he whispers in a cautionary tone. "I'll uncover your mouth, but you need to be quiet and let me talk. Nod if you understand."

My head slowly tilts up, then down.

"I've tried to warn you, but watching you walk home alone tonight makes it clear you don't get it. *You're not safe.* I'm not even safe."

"You've been the one following me?"

"I didn't want to see anyone else get hurt."

"The only person I'm worried about right now has his hands wrapped around my neck."

"I should be the least of your worries."

My fingers press into the moist soil surrounding a clump of shrubs. "Let me stand up and we can talk … I promise I won't tell anyone you were here."

"*Listen* to me—you can't trust *anyone* right now, remember that. I'm going to give you something … but don't let anyone see it until you've read it."

The warbled voice appears sincere, if not a little desperate—and for whatever reason I believe him. The tension in my body softens, my brain processing his warning. I feel him remove one hand, and I hear rustling beneath his coat. He pulls something out and slips it into my hand.

"Now, I'm going to release you, and you're gonna remain on your knees while you count to fifty. Do you understand?"

I nod again, feeling his fingers peel away from my face and his body separate from mine. I drop what he handed me into the gift bag I'm still holding, ready to obey his request—but then a sudden screech of tires hurtles me to my feet.

Headlights flash on, and a large black SUV races toward us. It comes to an abrupt halt on the opposite side of the street, stopping partially on the sidewalk, another following right behind it. I watch in disbelief as FBI agents pour out and pin my abductor to the concrete. They wrench his arms behind his back and snap cuffs around both wrists. There's an unexpected vortex of emotion as I watch him rock from side to side. His neck hinges upward, but I still can't see him clearly through the blackness. I inch closer to get a better view. He glances up again, affording a shadowy glimpse of his face, and it staggers me to my heels—*oh my God, it's Kyle.*

They lift him to his feet and push him toward the open back door of the truck. For a brief second, he looks directly at me, and I feel something I probably shouldn't for the man who has been haunting me for weeks—*gratitude.* One of the agents rests his hand on my shoulder. "Ma'am, are you okay?"

I shudder and swipe the loose dirt from my pants. "I'm … I mean … yes, I'm fine."

"Do you need emergency attention?"

"No, he didn't hurt me."

"I need to get your name and phone number," he says, and I offer both up.

"I live next door," I add.

The agent hands me his card, then walks away.

The commotion finally subsides, and the SUV rolls off. Still stunned, I hurry to my front porch, surprised for a second time tonight when I find Mason sitting on the top step, his arms folded across his knees.

"You knew he was following me?" I ask.

"They were watching him."

"Why didn't you tell me?"

"The FBI has taken over the case. They had a feeling he might come for you."

"He was trying to help me."

"You don't know that," Mason says. "They're gonna interview him tonight and I'll let you know if I learn anything."

I climb the stairs and maneuver around him, then unlock my door. He stands and I turn back toward him. "I need to get some sleep," I say.

He looks at me and I know exactly what's up; he wants to check my place out. It's almost as if he has a parentlike need to make sure I'm okay. "I'll be fine," I say, letting him know he can take off.

"You were just attacked outside twenty feet from your house. I'll feel better if I know you're safe."

"They just took the guy away like a zoo animal; why do you think someone would be in my house now?"

"How do you know he was alone?" Mason asks.

I press at my forehead with my thumb and middle finger, then push through the door and hold it, gesturing for him to come in, snapping the door shut behind me. I watch as he robotically does what he does, checking locks and windows, examining rooms and closets. He climbs the staircase and I remove my coat and out of habit go right to the kitchen, filling the kettle with water and sparking a flame. Feeling the weight of a thousand pounds of concrete crushing down on me, I finally give in and swallow a Xanax.

Mason treads back downstairs, heading toward the door.

"Feel better?" I ask, reaching for the handle to let him out.

He looks straight at me—no, it's more like through me, examining me. "Worrying about you has become a full-time job," he says.

"Then don't."

I expect him to charge outside, but something very different happens. He reaches for me, takes my hands into his, pins my arms to the wall. He heaves his body as close to mine as he can without actually touching. Our eyes fasten—faces so near that I can almost taste his minty breath—*and I gasp*. His lips press into mine and my pulse accelerates—I feel something between my thighs that I haven't felt in a very long time. But then I push him away, and he steps back, his breathing so rapid I can see his chest hammering through his fitted tee.

"What's wrong?" he asks.

"It's not that I don't want to, it's just that … my life is messy. I'm messy."

He takes another step back and raises his hands as if to say he understands, then slips through the door. I snap the dead bolt and set the alarm—then with my back leaning against the wall, my heart *ba-da-bumps* as I inhale traces of him. I'm not even sure what to make of the last two minutes, but my God, I wish I could feel that again. *Why did I stop him?*

Deflated, I'm about to head upstairs to change when I remember the bag. Taking it into the kitchen, I sit down at the table—first removing Frankie's gift, then the folder that Kyle had given me. Curious, I open it to find the words *Bank of Milan*, followed by several pages. As I leaf through the document, it doesn't take long to recognize what I'm looking at. These are deposits, and in the bottom right a handwritten note in black pen that reads *Silverstone, Summit Landing, Seventh Street Plaza, and Iron Properties.* All three are Parker Hill & Lee clients.

CHAPTER FORTY-ONE

I arrive at Frankie's porch stalked by a blast of wind. The bark of a small dog approaching from across the street draws my attention; I look over and watch as the furry little legs trot out of sight, and then I turn back and knock again. I'm about to give up when I hear movement on the other side of the red door. The porchlight flicks on and a middle-aged woman with a short caramel-brown bob appears, wearing blue scrubs, a white sweater, and a welcoming smile.

"Can I help you?" she asks.

"Hi there, I'm Emma … I live next door." I gesture toward my house and smile.

"Oh yes, Jacob let me know you might stop by. I'm Mary, his home nurse."

"Nice to meet you, Mary. Is he awake?"

"We were just about to get him ready for bed. Come on in, I'm sure he'd love to see you. It will have to be brief, though. The medication makes him drowsy."

"I won't stay long," I say, stepping in, holding the wrapped gift.

"Hold on, Emma—I just brewed some tea. Would you like a cup?"

"Thank you but no."

"All right, then, I'll be right back," she says, slipping into the kitchen.

Jacob's construction company recently renovated Frankie's house, and this is the first time I've been in here since it was finished. The original oak floors have been stripped and stained, and the wallpaper was removed and replaced with a fresh coat of pale gray paint, which makes the room appear much larger. A new chenille sofa is flanked by cream swivel chairs and a black coffee table holding a glass vase filled with purple orchids.

Mary returns carrying a tray with a navy mug and a plate with two sugar cookies. "He's in the family room watching the game."

I follow her down the hall, walking toward the warm glow at the back of the house. Inside, the room is a comfortable temperature, and Frankie is sitting in his well-worn recliner. I notice his gun display case hanging on the wall and want to make sure that he is completely lucid after his hospital stay. "Who's winning?" I ask, tapping his shoulder.

"Emma, if I knew you were stopping by, I would have done my hair." He chuckles.

"You gave us quite the scare," I say, leaning down to kiss his cheek. Mary sets the tray on the end table and fluffs his pillow.

"I'll go wash the dinner dishes and get your bed ready," she says, turning to leave.

As soon as she disappears down the hall, Frankie pulls out a small bottle of bourbon and pours a generous splash into the cup.

"Frankie! You just got out of the hospital," I say in a hushed tone.

He shoots me a playful grin and damn but this man is a powerful force. He's recovering from a hospital stay and still he looks as strong as ever sitting in his chair. "Haven't you heard of flavored tea?" he asks, taking a sip.

"No, no, no … we need you; *I need you* to be around for a long time. You can go ahead and finish that one, but I'm taking the bottle with me when I leave. Now … tell me exactly what the doctors say happened."

Frankie takes another long pull and then leans back. "They don't know. I came back from my run that morning, scooped the green drink you left for me and drank it along with a plate of eggs. I was only halfway through my breakfast when my stomach lurched and then my chest tightened and I knew something was wrong. My vitals were all over the place in the ER, so they admitted me. My heart was a little wonky so they put me on some meds temporarily, but now I feel better than I have in years."

"Frankie, I didn't leave a drink for you that morning. I was late for work, which is why I couldn't stop to talk. Remember?"

His expression hardens. "Are you sure? It was on my porch just where you always leave it, so I assumed …"

My head dips; I furrow toward my lap and squeeze the wrapped gift. *Oh God, this couldn't possibly be related to what's happening to me, could it?* I look up, forcing a smile. My hands rock as I hand the package to him.

His eyes widen. "What's this?"

"Just a little something to help pass the time."

Frankie tugs the bow loose, then peels the tape until the paper separates and the book is revealed. "It's perfect, I love it," he says, pulling it toward his chest. "I'll start reading it tonight."

"I hope you enjoy it," I say.

"You just reminded me—I have something for you too. It's not a gift, though—your friend dropped it off for you the day before I went to the hospital. I'm really sorry, she said it was important, but that morning you were in such a hurry and I couldn't get your attention. With everything that happened, I completely forgot about it until just now."

A shameful blast of warmth flushes my face as I think back to the morning I ignored Frankie's wave, just so I could get to work early. "Which friend?" I ask.

"The girl I nearly shot on your side yard last month."

My stomach twists. *He's talking about Jessie.* I sink into the chair. "What did she leave for me?"

"It's sitting over there on the sofa table, the large white envelope."

I look over and spot it immediately. Curiosity occupies my thoughts, and now I find it hard to think about anything else, but my attention remains on Frankie. We chat and watch the game, but my gaze keeps sweeping back to the table. And then I notice Frankie's eyes growing heavy, and I take the cup out of his hand. I slip the whiskey bottle into my bag and lean in for a hug. "I should let you get some rest," I whisper.

His eyes open just slightly. "I'm sorry, the medications make me drowsy." His lids fall shut, and I kiss him good night. I let Mary know that he's ready for bed, then grab the envelope and rush home.

I flip on the kitchen light and set a glass on the counter. I squeeze lime into a mix of vodka and tonic and swallow the first gulp, anticipating the bubbly citrus burn. Taking both the glass and the mysterious delivery to the living room, I drop to my knees. Leaning closer to the ottoman, I skim my finger below the sealed fold, then lift the flap and peer inside. There's a one-page note with a memory stick taped at the bottom. I begin to read.

Emma,

I'd like to say that I was wrong, and in a very big way I was, because it's much worse than we thought. The answers to our questions are contained in the memory stick that I've attached. I'm meeting with Detectives Mason and Foley tomorrow afternoon, and once I do, they too will know everything I've learned.

Maybe when the truth is finally unmasked, there will be some closure for the families.

I hope one day we can reconnect.

Jessie

My eyes leak as I reach for my laptop and power it up. I slide in the flash drive, apprehensive about what I might find as several files and documents come to life on the screen. I review them one at a time, and with each new revelation my heart skips another beat. There are pages of emails that appear to be from Dean but that were originated by Claire, impersonating him through a fictitious address. There are lists of numbers, and what looks like deposits made to several different bank accounts. The last page is Jessie's summary, with a total at the bottom—*$11,702,011*. I collapse backward, my hands cupping from below my jaw to the bridge of my nose as I finally grasp what she had been trying to tell me. It's not the stranger in the shadows that I should fear; it's the familiar smile right in front of me that should send terror through my marrow.

I throw down the rest of my drink, tipping the glass until every last drop grazes my tongue, hoping that the cocktail will trick me into believing none of this is real. *But I know better than that.* I close my computer and lie back on the couch with a dull ache building in my gut. Jessie may not have realized the danger she was in, but I certainly do, or at least I do now. Gramps once said *never underestimate evil disguised as kindness, because the devil was once an angel.* That sentiment has never been more true than it is now.

CHAPTER FORTY-TWO

An impressively decorated cake with white icing and silver candy golf clubs rests on the reception desk. It's an odd thing to see this early in the morning, but with my insatiable weakness for buttercream, it's unusual in a good way. Most days Ronni is already in position and bursting with smiles when I arrive, but today her chair is empty and the halls are quiet. I slip into my office and drop my bag, then plug my laptop into the charger. I pull the cord on the shade and take in the pale blue sky, adorned with clusters of vivid clouds and an airplane making its descent in the distance.

The air in the kitchen is replete with the delicious scent of freshly brewed coffee. A basket filled with bagels and a tray of fruit are displayed on the break table, along with a plate of flavored cream cheese and napkins. Ronni bounces in, holding a carton of fresh orange juice, placing it next to a stack of plastic cups. She's wearing a lemon-yellow blazer with a slimming blue skirt, and rocks every stretchy inch of her sexy ensemble.

"What's all this?" I ask.

"Logan's birthday," she says, scooping a bag of square plates and napkins from the chair. "I ordered balloons and a gift certificate to his favorite restaurant in Newport. I hope you'll be here to celebrate with us after lunch?" she asks.

"I wouldn't miss it," I reply.

"Perfect. Now, I should go hide the evidence before he arrives," she says, slipping out into the hallway.

I collect a clump of red grapes and return to my office, dropping into the chair so I can organize my day. I've just finished reviewing a lengthy lease agreement when, through my partially open door, I see Claire saunter into the office, wearing formfitting black pants with a white blouse and nude pumps. The leather bag draped over her shoulder appears to be new and likely costs more than I make in two weeks. Pretending everything is fine will take an Academy Award–winning performance, but I won't have to keep it up for long—before the day is over, I plan to tell Logan everything.

"Emma," she calls out, changing course and moving in my direction.

"Hey," I respond, and it takes a lot not to tell her everything I know.

"I was just thinking—we should go out for sushi this week."

"Sure, sounds nice," I respond. *Not happening.*

"Great—I'll make a reservation at Maki's for Thursday night at six o'clock?"

I'm about to tell Claire that I have to get busy when a roar of voices arrives in the lobby, chatting with Ronni. One I recognize as Logan; the other two are most likely partners coming in behind him. Claire spins and looks toward the front desk. "Seems like we have a full house today."

"There's a partners' meeting this afternoon, so I suspect all the heavy hitters will be in."

She turns back my way. "You know, I was told that if January tenth had never happened, I would have been named partner next. *You're welcome*," she says with a maniacal grin.

I choke out a cough, reach for my mug, and take in a sip. "Wouldn't life be so different if that day had never occurred?" I ask, wanting to slap the smug look off her Botoxed face.

She inhales deeply and releases her breath, her features sharp. "I should get some work done."

"Me too," I respond, standing to push the door shut behind her.

The morning is more productive than I had expected it to be—somehow I manage to push aside moments of fury, thinking back to the information Jessie had collected. I finish the salad I brought for lunch and am about to hit *Send* on a long email I had been crafting for a client when I hear Ronni flushing us out of our offices for the celebration. I don't feel much like cheering for anything at the moment, but I play along, if only to make Logan feel special.

The conference room is buzzing with chatter. Every seat is taken, and even the wall space is occupied by leaning bodies engaged in casual conversation and laughs. The cake sits in the center of the table with matching napkins and plates, and a black gift bag with teal tissue is beautifully displayed alongside it. Logan enters last, and the room erupts into a spontaneous round of "Happy Birthday." But as quickly as it began, the chorus of voices tapers off, the collective attention of the party diverted, staring in stunned silence at what's taking place in the lobby.

A noisy cluster of agents in navy jackets swarms in, the letters

FBI stenciled in large yellow letters across their backs. Showing no remorse for the interruption, two agents step into the doorway and call out a name. *"Logan Parker!"* I collapse onto the credenza—a wave of confusion churning inside my head. *What could Logan have done? Those iron bars must have given Kyle loose lips … but he couldn't possibly know about Claire's involvement, or she too would be marched out of here.* The crowd splits in two and shuffles toward opposite walls as if parting like the Red Sea, until only Logan is left standing in the middle of the room, with a look of shocked resignation. I shoot a glance at Claire, her body stiff, her face expressionless.

Cuffs are latched from wrist to wrist right there next to the gorgeous cake, and the humiliated partner is paraded into the lobby and escorted out toward the elevators. Other agents flood the offices, taking Logan's computer, laptop, and briefcase. The Accounting Department wing is thoroughly scoured, and by the time they're finished, not a single electronic device or document remains. The rest of us are kept at bay in the conference room by an army of agents—every set of eyes fastened to the unimaginable spectacle of activity. I watch as Claire maneuvers closer, squeezing between me and another associate. She leans in, her hand cupping my shoulder, and whispers, "A criminal with a brain would never leave evidence at their office."

I want to tell her that no, they wouldn't—they'd hide it in their wall. But I don't, of course. Rather, I raise my brows as if in agreement. She smiles and winks, like the poisonous spider she is—satisfied with the web she has spun.

CHAPTER FORTY-THREE

Fifteen minutes after I leave the office, the sky opens up—I keep walking, my hair wet and heavy against my shoulder blades. Pedestrians gawk; my clothes are dripping, and I can feel my mascara melting into half-moons. I stumble on, trying to figure out what I just witnessed. Logan is corrupt, and I missed it; it appears I've missed a lot of things lately. I don't consider myself to be naive, but I've been fooled this time.

My phone rattles against my laptop. Digging through my tote, I find my cell—Mason's name is on display. I study it for a second, then swipe the moisture from my finger and accept the call, lifting the phone to my ear.

"Emma? Where are you?" he asks in a restless tone.

My eyes linger on the sidewalk as I trudge up Boylston. "I just left work. I'm walking home."

"It's really coming down out here," he says.

"Is it?" I ask, with an eye roll so flippant he might be able to see it through his phone.

"I'm just down the street from the Pru. I need to show you something—it's important."

I stop in the middle of the sidewalk, searching through the jumble of umbrellas for someplace where a dripping-wet girl might blend in. Long strands of soaked hair whip around as I survey an area I know all too well, but suddenly can't remember. Then I spot a familiar blue-and-white awning. "The Station Coffee Shop," I say.

"I'll be right there."

———

The aroma of freshly ground beans drifts through the small diner. Ordinary coffee, the kind that makes me think of my grandparents when I was young, waking to their favorite morning ritual dripping into a glass pot, the clink of a teaspoon gently blending cream into the rich brown liquid. *I've never wanted a hot cup of anything more than I do right now.*

It's a small place, white subway tile capped by an intricate silver pressed-tin ceiling and blue-and-white vinyl booths stretched along a wall of windows. I slosh in and remove my coat, taking a seat at the far end of the restaurant. A stocky male server slips by me carrying plates of scrambled eggs and French toast, and just as he passes, I notice Mason outside. He wrenches the door open and looks around, then walks my way and slides in across from me. I lean back and ignore the water collecting on the vinyl. Mason looks at me as if he's *not* staring at a swamp specimen, and yet he is as handsome as ever. *Kill me now.*

His lips curl, deepening his dimples. "How are you doing, Emma?"

"Did you know it was going to happen today?" I ask.

"I learned about it this morning. Agent Riley called to let me know that the raid and the arrest were gonna take place today."

"And you didn't think to warn me?"

"Foley and I were on a plane about to depart South Carolina when he called."

"What were you doing in South Carolina?"

"We were alerted to a missing person's report that might have had a local connection."

A cheery round-faced kid holding a tablet stops by, his tight, strawberry-blond curls cut short. "Ready to order?" he asks.

"Just two cups of coffee," Mason says, deciding for both of us. The man nods and taps his pad, then scurries away.

My hands clasp in front of me on the table and I let out a nervous breath. "Was it related to Dean's case?" I ask.

"That's actually why I wanted to see you," he says, pulling out a large book from a plastic sleeve and sliding it toward me. "I've earmarked the page. I want to know if you recognize her," he says.

"The missing girl?"

"That's right."

I drag my finger along the spine, then pull open the leatherlike cover where it's been marked. I scan through the colorful images of just-barely adults smiling back at me—that fleeting look of innocent hope reflected on each young face. My eyes come to a stop on one in particular; her features are vaguely familiar, yet different, and it actually takes my breath away—*she's beautiful.* Blonde with bluish-green eyes, and high cheekbones with a wide smile. The name underneath reads *Allison Claire Ryan.* I look up, confused.

"Now turn back one page," he says.

I hesitate for a long beat, afraid of what I might see—then

slowly flip over the thick glossy paper. As the image comes into focus, my hand flies to my mouth, smothering a scream. The photograph is small, but the face is one I recognize immediately—shiny blonde waves and a self-assured smile. But it's the mesmerizing clear blue eyes that I can't stop looking at. It's unmistakably her—the friend that I've known and loved for so many years. But below the image, in crisp black font, is another name—*Libby Nicole Reed.*

The room whirls and my stomach sways. "Oh God, it's her—they could be sisters, almost twins actually."

The server returns and sets a cup down in front of each of us. I drop in a packet of creamer and stir, waiting for Mason to go on. He leaves his black, taking a couple sips before continuing.

"We found enough former students and a guidance counselor from their high school to fill us in on their history together. Allie's parents and sister were killed in a car accident when she was fifteen, leaving her financially stable, but emotionally raw. Libby was so attached to Allie that she practically moved in with her. The two girls were close for a while, and so similar in appearance that they were sometimes confused for each other. They even had matching tattoos. But eventually Allie began to see the real Libby and wanted nothing more to do with her. She attempted to sever the relationship, but Libby was both angry and jealous; she had no intention of walking away empty-handed."

I grasp my mug, embracing the warmth, then sit back and listen. Mason goes on for a while. His story about these two girls could fill a novella, and I absorb every detail. Hearing that Claire stole Allie's identity, and is going by her middle name, is enough to send me reeling. When he's finished I reattach my jaw, but I can tell there's something more.

"Emma, I wanted you to see the yearbook because I thought it was important—but as I told you, the FBI now has this case. The problem is that Claire, or Libby, covered her bases with precision, right down to subbing personal items with Allie's DNA in her home. The US Attorney has nothing to connect her to the crimes that Logan and Kyle perpetrated, regardless of what they claim or what we believe to be true. This makes her even more dangerous, so I'm hoping you will stay clear of her. Foley and I have been assigned another case that will require us to leave to Seattle in the morning. I'm not sure when we'll be back."

Hearing that he's leaving sends a pang of sadness through me. I swallow the emotion and immediately stand to leave. If I try to say anything, my face will soon be as wet as my blouse, and I really don't want him to see that. So I keep it simple. "Thank you for everything."

We lock eyes for a few seconds longer, and I can tell he has more to say, but he holds back, perhaps respecting my need for space. I grab my coat and hurry down the aisle, pushing through the heavy door, my fingers already dialing Amy's number.

———⌘———

The rain has stopped. I drag my soggy body through the city, blending in with every homeless person I encounter—I wouldn't be surprised if someone were to offer me a dollar bill or a Dunkin' Donuts gift certificate. I asked Amy to meet me at my place—I didn't give her any specifics, but I pleaded with her to drop what she's doing and to come right away. By the time I approach my house, her car is parked out front—so I tap at the window and gesture for her to come inside.

She follows me in. "You're scaring me," she says.

I flip on the lights and hang up my coat, then sweep my damp tangled hair into a knot. We walk into the kitchen; I pull two glasses and clunk them on the table, then grab the vodka and seltzer.

She stares down at the bottle and then back up at me. "Okay, so this is gonna be a serious discussion," she says, watching as I pour.

My hands rattle as the day's events come flooding down my face.

"Oh God, tell me what's wrong, Emma."

"Claire stole the identity of her childhood friend so that she could erase her already budding criminal record, and then used her grades to get into law school. The rest, as they say, is history," I say, downing a large gulp.

"Let me see if I can guess the rest. She convinced Logan to participate in a billing scheme, and my husband figured it out."

"Pretty much. And you can imagine how well Claire would do in jail, but you gotta give the devil her due. She knew that her friend had an identical tattoo, and they were similar in appearance and build. I'm guessing she lured the real Allison Ryan to Boston so she'd have a body that would pass as her, and then substituted personal items in her bathroom with hair and saliva so they would get a DNA match."

"And Dean was the scapegoat."

"Yes, ma'am. And now she can walk away from her life in Boston and live as herself, Libby Reed."

Amy takes the bottle of vodka and swigs. "Where the fuck are the fire-breathing dragons when you need them? If ever an evil bitch needed a flame to the ass, it's her."

"As of right now they can't charge her with anything. And by the way, I learned that she's gonna be taking an immediate leave of absence. I'm guessing that's the last we'll see of her."

"Unless …" Amy says with a slow drawl.

"Unless what?"

"Unless you expose her."

"So far a team of experts hasn't been able to do that, so how do you suppose I do it?"

"Go to someone who knows how a crime like this works and ask him how to trip up a criminal mind," she says with a wink.

I clink my glass against hers. "I like the way you think," I say, knowing that the first call I'll make tomorrow morning will be to the Massachusetts Correctional Institute to request a visit with Dad.

CHAPTER FORTY-FOUR

"In my dreams, I grip her neck and squeeze." That's what I say to Dr. Bradley when I call for an unscheduled session. It's been a week since I met with my father, and oh what a meeting it was. I've been a busy girl. But the nightmares keep coming and she's in every one of them, so I'm thankful when Dr. Bradley agrees to fit me in today.

On the way I stop by the tea house. The glossy-lipped teenager behind the counter hands me my cup and a coupon for a free breakfast sandwich. I grab my drink and hustle to the old Colonial. Climbing the rickety staircase, I balance my cup as I grip the railing and slip in, plopping down into the cushy chair outside his office. The thin drywall is no match for his booming voice, and I hear every word as he wraps up his call, as clearly as if I'm sitting in the room with him. For a moment, I wonder who might be sitting out here listening when I'm on the other side of that wall, laying bare my soul.

The handle twists, and Dr. Bradley's large frame fills the open space. "It's good to see you, Emma. Come in."

I waste no time striding into his office, settling into my now-familiar seat next to the fireplace, and as always, he sits across from me, skimming his legal pad. "I see the bandage is gone," I say, gesturing toward his hand.

He looks down, bending his wrist from right to left. "You remembered. And yes, it's better. Thank you."

I manage a weak smile.

"Tell me what's going on, Emma."

I adjust in my seat and then clench my hands into each other. "Have you been watching the news?" I ask.

"I have. I saw that another arrest had been made in the case involving your colleagues."

"It happened in front of the entire office. It happened in front of her."

"In front of who?"

"Claire," I say, reaching for my tea. I don't tell him about the recent revelations; I need to keep this session focused on me, but I can't help myself. I hold the paper cup close to my chest and inhale the scent of vanilla and cinnamon spices.

"Tell me why it bothers you that Claire was present."

"Because she probably should have been arrested too," I say.

His eyes widen. "I don't understand. Why would you say that?"

"Turns out my good friend is a clever storyteller; you might even say she's a savant of sorts. I'm only now realizing how shrewd she really is."

"Emma, this isn't your problem. Leave it to the authorities, and let's talk about getting you healthy."

"I spent a week in jail because of her—she was willing to see me lose my freedom so that she could keep hers. I think I was a target from the day she met me."

"Why would she do that to you?"

"She used to ask me about my father's case; looking back, she was oddly interested in it. And now I know why."

"You said your father has been in prison for years."

"She used to go with me to visit him—in fact, she insisted. I thought she was being a friend, but now I realize she just wanted to learn his game and execute it on a much higher level. She wasn't there for support; she wanted an education. Only she set her sights a little too high. She and Logan underestimated Dean Wolfe—it took a while, but he figured it out and was about to expose them. I think they were desperate and decided to do whatever it took to keep their wealth, and their freedom. I don't think anything was off-limits. Not even me."

Dr. Bradley scribbles notes, then stops me. "You appear to be a bit manic today. I think we need to revisit the antidepressant medications we discussed in our last visit. This class of drug can help with anxiety, and in my opinion that would be a good option for you now."

"What you're observing isn't mania—you're looking at *fury*. How many people have to lose their lives before someone speaks up loud enough to make everyone else look in the right direction?"

Dr. Bradley puts down his pad and folds his hands across his broad chest. His voice is deep and soothing; when he speaks, I want to listen. "My only concern right now is you, Emma. You've made good progress managing incredible loss and also settling into your new position at the firm. Arrests have been made, and the professionals have this piece of the tragedy under control."

I finish my tea and toss the cup into a small bin; he looks at his cell. "Hold on just a second," he says, typing a message.

I push back in my chair, once again admiring the art. My gaze shifts to his desk and I see the stack of books, and I study the titles, waiting for him to end his text. He says my name and I turn back toward him.

"I'm sorry, my next patient was running late but he's almost here now. I wish I had more time."

"No, it's my fault—I put you behind schedule," I say, standing to leave. As I turn to walk out my tote catches the end table, sending his mug of coffee flying. Embarrassed, I drop to my knees, but Dr. Bradley stops me.

"It's fine, Emma. It's just a drink. I'll clean it up."

Feeling the need to do something, I pick up two of the larger pieces. The words Clemson and Tigers are now separate shards of ceramic dripping in warm coffee. Not sure what else to do, I gently place them on his desk, mortified that I can't seem to get out of my own way these days.

"I'd like to see you in a week—you have my cell in case of an emergency, so make sure to use it," he says.

"I will," I reply. He yanks the pewter handle and I step out, then look back. "I'll see you next week."

"See you then, Emma."

I head home eager to change and go for a mind-clearing run. But just as I approach my street, an image flashes in my brain and I stop cold, my hand covering my mouth. How did I not see this before? The face in the Uber is now as clear as if he is standing in front of me. *I remember.*

I dial Agent Riley, and within the hour he's at my door.

By the time the FBI leaves, the truth has been laid bare; the entire investigation to date methodically described in excruciating detail, and I absorb every word. But it was *my* revelation, the tiny little image that rose to the surface and revealed itself to me today, that changed everything.

CHAPTER FORTY-FIVE

When I arrive at the park, it's already populated with early risers going through their typical morning routines—runners on the trails, dog walkers, stroller pushers, and the occasional joyous yelp of a toddler stretching its tiny legs. My last visit here was when I met with Mason—and despite his interrogative eyes I could tell there was something good about him, and I felt safe. Today, though, everything I've learned sits just beneath the surface of my thoughts, kicking my adrenaline up an uncomfortable notch.

I find the bench where Claire and I used to meet up every Saturday—first, as a quiet refuge from the grind of law school, but eventually it just became our happy place. I see her approaching in my direction and as usual she is fashion-magazine ready in stylish gray ankle pants, black flats, and a plaid charcoal blazer, her blonde hair swept into a sleek ballet bun. I notice her carrying a drink in each hand—she's thoughtful that way—stopping for my favorite tea latte is typical of her. *That's* the person I've known for all these years. It's what's been buried down deep inside her, the grifter I never really knew, that terrifies me.

She stops in front of me and smiles, a gentle lilt to her tone. "Sorry I'm late. The Uber took a little longer than the estimate," she says, sliding in next to me.

"You're fine," I respond.

She swivels in my direction and I can feel her examine me. "Is everything okay, Emma?"

My fingers roll into a fist and tighten, the honest response to that question lodged in my throat. Claire appears to notice, and breaks the tension. "I brought you a chai," she says, handing me one of the large paper cups.

I force a grin and take the tea into my hand. "Thank you." *Not a chance that I'll be drinking this thing.*

"I was really glad you called yesterday. I wasn't sure how you were feeling with everything that's happened," she says.

"I know, and I'm sorry. I've been preoccupied. Taking on Dean's cases without a proper turnover of his files has been a lot. It's only now that I finally believe I know what's really going on."

Claire sips from her cup and smiles. "It's not rocket science, Emma. I have no doubt that you've been able to get up to speed by now."

God, could she be any more obnoxious? I nearly laugh, but I hold it in and smile. "I heard you're planning on taking a leave of absence from the firm."

"That's right. Dealing with the constant gossip and the rumors—all of them untrue, by the way—has been exhausting. So I've decided to take a trip."

"Where are you going?"

"I was thinking Portugal—I've always wanted to learn the language."

"What about Logan?"

"What about him?"

"Wouldn't it be hard to be so far away from him?" I ask.

She cocks a glance directly at me, one brow lifted. "What are you talking about?"

"Well … you've been sleeping with him for years, so I just assumed you'd want to be there to support him now."

Claire stiffens, her glare a violent punch. "Why did you ask to meet with me, Emma?"

Her voice has shifted to a low and pointed pitch, her wrath bubbling to the surface. I've thought about this moment a lot recently—all the things I could say on behalf of each life she has ruined. But then it came to me—Claire doesn't *feel*, she only *wants*. My dad was right—I would need to think like her.

"I know it was you who left the message threatening to file a complaint against me with the bar, letting them know that I withheld evidence in the Christian Wilkes pro bono case." I search her eyes for a reaction, and a flicker of acknowledgment belies the defiance in her voice.

"Oh, Emma, no one ever has to know about that little legal hiccup. It's really up to you."

"I didn't withhold anything, and you know it. I wasn't told about the prior incident until after the hearing for a new trial because he hadn't even remembered it himself. It wasn't relevant anyway, he was eighteen years old when it happened, and his girlfriend was seventeen and a half. They had been dating for three years without any problems until a fight at their senior prom. Besides, it happened twenty-five years before his arrest for a murder he definitely didn't commit."

"That's the thing, Emma. History is up to interpretation depending on who's telling it."

I'd have to burrow below ground to stoop to her level, so I draw in a meditating breath and stay above the belt. "I'm sure you're a master at that game."

Claire ignores the comment, but I notice a sag in her posture. *I'm getting to her.*

"By the way, I finally met Jessie—I understand why you liked her so much. I liked her too. You never told me how good she was with computers. I guess you underestimated her talents."

"Jessie had no right getting involved; she's always been weak and pathetic; I'm sure she was jealous of all the attention my story was getting. Seems I have a type when I pick friends," Claire says, finishing her drink.

I sit on my hands to keep them from slapping the mean off this girl. "When Jessie visited you back in December, you wanted to order dinner online from the little Italian place on the corner. You apparently got busy with a phone call and asked her to finish the order you started on your laptop, so you gave her the password. And she remembered it."

"Emma, where are you going with all this?" The frivolity in her tone softens into what might be a tinge of angst.

"Jessie asked me for help finding your personal laptop so she could see for herself what really happened to you. All she needed was access to your place, and I gave it to her."

"Get to the fucking point."

"You've probably guessed by now that what she was looking for, and what she finally discovered, were two very different things. She shared it all with me. Turns out, you aren't all that bad with tech-nology yourself. I have to say, I was impressed. Sending emails to yourself from an account you created to look like they were coming from Dean; ordering diamonds online using his credit card, but picking them up in person; and most impressive of all, convincing Kyle to transfer all that siphoned money into offshore accounts, well, that was just brilliant. But you didn't count on Dean figuring it all out, did you? And I'm willing to bet Alex Ford was about to confirm his suspicions, which is why he needed to disappear."

"What does any of this have to do with you?" she hisses.

"You know, I've been asking myself something for a while now—how did you do it exactly? Was it you or Logan that drugged me, stripped me of my clothes, and put me to bed be-fore stealing my gun to use in your malicious plan? And which one of you brought it back? You were the only other person who had a key to my place. I know you were there that night."

Claire's grit wilts into a pathetic sigh. "You're not a half-bad lawyer, Emma, but don't flatter yourself. Neither of us touched you that night."

She sounds so convincing, even to me. I sit up straighter, curling my fingers into each other, clasping my hands together beneath my chin. "You stole the identity of a childhood friend so you could get into law school—then killed her so you would have a body to use in this scheme. You took Dean's life and his reputation—a man who did nothing but teach you, *believe* in you. You destroyed Jessie to keep what she learned hidden. And then Alex—sacrificed simply so you could come back to life. Those are the facts."

Claire gets to her feet and looks down at me. "This is my cue to leave," she says.

"I'm not done—sit back down," I demand.

"What did you just say?" she asks with an indignant growl.

"Let me rephrase. I said *sit the fuck down*, or my next stop is to the Boston PD."

Claire lowers herself back onto the bench, her eyes stabbing at me with an incensed glare. "I asked you what you want from me."

"I know you tried to frame me for the murders, and if it wasn't for some really good detective work on the part of Foley and Mason, I'd still be sleeping four feet from a metal toilet."

"Oh, Emma, stop being so dramatic. The investigation is closed, and Logan and Kyle are headed to prison—*as they should be*. The Feds have seized the offshore accounts. Case solved and a price paid, so you don't have to sing that song anymore."

I turn toward her. "Not all of them."

Claire's forehead creases. "All of what?"

"The FBI didn't seize them all, did they? I was told about the accounts in the Caymans, but they don't know about the one in Milan, do they?"

The corners of her mouth arch into a snarl, and it makes me wonder how I've been so blind to who she really is all these years.

"I told you, I've already been cleared of any involvement in Logan and Kyle's crimes," she says.

"That's right, I heard that. You played your hand very well. And … the truth is, I'm willing to forget about everything."

She studies me. "In exchange for what?"

"Put in writing that you know I didn't withhold evidence in the Wilkes case, and give me the password to the Milan account so I can return that money to the clients."

"How do I know this isn't a trap? Or that you won't take the money for yourself?"

"Your question is fair. I suppose if I don't share what I know with the FBI, that implicates me too. As for the second, you're the only thief in this conversation."

She stands again and tosses her cup into the bin. "The password is in my safe-deposit box—it will take me a couple days to get it, and then I'll call you with it," she says, turning to leave.

I swallow her lie and feign a smile. "Hey, Claire?"

She pivots back.

"You should know that if anything happens to me, my will has been amended to provide the FBI with a flash drive that will lay out everything Jessie uncovered."

She looks down at me for a long moment—her thin smile so evil, I half expect horns to erupt from her scalp. "Bye, Emma."

"Good-bye, Claire," I reply. She doesn't look back and I wonder if she heard me, but it really doesn't matter now. I watch as she fades through a cluster of trees, then turn my gaze back toward the river, feeling my insides rattle. I hold out my palm and catch a tear, then press my hands down on the sides of the bench and allow the rest to spill down onto my jacket. I hear the sound of a jet in the distance and look up—I notice wispy strips of clouds, and for a moment it makes me think of the thin ribbon of smoke I used to watch rise from my grandfather's cigar. I imagine him looking down on me right now with a grin of approval, knowing that he taught me to always act with kindness, but when necessary, to be prepared to outmaneuver evil.

CHAPTER FORTY-SIX

Libby

The sweet blend of jasmine and orange polishing oil invades my senses as I step through the thick gold-framed doors, held open by a tidy-looking doorman in a crisp blue uniform. I smile with the zeal of a delighted child on Christmas morning seeing her first dollhouse—far better than anything a tiny mind could have imagined. Gliding through the lavish lobby with purpose, my heels *click-clack* against the gleaming white tiles. Stopping just short of the reception desk, I gaze up toward the second-floor balcony, admiring the two impressive winding staircases adorned in scrolled wrought iron and separated by a contrasting black marble walkway. Despite my best effort to appear as if I'm accustomed to such elegance, my face grows warm with excitement, anticipation swelling in my chest— *the online photos did not do this place justice.*

The desk clerk smiles as I approach, and I return the gesture, although my cheerful expression is aimed inward. Sure, the last couple months have been a bit messier than I originally planned—*a hell of a lot messier, actually*—but none of that matters anymore. The point is that I made the necessary adjustments, and here I am. I won't be able to return to South Carolina as myself, albeit a wealthier version, not yet anyway. Years of planning and executing in great detail have earned me the lifestyle I crave, and now it's time to collect. I whip a golden wave behind my ear and slide my rose gold leather tote onto the counter.

A slender man with olive skin and chestnut curls stands behind the front desk with a wide smile. "Hello, welcome to the Grande Milan. Do you have a reservation?" he asks.

"I do."

"Last name please," he says.

My mouth begins to move but the wrong syllable starts to form, almost spilling out. I catch myself and smile. "Reed. Libby Reed," I say carefully, scrutinizing his expression, searching intently for a reaction as if this stranger could possibly know my secret.

"Ah yes, Ms. Reed. You have a suite on the eleventh floor."

I nod in sync with the audible breath I release, my mind absorbed with thoughts of fluffy hotel robes and morning room service trays filled with brioche and espresso. "Perfect," I say, handing over my credit card.

"Now I'll just need to see your ID."

I extract the card from my phone case and stare at the younger version of my face leering back at me; an involuntary grin spreading wide as I take in the brash self-assurance in her ambitious eyes. It's almost as if they knew all along that life would culminate in this one spectacular moment in time. I haven't used my real name in so many years that seeing it in print again, or even hearing it leave my own mouth, causes my posture to stiffen. I gladly destroyed all reminders of my life as Claire Ryan—being her had become so complicated that I was relieved to finally see her go.

I slide my South Carolina driver's license toward the clerk with pride; he glances at the card, then back up at me.

"Thank you, Ms. Reed. Here's your room key. Breakfast is included—the restaurant opens at seven o'clock."

"*Grazie*," I respond, slipping the tote over my shoulder and tapping my fingers on the veiny marble countertop before heading to the elevator. A bellman scoops up my luggage and places it on a cart, hurrying after me. I wait for the heavy elevator doors to slide open, then step in.

My jaw swings wide at the sight of the room. Falling onto the bed, I swipe along the velvety soft duvet, then jump to my feet again and stare at the oversized tub that I plan to soak in later tonight. After flipping on several lamps, I remove the bottle of Lagavulin I purchased on my way from the airport, taking a moment to admire the label, then pour a good measure of the sixteen-year-old, single-malt scotch into one of the glasses from the selection of Italian crystal found behind the wet bar. The oval-shaped vessel is smooth against my lips and I welcome the burn swirling down my throat.

Scooping up the bottle and glass, I saunter toward the slider, nudging it open with my left elbow. An early-spring chill hangs in the night air, so I grab a sweater and wrap it around my shoulders, then plop down on one of the two chairs looking out toward the city. A church bell chimes in the distance and for just one second,

I imagine the God so many people feel compelled to pray to, and wonder if he'll forgive my sins; but then I hear a noise and lurch upright. I scan the space but see no movement—I stand for a few minutes listening intently but all I hear is silence. A powerful *woosh* escapes my lungs—I hold my hammering chest, waiting for the thumping to subside.

Returning to my chair, I finish off the glass of whiskey, then pour another. Leaning back, I watch as the shimmering city comes into view, immediately lost in the tangle of lights. The soothing effect of the alcohol sinks in and I extend my legs, crossing them over each other. I rest my eyes and nearly drift off when another sound jars me upright—but just as I rise, a hand whips around me, clenching my forearm, causing me to gasp. A scream climbs from my throat, but it's muffled by a hand wrapping over my mouth. The grip is powerful—I twist, breaking free and leaping to my feet, spinning around, ready to strike. But then I see him—Dr. Bradley is standing in front of me.

He holds up both hands. "I frightened you—I'm sorry, I only meant to surprise you," he says.

"Are you insane, Mark, why are you *here*? You're supposed to meet me in Morocco. It's almost ten o'clock."

"Would you prefer I waited until daylight to visit? Perhaps pick up some Danish and a cappuccino?"

Dismissing his sarcasm, I hold my chest, waiting for my unruly pulse to return to normal. "No, I'd rather you follow the plan. It's safer in Morocco."

"You mean, the same way *you* followed the plan?" he asks with a wink.

"I had to improvise and you know it—Kyle turned out to be weak, and that idiot Logan was incapable of putting the kid back in his place. I had no choice but to come back and make sure no one was onto us. And they're not, so you're welcome."

Without waiting to be asked, Mark points toward the amber bottle. I walk back into the room and grab another glass, then return to the balcony and hand it to him. He splashes in a generous pour and leans back on the railing, then swigs a large gulp and shudders.

"Tell me why you're really here—the truth," I say.

His playful expression turns somber. "Emma came to see me for an unscheduled visit."

"What did she say?"

"That you probably should have been arrested along with Logan."

"This coming from the girl who sat feet away from you for the last three months, staring into your face while pouring out her pathetic little heart—without ever realizing you were the one who carried her to bed and changed her out of her clothes. You confirmed that she has no memory of that night, and no one can connect either of us to the crime. Besides, Logan and Kyle only know me as Claire, so we're good."

"And the money?"

"The US currency that I was able to get my hands on was converted into diamonds. I have an appointment at the bank tomorrow morning to withdraw the rest, and a train ticket to Madrid, and then I'll make my way to Morocco within the next three days."

Mark walks over to the suitcase and begins rifling through it.

"Um, excuse me—what are you doing with my bag?" I ask.

"I'd like to see them up close," he says.

I let go of an especially long sigh, then maneuver around

him and make my way to the closet. He follows so closely behind that I can feel the heat of his breath on my neck. I tap the small illuminated buttons until the latch clicks and the safe door snaps open. Fishing around, I grope for the tiny black velvet bag and take it out, once again surprised by its weight. I pull open the silk cord, tilting the bag toward him. His eyes grow wide and he nods, as if to acknowledge the magnitude of what we're looking at. Even now it's difficult to imagine how so much wealth can be reduced to a cluster of dazzling little rocks, but that's the beauty of diamonds, after all. It's a remarkable way to carry millions of dollars in the palm of your hand. I return the bag; then click the heavy metal door back into place, entering a new combination code.

"The view is really something," Mark says. He returns to the terrace, dropping into one of the two lounge chairs. I watch as he leans back—his eyes gently closing in delight, his body visibly unwinding in the evening breeze. He's a beautiful man, always has been. I've known him for many years—we met after I was incarcerated as a teenager. Part of my early release agreement mandated that I participate in a post-confinement therapy program. He was fresh out of the grad program at Clemson, and new to a small, state-sponsored practice working with teens. As fate would have it, he was assigned to me.

To be honest, I didn't mind working with Dr. Bradley; he was easy to talk to, and I could tell that he understood me from the start. It wasn't long before the professional barrier between us was cracked wide open and our sessions moved from a tiny office in a sketchy part of town to his bed on the second floor of the room he rented downtown. There was nothing romantic about our relationship, but the sex was fire and a lot more enjoyable than having my complicated brain poked and prodded.

When I moved away from the south to begin my new life, I had no choice but to lose all contact with my past, and that included Mark. But one day while researching a case for Emma, I came across an article that spun my head; even after ten years, I recognized him immediately. Turns out he got himself into a bit of trouble, lost his license, and was left practically unemployable after one of his patients filed a malpractice lawsuit against him. We probably never would have crossed paths again, but when it became evident that Dean was about to expose the billing scheme, I realized that the answer to my problems had just fallen into my lap, in the form of a desperate man with nothing left to lose. *And that was that.*

"It's nice out here. Join me," he calls out.

"We're so close, now is not the time to draw attention to ourselves. You need to leave, and I'll meet you in three days. *Placating this man is beginning to get on my nerves.*

"Sunset in Casablanca," he says with a grin.

"That's right," I say, reaching down and taking his hand, guiding him toward the door.

Mark leans in for a kiss, and I acquiesce, then close the door behind him, fastening both the deadbolt and security bar.

CHAPTER FORTY-SEVEN

I t's just after noon when I enter the Bank of Milan, anxious to begin my new life. I originally scheduled the appointment for yesterday but was told that the international accounts manager wouldn't be available until this afternoon. So I spent the day selecting a new outfit for the occasion. I needed something sharp—it's not enough to simply exude classy wealth, which I can certainly manage—*I have to look the part*. So I chose a white tailored Valentino cap-sleeve dress, a tan Celine handbag, nude Manolo Blahnik pumps, and oversize tortoiseshell Prada sunglasses. Noticing my reflection in the floor-to-ceiling glass windows, I impress even myself.

I'm escorted into a large corner office, the walls adorned with white wooden paneling and postwar paintings framed in gold. A slight man sits at a large wooden desk and types into his computer. He looks up and politely stands; he's wearing a blue suit fitted to his slender body and small round glasses, his dark brown hair cut short. He reaches out his hand and I move closer, returning the greeting.

"Ms. Reed, so nice to finally meet you."

"You as well," I say, taking a seat across from him.

"I understand you'd like to make a rather large withdrawal today?"

"That's right—I have an investment opportunity that will require me to move quickly, so … I need my funds to be liquid."

"Well, we certainly are sorry to lose your business, but I can definitely help you with this transaction. I'll need your passport."

"Of course," I say, handing it to him. He begins tapping on his keyboard and I allow my mind to drift. There's a moment when I almost feel guilty, but it wasn't as if I targeted Logan exactly; his vulnerability when I needed it most was, quite simply, serendipitous. The idea was born one night some years back—we were working late and everyone else had gone home. When we were done, we decided to stop for dinner and a drink before calling it a night. That was when I learned that his marriage wasn't all it pretended to be, which presented the opportunity I'd been looking for. His wealth would of course be divided if they were ever to divorce, so I convinced him that together we could grow a separate fund, and half of that would be his alone. Tax-free, no less. He didn't require much persuading, because as it turned out, money wasn't his greatest weakness—what he really wanted was *me*. I had him at that point—*he would do anything I asked.*

"Ms. Reed …?"

"Sorry, I was distracted … What was it you were asking?"

"I was wondering when the cosigner would arrive."

My breath catches. "Cosigner?"

"Yes. The account has a two-party in-person signing requirement for any withdrawals."

"There must be some mistake—this account was set up in my name alone. Please check again."

"Of course, let me take another look," he says.

I feel the tendons in my neck flare and I stand, my dress sticking to my skin.

"I'm sorry, Ms. Reed, but I've confirmed that withdrawals can only be made from this account with you and your cosigner here together."

I drop back into the chair and lean in on my elbows, starting to lose patience with this idiot. "This is *my* account. There are no cosigners."

"Why don't I just give her a call and we'll get this sorted out?"

"Her?"

"Yes. The co-owner of this account. Her name is … let me see … oh yes, that would be a Ms. Claire Ryan. Her number is right here."

My legs go limp, and I feel the blood drain from my face. *Fucking Emma.*

"Ma'am? Are you okay?"

A shrill pitch whistles beneath my skull—panic zipping from knee to neck. He picks up the phone, giving me a quizzical look, and I know that I need to get out of here. I seize my bag and gesture to the banker. "You know what, I have to be somewhere in about twenty minutes. I'll come back tomorrow, and we can clear this up."

I watch as his fingers continue to touch numbers, and the room spins. I work to keep my balance as I slide the chair under the desk and start to slowly back up. "Thank you for your help," I say, striding briskly out of his office and down the hall. I push through the exit and onto the sidewalk, struggling to fill my lungs. *Think, think, THINK.* I struggle for oxygen, but I have to keep moving. I trudge step by heavy step back toward the hotel, the gleam of the golden doors visible in the distance. I nearly let defeat consume me, but a thought sparks—*they expect me back tomorrow, so that gives me just enough time.*

⤖

The large hotel doors part to the sound of metal gliding on tracks, and I know I have minutes, not hours, to empty my room and find an earlier train out of here. I push the elevator call button and stand with three other hotel guests waiting for it to open. I hear the chime and swing my arms wide as the doors move, jumping in and slapping the eleventh-floor button, watching irritated expressions as it closes without letting anyone else in.

I hurl my body toward my room and wave my card over the lock, relieved to hear it unlatch. I push it inward and grab my suitcase, already packed for my trip tonight. But then I catch a glint on the carpet. I crouch down and pick up the tiny object, holding it between my fingers—it's one of the diamonds. I lurch forward and begin digging through my suitcase, tossing clothes to the floor, searching for the tiny bag, and my head drops backward. *They're gone.* I'll crack his neck with my bare hands, but right now I need to get to the train station.

I put the suitcase back together and drag it to the elevator, exiting into the lobby. But I'm only a few steps in when I hear a voice call my name, and I feel a hitch in my throat.

"Libby Reed—*fermata dove sei! Tu sei sotto arresto!*"

My hands flutter, and I look around. The man in the corner is casually drinking an espresso, but he studies me with a curious expression. The clerk at the front desk pretends to busy himself, but he doesn't lift his gaze. The couple sitting on the couch to my right is watching with open jaws. I hear my name again and pivot slowly toward the voices. It's then that I see her—Emma standing alone, just to the side of a group of what looks like Italian authorities and one US FBI agent. She takes a step toward me, and my stomach contracts. She keeps walking; it feels like minutes between steps, but soon we're standing shoulder-to-shoulder. She leans in and whispers. "They couldn't connect you to the stolen money, Libby. That is, *not until now.*" *Hearing her say my real name stings.* I watch the expression in her eyes as she steps back, and my head dips. I'm not entirely sure what I'm feeling now ... fury, yes; fear, maybe. But misjudging Emma's grit and determination will be my greatest regret ... always.

CHAPTER FORTY-EIGHT

Emma

THREE MONTHS LATER ... JUNE.

A
t times when it's quiet, and I'm alone, I find myself thinking about her. It happens less often now as more time passes, but when it does, I wonder how I missed every little sign—*there were so many*. The subtle but persistent curiosity over my father's crime, as if genuinely concerned about him, when what she was really doing was taking notes—studying him, learning from his mistakes. Or the family she never introduced to me, claiming she was too embarrassed of their snobbery, when in reality she couldn't expose the identity she had stolen. And the many nights out we shared over the years—realizing that she rarely offered to pay. There never was a trust fund, her elaborate lifestyle just a smoke screen masking her mind-numbing greed and debt. I realize now that Claire—I still have a hard time referring to her as Libby—was a chameleon, revealing only the person she wanted to be, never who she actually was.

I think a lot about Jessie and Allie, the value of their lives measured with dollar signs. Nothing but pawns in a wicked scheme, necessary sacrifices to keep Libby Reed and Mark Bradley on the right side of prison bars—my heart will never stop aching over their loss. I want to feel sorry for Logan ... I don't know how he let Libby convince him to turn on his family and his clients, but just like with my father, it really doesn't matter—he is a thief and he will pay the price for his crimes, but someday he will walk free.

On the other hand, Dr. Bradley *is* a killer. What he wasn't was a therapist, not anymore anyway—he lost his license years earlier. Ironically, though, he somehow helped pry loose the demons of my past. It was the Clemson mug that finally lifted the fog. I realized his connection to South Carolina, and then the vague image in the Range Rover became clear. I suddenly remembered seeing his photo on Claire's phone that night at the pub; it was only seconds really, but it was him—the mysterious Walgreens guy. Only that's not how they actually met; they had known each other for years. In the end, Claire convinced him to help rid her of the threat Dean posed, and Allie was a necessary piece to her diabolical puzzle. The Italian authorities secured his arrest prior to boarding the train that held his freedom, and now he'll spend the rest of his days wishing I had never stepped into his office.

Kyle was a different story altogether. There was enough of a digital trail to convince the FBI that he had been coerced into participating. I hope that he finds some kind of peace in knowing that I testified to make sure his part in exposing the crime was known. He'll be released in three years and will still be a very young man who can turn his life back around.

The long-overdue celebration for Dean finally arrives on one of those perfect New England summer mornings when the world seems to be on pause, and the air is crisp—before humidity cloaks the city in a steamy blanket of heat. Amy invited me to speak, and although I wasn't sure I'd be able to do it, I agreed.

The truth is, I didn't know everything about Dean, but I knew a lot. I talk about the time he invested in his law students, and how he taught them to look at people as individuals, and never to judge or assume. I talk about his passion for helping the wrongly accused, and how he showed me that by working with the Innocence League, I would learn to appreciate my freedom in a very different way. He couldn't have known how that sentiment would eventually take on an entirely new meaning in my life.

There are so many good things about Dean to share, but I don't tell them everything. I leave out the small detail that while mourning him, I somehow allowed myself to fall for someone, and that I knew he would approve. I haven't talked to Mason since the arrests and extraditions back to the US. I realize now that my feelings are one-sided, but just knowing that someone like him is out there is enough for me.

After the service we gather at Amy's house to share Dean's favorite meal—chicken marsala and Caesar salad catered by Di Bucco's. There are no more tears; he wouldn't want that. Rather, we sit around tables filled with photographs, reminiscing about his life and laughing until our jaws ache. Colleagues from the firm stop by to offer condolences, and friends take turns sharing stories about fishing trips to the lake and weekend biking excursions.

When the crowd finally dissolves, I stay behind; Amy and I

have grown close. We assemble a crib and fold tiny laundry, tucking it neatly into a beautiful white dresser. A week ago I helped her paint one wall pale blue, dotting it with cottony clouds, preparing for the arrival of Matthew Dean Wolfe. Dean never knew about his son—the pregnancy was confirmed nearly two months after he passed. I'm hoping he's looking down and feels some sense of comfort knowing that I'll always be there for his little guy.

It's close to nine o'clock when I decide it's time to head home, remembering the work I need to catch up on. I order an Uber and pack up my bag to leave. Amy stops me. She doesn't need to say anything; her eyes say enough.

I smile. "It was a beautiful day."

She wraps her arms around me. "It was perfect."

I take her hand and squeeze.

"Looks like your car is here," she says, sliding the door open.

We hug one more time, and then I make my way down the walkway, lifting my hand to wave before sliding in and pulling the handle shut.

The streetlamp between Frankie's house and mine has been repaired, a fountain of light casting a glow over my porch. I search for my keys—an evening breeze brushing against my neck. I'm about to unlock the door when I spot something resting on the mat. It's a small kraft paper bag with a box inside, tied with a pale green satin bow. I balance my tote and scoop up the package, bringing it into the house.

I pull the smooth ribbon and slide my finger below the tape, lifting the wrapping. My hands sweep to my cheeks, warmth climbing through me as I take in the silver bracelet engraved with the words *wabi-sabi*. I whip the door back open and peer out-side—Jet gallops up my steps and buries his nose into my thigh. My eyes water as I drop to a knee and stroke his neck. And then a familiar voice says my name and I look up. He's standing at the bottom of the staircase, with one leg propped on the first step.

"Don't do or say anything sweet because I might just get the idea that you like me," I say.

"I'll try my best," he says.

"I thought you were in Seattle with Detective Foley."

"I am, or I was, I mean I'm supposed to be. I heard about what happened in Italy and wanted to check on you. I'm going back in two days," Mason says.

"You came all the way back here just to check on me?"

"Yes, I did."

"Why?"

"Because I realized something while I was gone."

"What was that?"

He takes another step up. "I like messy. I might even prefer messy."

I breathe in as if it's the first time I've felt air in my lungs.

His hand slides below my chin, guiding me toward him, his lips barely parting until our mouths are intertwined. Our bod-ies press into each other, and at this moment I am sure of one thing—*tonight I'll finally turn the lights off.*

Made in the USA
Middletown, DE
01 February 2023

23650087R00203